You know, surprisingly, they don't sell a lot of brains in the local 24-hour grocery store around the corner from my house. And, believe it or not, they don't really like it when you ask about them. At least, not the sleepy college kid working the only open cash register the night I become a zombie.

"Hi, yeah, listen, uh . . . Tad? Tad, I'm looking for, well, see, my, uhhm . . . grandfather . . . is coming into town this weekend, and he really likes, well, believe it or not, he *loves* brains. Don't look at me like that. I guess they ate them on the farm when he was growing up or something, but . . . do you know where I could find any?"

"Tad," or so says the name tag on his chest, looks past me, around me, out into the parking lot, and everywhere *but* at me before finally saying, "Very funny." Then he stares at me, as if to say, without words, "I'm too smart to be punk'd. Even if it is two in the morning and there's not another soul around for miles."

"It's not a prank, Tad. Seriously. I looked all over the meat department, found tubs of chicken livers, something called 'chitterlings'—not sure I want to go there—even a big, gray cow's tongue, but . . . no brains. So . . . do you know where I could find them? I mean, I'm asking as a customer"—here I hold up the insanely fat roll of $20 bills Dad keeps in a cookie jar in the kitchen in case of an emergency (which, I think you'll agree, this is)—"so I'm really *not* trying to prank you."

He sighs, reaches for a curvy microphone next to his cash register, pushes a button at the ⌐⌐⌐⌐⌐ and says, "Harvey, I'm sending a live one back to the ⌐⌐⌐⌐⌐ of, get this . . . *brains.* . . ."

ZOMBIES Don't Cry

Rusty Fischer

MEDALLION
P R E S S

Medallion Press, Inc.
Printed in USA

ZOMBIES
Don't Cry

Rusty Fischer

Dedication

For my lovely wife, Martha, who's had to put up with my
zombie shenanigans for far too long now.

Published 2011 by Medallion Press, Inc.

The MEDALLION PRESS LOGO
is a registered trademark of Medallion Press, Inc.

Typeset in Adobe Garamond Pro

Printed in the United States of America

ISBN 978-1605423-82-1

10 9 8 7 6 5 4 3 2 1

First Edition

Acknowledgments

Rusty would like to thank the following for their invaluable contribution to the "making of" *Zombies Don't Cry.*

First, to Jamie Brenner with Artists & Artisans, Inc., who knew this book better back when it was still called *Have a Nice Afterlife.* Jamie taught me the importance of story, as well as knowing your audience. She also taught me that timing is everything and that writing a "timeless" book is more important than chasing a fad.

Second, to the good folks at Medallion Press. Finding a publisher is never easy; finding a publisher who actually cares about its authors, particularly in this day and age, is doubly so. I'm proud to have found a "home" at Medallion, where zombies are always welcome. Editorial Manager Lorie Popp has been particularly encouraging, and I'd also like to give a major shout-out to my "point person," Editorial Director Emily Steele, who has made the process easier than it should be.

Next, to my unofficial mentors on Facebook and Twitter. There are too many to list by name, but being able to talk about writing, publishing, e-books, print books, submissions, query letters, plot, and characterization with folks I've long admired—and read—has been a true inspiration. They say writing is a solitary venture, and that's true for the most part, but social media has really opened up my world and, I like to think, my writing is better for it.

Finally, to my family and friends, who have learned more about zombies than they probably ever wanted to. I never fail to get a kick out of hearing my in-laws, Helen and Gerry, asking about flesh-eating zombies or watching my mom, Colee, egging her teacher friends to buy her son's book about the living dead. (And don't get me started on trying to convince my dad, Rusty Sr., how well a book about zombies would go over at Rusty's Raw Bar.) They've been hearing about this book for so long, I hope they're not disappointed when the dead finally spring to life!

Contents

Prologue
Zombie Picnic

THE GRAVEYARD IS calm at this hour, an appropriately full moon shining down on acres of freshly mown lawn and miles of evenly spaced headstones. Their endless rows are surprisingly calming; it's almost like I'm staring at a big mouth with thousands of teeth smiling just for me. Though the air is chilly this time of year, it's clear, making everything clean, crisp, and high-resolution; death in hi-def.

I always thought this was a particularly nonspooky cemetery as far as cemeteries go. Most of the ones you see on TV or in the movies are purposefully creepy crawly, gruesome affairs, with crooked headstones leaning and fences broken and the graves overgrown with dried, dead bushes and looking, I suppose, about the way you figure a cemetery should look.

Here in Florida, they take their graveyards pretty darn seriously.

The fence doesn't creak when you walk by, there is no pack of feral black cats roaming the grounds, the grass is ballpark green, the headstones are all straight, a nice unbroken sidewalk runs the length of the graveyard, the grave markers are clean, and the flowers are all fresh.

I use the moonlight to inspect the contents of the picnic basket at my feet.

Four cans of Mountain Dew?

Check.

Plastic forks and knives?

Check.

Plastic plates?

Check.

Paper napkins?

Check.

Handcuffs if things go south?

Check.

Leg chains if things go really south?

Check.

Hatchet if things go really, *really* south?

Check.

ZOMBIES *Don't Cry*

Fresh brains?

Double-check.

I smile, shut the picnic basket, clasp it tight, and pat the top for good measure. Clouds move across the moon but, thanks to my new zombie vision, I can still see fine, thank you very much. (Even if everything looks a little . . . yellow. But that's okay; you get used to it after awhile.)

The grave at my feet is fresh. Half the folded white chairs are still lined up in the back with the rest stacked neatly on a metal dolly someone forgot to haul back to the funeral parlor come closing time. Well, no surprises there. After all that's gone down in the last few days, who can blame the gravediggers for being underpaid and overworked?

I don't need to look at my watch to tell me it's been nearly 72 hours since I turned him, so by now he should be just beginning to stir down there, six feet under. I sigh, grab the shovel I brought from the back of the truck, and start digging. It's hard work, true enough, but I like the constant motion. Zombies tend to get a little stiff after awhile, so anything we can do to keep moving, to keep our joints from freezing up and stiffening out, well, more's the better, I always say.

I make quick work of the top layer of soil, step into the grave itself, and dig some more. I take my time; no use exerting myself before our big reunion. I form a kind of musical rhythm here in this empty graveyard on this moonlit night: shovel in, scoop out, over the shoulder, back again; shovel in, scoop out, over the shoulder, back again. Like that, over and over, until finally the rhythm is interrupted by my shovel hitting casket wood, giving off a shower of fresh, varnished splinters.

I step aside, squeeze alongside the casket, and use the hard end of my shovel like a trowel to carefully scrape away the thin layer of dirt covering the top. When the coating is gone and wood is all that remains, I lean on my shovel, stretch my back, wipe my forehead out of habit (zombies don't sweat), and listen for a minute or two.

I smile at the sounds of shuffling coming from inside; nothing too terribly urgent, just the generally spooky sounds of funeral tuxedo against coffin satin. (Trust me: once you hear it, you never forget it.) Just to make sure I'm dealing with a good zombie and not a bad one (yeah, actually, there *is* a difference), I tap the top of the coffin with my stiff new army boots. *Tap, tap, tap.*

I wait, glad for the still, autumn night, until I

hear the urgent response beneath my feet: *tap, tap, tap.* That's my boy. I use the end of the shovel to pry the casket open and listen to the hiss as the hydraulic cover slowly rises like the trunk of Dad's reliable old station wagon.

Inside lies a statuesque young man with pale skin, a blue tux, and the most deliciously delectable curl dangling across his marble white forehead. I know I haven't been a zombie all that long, but I actually think it's ruined me for regular guys.

Back when I was a Normal, I always had a thing for jocks. You know, the robustness, the ruddy skin, the muscles bulging out of sweaty gray tank tops, the suntans . . . the tan lines. But now? I gotta tell you, something about the pale skin, the 0 percent body fat, the no heartbeat, and those deep, dark circles under the eyes is *really* bringing it home for me.

And this one? This one's got all that in spades.

He smiles faintly, though aimlessly, perhaps in response to the moonlight flooding down rather than to seeing the girl who actually put him in the casket in the first place. At any rate, he certainly doesn't seem too panicked about waking up six feet under in a wooden box, satin-lined and expensive though it may be.

"Who are you?" he asks quietly. "And why are

you carrying that shovel? And where am I? And whose tux is this? And why is it . . . *blue*?"

Ah, Fresh Meat; always with the questions. I shoosh him with a pale finger to my gray lips, tasting fresh grave dirt and shovel splinters and swiftly wiping them off on my black cargo pants. Then I haul him out of the casket, drag him up out of the grave, sit him down, open the picnic basket, show him the fresh brains, and watch his eyes. Light. Up.

As he makes short work of the first brain, I sigh, filling in his grave a little more speedily than I dug it out and patting down the top layer so it looks relatively undisturbed. By then he's halfway through the second brain, and before I can say, "Hey, save some for me," he's sitting back in his musty tuxedo, patting his stomach and burping.

I crack open a fresh can of Mountain Dew and hand it to him.

"Thanks, Maddy," he says finally, sleepy eyes full of recognition, drowsy smile full of gray matter and gore. I shake my head, sigh, and join him on the fresh sod next to his even fresher grave. Hey, we're not exactly Leo and Kate on the bow of the *Titanic*, but when you and your boyfriend are both dead (sorry, *undead*), trust me, you take what you can get.

Part One
Two Weeks Earlier . . .

1
The Curse of Third Period Home Ec

My Home Ec class is cursed. Well, that is, if you believe my best friend, Hazel (who's always been a tad prone to histrionics, so—all I'm saying is maybe you shouldn't believe her).

We're now two weeks into Muffin Madness Month in Third Period Home Ec, but do you think that matters to Hazel? No, not one bit. How do I know? Because, while I'm stirring together the dry ingredients for our Mexican corn bread muffins, Hazel is *still* staring at Missy Cunningham's empty stool.

Just like she did yesterday, and the day before that, and the day before that.

And before she started staring at Missy Cunningham's empty stool, it was Sally Kellogg's. And before that, it was Amy Jaspers'. (Hmmm, come to think of it, there might be something to this Home Ec Curse after all.)

"Come on, Hazel," I say with mounting irritation. "Those eggs aren't going to break themselves."

"Ugghh." She sighs, sliding them over our flour-dusted cooking station so I can do the deed. "You know I'm a vegetarian. A *strict* vegetarian. Breaking eggs? That's like committing murder." When I raise an eyebrow, she counters, "Well, at least, poultry abortion."

Hmm, for a *strict* vegetarian, she sure didn't mind when I swung by to pick her up for school this morning with a bagful of Egg McMuffins on the passenger seat. I guess it's not really "egg abortion" once they're slathered on a hot steaming grill, fried in crackling grease, covered with Canadian bacon, and slid into a toasted English muffin with a bubbling blanket of American cheese.

I shake my head, not amused, and glance at the butter-stained recipe card before breaking in the four eggs. "Thanks for the help," I say, waving a floury hand in front of her eyes, which have glazed over completely while she's been staring at Missy's empty stool. "Hazel, seriously, enough with the whole Home Ec Curse thing, okay? It's been over a week of this now, me cooking muffin recipe after muffin recipe, you staring at Missy's empty stool. You're starting to creep me out already."

"Creeping *you* out?" She finally glances in my direction. "*You're* the one baking like there's no tomorrow, like nothing's going on here, like we're not in some kind of . . . *cursed* . . . Home Ec room."

"Cursed." I scoff. "Hazel, quit overdramatizing things. I mean, I know it's physically impossible for you not to make a mountain out of a molehill, but at least try. For me? Just this once? Statistically speaking, it's not even *that* big a surprise that we've . . . lost . . . a few students this year."

Hazel looks at me like I'm an alien pod person who's just inhabited her best friend's body and hasn't quite gotten a grasp of these things called human emotions yet. "*Lost*? What's that, some kind of code for 'not one, not two, but *three* of your fellow Home Ec students have *died* since the school year started'? Not gone missing, not run away, not gone on to star in an episode of *16 and Pregnant*. Died! As in, dead, forever, six feet under, worm food! And let me remind you, Maddy, it's only mid-October. That's, like, well, that's like one student a month! If that's not a curse, well, I don't know what is."

I'd look around to see if anybody is listening, but ever since our fellow students *have* started dropping like flies, Home Ec class really is a ghost town lately. Most students transferred out after Missy's accident last week, and the rest, like Hazel and I, really, *really* needed the easy A to round out our college transcripts. Otherwise, trust me, coolest Home Ec teacher on the planet or not, Hazel and I would have bugged out after "accident" number two.

"No, it's *not* code for anything," I finally answer, "but, I mean, accidents *do* happen." As I argue, I can't help but wonder who I'm trying so hard to convince.

"Yes, Maddy, accidents *do* happen—to old people, to sick people, to careless people, to reckless drivers, to stoners and drunks. But to little Missy Cunningham, who never crossed a bike path without a crossing guard in tow? To Sally Kellogg, who was so fat she could have fallen down a flight of stairs and bounced right back up without a scratch? And to poor Amy Jaspers, who, God love her, was so scared of her own shadow she only left her house to come to school and go right back home every day? Come on, Maddy. Wise up. I don't see why you're ignoring the facts. I mean, you're supposed to be the logical one in this best friendship. So why am *I* the one making the most sense right now?"

I give Hazel a knowing scowl and open my mouth to lecture her, but before I can, she sees where I'm headed.

"And, Maddy," she says, "please don't give me the 'I'm the coroner's daughter, I think I would know if our Home Ec class was cursed' speech again, okay? I've heard it three times this week, and I don't need to hear it again."

"Well," I say, using my frustration at Hazel's unreasonableness to mix the lumps right out of our muffins, "I *am* the coroner's daughter, and I like to think I *would* know if our Home Ec class was . . . cursed. There, I said it, but only because it's true, Hazel."

And it was. Back in August, Amy Jaspers fell into a ditch and broke her neck on the way to school one morning. Coroner's determination? Accident. Then, in September, Sally Kellogg choked on a chicken leg. Coroner's determination? Accident. And finally, last week, poor Missy Cunningham fell asleep while driving home after work late one night and drove into a light pole. Coroner's determination? Accident. It just so happened, all three girls were in our junior Home Ec class. (Emphasis on *were.*)

Hence, Hazel's new fascination with the fabled

Curse of Third Period Home Ec.

"Girls?" Ms. Haskins nods toward our oven timer, which indicates 15 minutes left. "Cutting it a little close this morning, aren't we?"

You know that one teacher in school who's cool enough to be your best friend? Who's hot enough to be your girl crush? Who's fashionable enough to be a guest judge on *Project Runway*? Who's smart enough to make Alex Trebek look like one of those clowns from *Jackass*? Well, at Barracuda Bay High School, that role is currently being played by none other than our Third Period Home Ec teacher, Ms. Haskins.

Ms. Haskins still has one of those young girl voices, a little throaty, a little scratchy, like maybe she could be a VJ on MTV or a spokesperson for a young, hip bikini company.

I mumble something about "stubborn lumps in our batter," and Ms. Haskins winks knowingly before moving on to the next table. The perfume wafting from her sultry departure quails on anything we could ever bake for her.

I look at Ms. Haskins as she walks away.

Hazel does, too. "At least Ms. Haskins is still in mourning," she says. "You could learn a thing or two about sensitivity for your fallen classmates from her."

I have to admit, ever since her Third Period Home Ec class became "cursed," Ms. Haskins' wardrobe *has* shifted from the fun, funky, vibrant red tones she wore the first week of school to a dowdier black-and-white and black-and-gray and black ensemble.

Today she has on sensible but stylish black pumps, a semitight gray skirt, a black beaded tank top under a matching gray, summer-weight blazer with black buttons. She always wears her hair up on cooking days, and today it's held in place with two black wooden chopsticks. And, of course, her glasses are black with sleek, stylish rectangular rims.

At last the muffins are done, and I open the oven to reveal a bubbling tin full of soft, crusty Mexican corn bread hissing steam and oozing another fresh A for dear old Table 2. The smell is enough to rouse even Hazel from her staring match with Missy's barren stool. She and I split the first muffin and share our approval.

Then I slice them, plate them, and promptly hand them over to Hazel. It's a tradition during "share time," the last 10 minutes or so of class when we go around the room sampling each other's mostly delectable muffin creations, that Hazel does the presenting.

Forget the fact that I did all the work, that I beat the eggs and sifted the flour and poured the batter and Hazel's done nothing but stare at Missy's stool all morning. This is Hazel's show, and I'm merely the assistant chef. After all, this isn't about Hazel getting us another A or Hazel pleasing Ms. Haskins or even Hazel helping me. As usual, this is *all* about Hazel.

Not that I mind all that much. In the 11 years since we've been best friends, ever since she walked up to me in my backyard one summer day and said, "I'm your new neighbor; we're going to be best friends. Any questions?" it's always been about Hazel.

Hazel the Girl Scout.

Hazel the wannabe fashion designer.

Hazel the head of Cheer Club.

Hazel the class secretary.

But that works for me. Hazel likes to be out front; I'm happy hanging in the back. Hazel likes to talk; I like to listen. Hazel likes bright pink; I like faded khaki. Hazel likes to make the introductions; I'm happy being quickly forgotten.

It's not that I'm a wallflower, per se. Far from it. I have my own style, low-key as it is, my own friends (okay, my own *friend*), my own passions, my own

pursuits. It's just that, well, none of them are quite as interesting—or quite so obvious—as Hazel's.

So we go around the classroom, mostly deserted now, the dozen or so students still brave, or stupid, or desperate, enough to sit in Third Period Home Ec sharing hooded smiles and muffin slices while Hazel works the room.

"Like the crusty tops?" she asks Table 4 with a flourish. "I added butter for the last five minutes."

Complete lie!

Mimicking pouring a can with her bubblegum-pink-painted fingers, she stage-whispers to Table 6, "The secret to the fluffy innards is leaving in *just* a little juice from the can of Mexican corn."

Also an utter fabrication.

At last we find ourselves lingering a few steps away from the darkest, coldest, emptiest corner of the room, and Hazel's show abruptly, unapologetically ends.

"Good luck," she whispers, already backing away from the dreaded Table 9.

"Come on, Hazel," I say. "Don't do this to me again. Just once it'd be nice if you came with me back here and had my back."

"No way," she says, inching back, back toward

the safety of Table 2 and our own little neck of the Home Ec class woods. "I tried that the first week of school, and he practically spit my pig-in-a-blanket back on the serving tray."

"Just . . . Hazel . . . please." My back is turned to Table 9. It's all to no avail. Already she's perched her ample rump on her tiny stool, arms crossed tightly across her chest and texting God-knows-who to keep from looking guilty (it's not working). And so it's up to me again to face Table 9 all by my lonesome.

Not that I blame Hazel, of course.

After all, it is here that Bones sits. Bones, he of the gangly six feet four, 160-pound frame, of the ever present white ski cap, even in Florida's trademark 90-degree weather, the shiny white track suit, and the spotless white sneakers.

But it's not his height or even his weight that earned him the nickname Bones. (Come to think of it, I don't even *know* his real name.) It's his nearly skeletal face. Pale as the white plate on which only a few slivers of our Mexican corn bread muffins now remain, his cheeks are hollow, his eyes shrunken, his lips razor thin and pulled back from his large, almost horselike teeth.

And his eyes—ugghh—they're this kind of filmy yellow, like maybe he hasn't quite gotten over some rare disease or something. I mean, I know I shouldn't make fun of a diseased person, and normally I *wouldn't*, but there's something so inherently unlikable about Bones that it's impossible to have any charity in my heart for him what. So. Ever.

I would skip Bones' corner altogether and get right back to explaining to Hazel why our Home Ec class *isn't* cursed, but it's not only how the muffins *taste* that affects our grade. Presentation is a big part as well. (Hence Hazel's weekly "come taste my world-famous muffins" tour.)

Out of the corner of my eye, I see Ms. Haskins watching my performance, so I stride right up to Bones who, high atop a stool at his station, subtly looks down on me. "Care for a nibble, Bones?" I don't know why I say it; it just comes out. Abject fear will do that to a person.

He snickers. "Anytime, Maddy. After all, you *do* look good enough to eat." His voice is deep, like black-hole deep, and dry; we're talking fall-leaf dry.

"Of the corn bread," I insist, deadpan, holding out the plate for emphasis.

He shakes his head.

"Your loss," I say under my breath as I turn around. I'm thinking, *Phew, at least that's over with for the week!*

Then he reaches his hand out to grab me, and it's like my arm's being dipped in ice water up to the elbow. The cold from his skin is jarring, not just unsettling or flinchworthy but actually jarring, and his grip is like a steel bear trap on my arm.

"Let . . . me . . . *go*," I whisper, struggling to break free. On my fourth or fifth yank, he finally unhands me and I would be sailing across the room if his better half, Dahlia Caruthers, weren't standing right there to catch me.

"Watch it!" She shoves me off of her and back into Bones.

I shiver again. It's like bouncing from one glacier to another. Gheez, they really need to work on the ventilation back here; these kids are freezing to death. (Maybe that's why they're so mean all the time.)

"Sorry. I was just offering Bones a taste of our corn bread."

Dahlia smiles, inching forward, her own plate held high. Whereas my plate is mostly empty, hers is almost completely full. I can see why. While, thanks to Hazel—or so she would have the class believe— our corn bread is fluffy and moist, tender and juicy, theirs is dry and thin, almost like Mexican biscotti left out for a month.

"Try a little of *this*," Dahlia says.

Though Bones is a decade out of style and centuries out of touch, Dahlia is on the cutting edge fashionwise, her violet bangs cut clipper-straight across her powdered white forehead, her lashes thick and black, her maroon lip gloss creamy and sparkly at the same time.

The weird thing is, and maybe *this* is why they're a couple but . . . *she* has yellow eyes, too. Don't get me wrong. They're much easier to take on Dahlia than they are on Bones, but who'da thunk the only two folks in Barracuda Bay High School with yellow eyes would hook up?

Her look is somewhere between Goth and glam, with a heavy dose of glitter and gloss for good measure. Today she has on high-heeled black wedges, burgundy hose, a leather miniskirt, and a sheer platinum bustier under a white leather jacket. Barely five feet five, she is Mutt to Bones' Jeff (or is it Jeff to his Mutt)? Either way, even though she's actually an inch shorter than me, she seems a foot taller, thanks, no doubt, to her brass balls and titanium confidence.

I notice that somehow Dahlia has managed to nudge me even closer to Bones. So now, with an oven on one side and a row of fake kitchen cabinets on the other, I am effectively hemmed into their dark little corner of our Home Ec universe. Over Dahlia's head I see Ms. Haskins bent over her grade book, her back to me, so I turn to Dahlia and grab a biscotti-slash-corn bread plank and take a bite to keep the peace and get out of this cold, dark corner alive.

Wow, it's bad. Deathly bad. Just . . . awful.

"Well?" she says.

I hear the stool slide out from beneath Bones. I can feel his eyes on my back as he stands to his full height; if we were outside, he might block out the sun.

I cough, then swallow dryly. "Not bad. I'm thinking maybe next time, less flour and more butter . . . you know, to make it a smidge flakier." (Did I just say smidge? I did, didn't I?)

I'm stammering, trying to find anything nice to say, when the bell finally rings. I smile, thinking, *Saved by the bell*, but Bones and Dahlia hardly budge. If anything, they move closer.

"Guys, seriously, didn't you hear? The bell. I'll be late to Art class."

Dahlia and Bones snicker as they gather up their books and stand to one side. Dahlia's yellow eyes grow small and suddenly cruel. The room grows ten degrees cooler, but between the two of them I might as well be standing in a walk-in freezer, so there's not much farther down the Celsius scale we can go here.

"Well," Dahlia says, "we wouldn't want *that* now, would we?"

"Quite right," Bones says. "The world needs more artists."

Dahlia looks around the room and settles her glare on me. "Yeah, Bones. Kind of like this class needs more warm bodies."

The laughter oozes out of them, like steam from fresh-baked Mexican corn bread (only colder, and deader, and not quite so steamy).

I open my mouth to say something, to defend my fallen classmates—Missy, Sally, and Amy—to preserve their honor against these, these . . . creeps . . . and they're practically daring me to. Like they *want* to talk about the Curse of Third Period Home Ec, like they can't wait to tell me something, anything, I don't already know.

It's something about their eyes, their beady yellow eyes, practically drooling (wait, can eyes drool?) over the chance to dredge up the Curse. But I don't let them. I *won't* let them; won't give them that satisfaction.

Instead I shrug and start to back away, not

realizing Bones has slipped a foot in the path of my retreat. I trip over it instantly, my hands instinctively dropping the plate.

The white plastic clatters across the floor, the noise sending Bones and Dahlia scurrying out of the room before Ms. Haskins can reach me. The last thing I see as they walk through the door is Bones bending down to low-five Dahlia's precious, perfect, pale little hand.

"Madison?" Ms. Haskins asks as I wipe corn-bread crumbs off my khaki skirt and put as many pieces as possible back onto the white plate before adjusting my peach scarf belt. "Are you okay?"

"Yeah, sure," I lie, flustered, eager to get to Art class, to stand up, to leave this chilly, dark corner of a room that, come to think of it, really *does* feel cursed. At least, at this very moment. "Clumsy, I guess."

She helps me clean up and we stand. I see the clock and rush past her. "I'll be late," I say, leaving her the dirty plate.

"I can write you a pass," she says, but I've already grabbed my denim backpack and am steaming out of class, head lowered, when I go down for the second time in less than an hour.

2
"Oooomph"

"Oooomph." This is what I say when I run into that yummy new kid on the way out of Home Ec. "Oooomph." Not "Excuse me." Not "Here's my number." Not even "We've got to stop meeting like this." Not something charming, clever, or sexy. Just . . . , "Oooomph."

But that's okay because as we both watch our books, papers, folders, and notebooks tumble to the ground in a whirling spiral of college-ruled paper and No. 2 pencils, he stands there helplessly and murmurs something like "Murrumph."

I look for Hazel for some help, but she's already on the way to Cheer Club practice by now. We're jostled by other kids a good dozen times as I watch the new guy's big, pale hands carefully separate his papers from mine. Not that he has many; I mean, the kid *did* just transfer here from Wyoming or Washington or some godforsaken place.

"I'm usually not so clumsy," I lie as he hands me my Home Ec handbook.

"My fault entirely," he says while I hold out his Barracuda Bay High schedule sheet. "I've been doing this all day."

"Really?" I quip before I can clamp my mouth shut. "And here I thought I was special."

He snorts, then looks self-consciously down at his ratty size-jumbo sneakers. Even though we're kneeling, snatching up and separating the last of our loose-leaf papers, he's tall; not Bones tall, but then who is?

He's slender but tight, like he's coiled to pounce on something—or someone—nearby. (*She wishes.*) His skin is pale and smooth but hard like marble, with a faint dusting of hair across the backs of his hands. He smells like cologne; something good but not *too* good.

He's dressed down for his first day: faded jeans and a rugby shirt with brown and blue stripes. It's tight across the chest but loose around the waist, and I only realize I'm staring when it's been silent for awhile and the halls are practically empty.

"Shit!" I stand at attention.

He follows me as I stand to my full height, but then he keeps going, a head or so higher once he's finally stopped unfolding.

"I'm going to be late." He looks stranded, helpless, the walls of Barracuda Bay High suddenly a maze, his books all stacked wrong and his schedule knotted.

I take pity and say, somewhat irritated (though trying to hide it), "Where's your next class?"

He frowns, unraveling his ruined schedule from between two teetering textbooks. "Art," he says without enthusiasm.

"Really?" I ask, tugging on his sleeve and steering him toward C-wing before falling into stride with his long, thin legs. "Me too."

"Not by choice," he adds defensively.

"Don't worry." I sigh. "Your heterosexuality is still very much intact."

"No, I just mean . . . you know what I mean."

"Art's not too big in Wyoming?" I say, rounding the corner.

"Nothing's too big in *Wisconsin*," he says, correcting me without formally correcting me, "except hunting, fishing, and . . . more fishing."

I smile and rush into class, dragging him across the threshold right before the final bell rings. Mrs. Witherspoon raises one gray eyebrow above her ridiculously round, incredibly red tortoiseshell glasses, until she sees the big kid lumbering behind me.

Then she winks, clears her throat, and announces theatrically (her default setting), "Cutting it a little close, aren't we, Maddy dear? Well, since you and your new friend are so late, I'm afraid you'll have to take the two last seats in the house. I hope you won't . . . *mind.*"

As I walk past, I try to avoid the jealous stares of all the other Art Chicks shooting me daggers, but there's something about walking into a class full of frustrated feminists with a big, tall, strapping jock by your side that makes me want to jump up on one of the black lab tables and shout, "In *your* face! In your *face*!" I restrain myself and slide into my chair.

The new kid sits stiffly to my left as if he'd rather be anywhere else in the world. His chiseled face is Midwest pale above his weathered collar, and I notice as he blinks rapidly that his eyes are an almost chocolate brown. Between that and the thick black hair, he might as well be a giant chocolate chip cookie. He fiddles with his books as Mrs. Witherspoon calls roll, and when she gets to the Cs and calls out "Crosby, Stamp," I can literally see the blush creep from his throat to his taut Wisconsin cheeks.

"Yes, ma'am," he says politely, eliciting twitters from the tough artsy crowd.

She smiles and corrects him. "My mother is called 'ma'am,' Mr. Crosby. So you shall call me *Mrs.* Witherspoon. Stamp, I'm sure you know the drill by now. Please stand and introduce yourself."

He groans so only I can hear him, and I kind of want to pinch his cheek while standing up and demanding Mrs. Witherspoon give him a pass just this once. I do neither and merely watch with the rest of my smitten Art Class sisters (plus the resident moody male, Dmitri Collins, who could be smitten, or bored, or asleep—It's hard to tell what with all the eye shadow).

Stamp stands to his full six feet (and then some). "My name is Stamp Crosby. I just transferred here from Waukesha, *Wisconsin*. I'm the new kicker for the Barracuda Bay Marauders." When we don't all stand up and cheer and flash our jugs, he sighs and says, "You know? Your school football team?"

That gets a few laughs, and I notice a few of the

Art Chicks start to swoon. (Witches.)

Thankfully, before he's allowed to go on in his entirely charming way, Mrs. Witherspoon clears her throat. "Thank you, Stamp. Very . . . interesting. Now, if you'll kindly take your seat, I'll explain today's assignment . . ."

Mrs. Witherspoon gives him a square clump of brown modeling clay and a picture she's cut out of some pet magazine that shows a fluffy little cat curled up in a soft, cozy bed. "Interpret this," she says cryptically before moving on without a backward glance.

Stamp shrugs in my direction and begins creating an exact replica of the picture. I watch his large fingers dabble with the clay, lots of it getting under his bitten-to-the-nub fingernails and the frayed edges of his rugby shirtsleeves. He's one of those guys who sticks his tongue out when he's concentrating, which I can't say I mind all that much.

Halfway through class, he's done with his cozy kitten and about to raise his hand to call Mrs. Witherspoon over, when I stop it in midair. "She said 'interpret' it, Stamp, not *copy* it exactly."

"What's the difference?"

I point to my own glob of clay in response. The

magazine picture taped to my workstation is of a simple tennis shoe, but my piece of clay has been twisted and molded and bent to look like a single shoelace coiled into the pose of a striking anaconda.

"What the heck is *that* supposed to be?"

I frown, looking at it with a new pair of eyes. "Well, it's *supposed* to represent the commercial oppression of the American shoemakers who hire cheap immigrant labor to manufacture their capitalist ideals of consumer confidence . . ." My voice trails off as his mouth opens wide and his eyes glaze over. I reel it back in and say, "Anyway, when Mrs. Witherspoon tells you to *interpret* something, you're not supposed to just totally re-create what you see. You're supposed to illustrate how the kitten makes you *feel*."

He nods, shrugs, nods again, says, "huh," really loudly like maybe he's in a room by himself, and then leans in, body heat shimmering off of him in warm, golden waves. Finally he murmurs to himself, "How do I turn a piece of clay into . . . happy?" He frowns at the prospect but then turns his clay cat into a (wait for it) smiley face. You know, the kind that Walmart used to use before it got too cheesy even for them?

When Mrs. Witherspoon finally rolls around to check out our table, she is *not* amused. I see the righteous indignation roiling inside of her, back there behind her big red glasses and above her flouncy red scarf. As she raises a trembling finger and gets ready to chew Stamp a new one, I momentarily catch her eye and, with pleadingly blinking eyelashes successfully derail her—at least for today. (You're on your own tomorrow, Stamp.)

She sighs, bites her lip, and says, "Very nice, Stamp. Very . . . *adequate*."

When she's gone, he looks at me, unconvinced, leans in, and whispers glumly, his breath Tic Tac fresh, "She hated it."

I snort a little and inch even closer. "There's always tomorrow."

He's laughing as we clean up our clay, but since he's a guy, and new, and a guy, his so-called cleanup takes many minutes fewer than mine, and when the bell rings, I'm still elbow deep in muddy, clay-filled water at the sink.

I try not to look too desperate as I glance toward our table, sending violently strong ESP waves across the room for him to *Wait up, Stamp! Wait up!* but already that Art class hussy tramp Sylvia Chalmers has his schedule in hand and is leading the way out of the room. I hang my head, dry my hands, and grab my books from our table—*our* table!

As I exit the class, Mrs. Witherspoon doesn't bother to look up from her latest copy of *American Photographer* when she whispers, "Careful, Madison. That one's got heartache written all over him."

I snort, linger by the door, and remind her, "Weren't *you* the one who told us every artist needs a broken heart to be any good?"

3
Rubbing the Grave

DAD'S STILL NOT home from his swing shift at the Cobia County Coroner's Office when I get home from school later that day, so I grab two apples from the fridge and eat one of them while standing over the kitchen garbage can. Although I dropped her off not five minutes ago, Hazel starts texting me before I can toss the apple core into the trash and reach for my phone.

What r u up 2?

I text back: *Wuz gonna do some rubbings in da g-yard.*

Two seconds later: *LAME! Call me l8r!*

I shrug, not really planning on it. (In case you haven't already noticed, a little Hazel goes a *long* way.) I grab my sketch pad and an old leather satchel hanging by the front door, walk outside, and lock up behind me. By now the sun's starting to think about setting, and already the mid-October air feels crisp and blue.

I wedge my oversized pad of expensive onion-skin paper beneath my arm, sling the satchel over my shoulder mailman-style, and start trudging down Pompano Lane toward the Sable Palms Cemetery, conveniently located at the foot of the hill.

Yes, I admit, it *is* a little strange to live up the hill from a cemetery, but not when you have a coroner for a dad. In fact, you might say it's fitting since most of Dad's customers, as he likes to call them, are currently resting in Sable Palms. Or, as he likes to say, even when he doesn't want to, he seems to bring his work home with him.

I pass Hazel's house on the way down the hill, trying to ignore her as she waves frantically from astride the StairMaster in front of the big picture window in the family's den-slash-home gym. Finally, I wave to keep her from bounding out of the house and following me down to the cemetery. (If there's one thing Hazel hates, it's being denied.) I can almost hear her delighted squeal through the hurricane glass.

A large cul-de-sac sits at the foot of the hill, on the other side of a two-way stop sign where Pompano Lane meets Mullet Avenue. I don't bother looking both ways, or even one way, before crossing the wide, empty street. This time of day, both streets are deserted, and even if they weren't, the cemetery is so quiet you could hear a well-oiled bicycle coming from 60 paces and crawl out of the way twice before it got there.

Only one of the big metal gates is still open. I spot Scurvy leaning on a dirty shovel, tapping his watch (though giving me a dirt-rimmed smile) as I slink through the open side.

"Cutting it a little close today, aren't we, Maddy?"

I hand him the extra apple from my leather satchel. "I don't know what it is, Scurvy, but that hill keeps getting longer and longer."

He ignores the lame excuse, takes the bribe, smiles, and downs the apple in four large bites. He tosses the core over the large wrought iron fence, and we both watch it land in the bed of his rusted-out, once-upon-a-long-long-time-ago lime green Chevy truck. It clatters around with the extra dozen shovels, hoes (not what you think), and hammers he keeps back there just in case.

Scurvy is the local gravedigger, and since he and Dad spend so much time together—coroner, grave-digger, dead bodies, funerals, cemeteries; you do the math—he's good enough to let me wander through the cemetery most evenings so I can do a few grave rubbings a week.

Scurvy is all of 28. Despite his scruffy name, he's anything but. He's tall and broad, beefy in his tan-on-tan cemetery uniform, arms bulging and skin ruddy from digging graves or landscaping or whatever it is he does all day.

His real name, according to Dad anyway, is Paul Delgado, but everybody in Barracuda Bay calls him Scurvy on account of his unfortunate teeth, which, as the name implies, are crooked, yellow, and big enough to resemble the headstones Scurvy tends to all day long.

As he fiddles with the large, jangling keychain clipped to his faded leather belt, Scurvy eyes my sketch pad eagerly and asks, almost shyly, "Got any good ones lately?"

I smile and flip the pad open to the middle, where I've carefully folded one of my latest grave rubbings. I hand it to him gingerly. Even coated with a special polymer from the art supply store, the paper is brittle and the thick black chalk easily smears.

"This was a . . . a . . . recent one," I explain without really explaining.

I don't need to. He reads the name above the brief dates—1994 to 2011—and says, "She was a friend of yours, right?"

"Amy Jaspers? Not really, but . . . we did have Home Ec class together."

He stares at the rubbing, his forehead wrinkling, his leathery tongue licking his tombstone teeth. "I gotta tell ya," he finally says, "I've been doing this since *I* graduated from Barracuda Bay, Maddy, and there's a big difference between digging a grave for some old geezer who's lived a long, full, happy life and some young teenage girl who gets cut down in her prime."

Then he looks me up and down, and then past me, into the dark, still graveyard. "You take care of yourself, Maddy. I know you kids don't believe in things like curses nowadays—"

"Oh, you'd be surprised," I murmur.

"But between you, me, and the headstones, something's not right about this town; hasn't been since the school year started."

With that, he carefully rolls up the rubbing and hands it to me before trundling through the open cemetery gate. "Same deal as always," he shouts over his shoulder, leaving the gate open just enough so I won't get locked in but tight enough so I can squeeze through and push it closed myself when I'm done. "Lock up when you're done." I count to six before he snickers and adds his nightly joke, "And don't forget to turn off the lights on your way out!"

I wait until I hear his engine fire up and chug off before I turn toward the newer part of the cemetery. The satchel full of masking tape, scissors, charcoal strips, and other grave rubbing necessities isn't heavy so much as it is awkward, so it's good they buried Missy Cunningham close to the cemetery gates.

I find her grave a few rows away from Amy's and a few more away from Sally's. Three high school classmates, three months, three grave rubbings, three identical dates: 1994 to 2011. (It doesn't help that those would be my dates, too . . . you know, if I died tomorrow.) I shake off the shiver, try to put Hazel's and now Scurvy's words out of my mind, and look at Missy's simple but honorable headstone.

It's granite. Most of them are these days. And there's a tuba etched on a brass plate in the corner (she was in the band). But it's the dates that get you the most: 17 short years. I don't care who you are—

rock star, millionaire, supermodel, or second chair tuba player for the Barracuda Bay High School Band—that's not enough time.

I sit down, dig into my satchel until I find a soft wire brush, and then clean off the face of Missy's headstone. It doesn't take too long, and it's important that it be free of debris, especially here in Florida, where fresh (and even not so fresh) seagull droppings can turn a simple grave rubbing into a Jackson Pollock print in no time.

Next I tear a fresh sheet of onionskin from the sketch pad and tape it at the top and around the sides of the headstone so it stays stationary. Finally, I sit in front of the tombstone, crossing my legs over one another and slowly, systematically rub across the stark white paper with a fresh piece of charcoal.

By the time Missy Cunningham's name has been etched into the clean, white paper, the sun has gone down and the streetlamps ringing the paved sidewalk around the cemetery have all flickered on, one by one. It's still not enough light to see by, but as long as I set up the rubbing before dark, all I have to do is keep rubbing, so I'm still in pretty good shape.

Crickets are chirping and my stomach is rumbling by the time I'm through with the etching. I carefully peel off the tape, roll it up, and slide a rubber band around the crisp onionskin tube to keep it smooth, tight, and, above all, clean. But even when I'm done and hungry and should be back home greeting Dad at the door with something fresh and hot out of the oven (yeah, right), I can't stop staring at those short dates right under Missy Cunningham's name: 1994 to 2011.

"Tragic, isn't it?"

I turn, even in my panic careful to keep the tops of my sneakers from smudging the fresh rubbing, only to see stupid Bones sitting on a nearby gravestone, watching me with his beady yellow eyes.

Leaning on the next gravestone familiarly, Dahlia smolders at his side.

"W-w-what?" I ask, rapidly standing up and dusting off my jeans, the memory of that morning's tumble in Home Ec still fresh on my mind.

Bones doesn't move, only sits there in his ridiculous white track suit. "I said it's tragic, dying so young like that."

"I dunno," Dahlia says, menace in her radiant yellow eyes. She's changed into a formfitting black sweat suit that accentuates all of her petite curves, and silver sneakers that add an extra inch to her height. "Some girls just . . . deserve . . . to die young."

"N-n-no one deserves to die that young, Dahlia," I say over the blood pounding in my ears.

"I dunno," Bones says. "I mean, it's not like anybody really misses her. Maybe it was good Missy died so young. Who wants to live a sad, lonely old life?"

"Of course people miss her." I stand my ground. "Her parents; I think she had a younger brother; I *know* she was one of Ms. Haskins' favorite students."

"Look at her grave, Maddy." Dahlia points almost accusingly at the stone.

I hold up the rubbing and say, "I've spent the past two hours looking at her grave, thanks."

"No," Bones says, "she means, *really* look at it."

Their gleaming yellow eyes, darker, brighter, angrier now that the sky has grown black, leave no room for argument.

"W-why?" I ask, gathering my things without making a big show of it.

"Just . . . *do* . . . it," Dahlia says.

So I do, and even before I turn all the way around, I see what they mean. Upon closer inspection, the headstone's not real granite; it's fake. Like the fake flowers in the fake brass vase screwed to the fake granite tombstone.

"Okay, so her parents weren't millionaires. Doesn't mean they don't care."

"Look at the grass," Bones says. "No one but you's even been to this grave this week. You'd think, someone dies that young, kids from school would flock here, weeping and leaving teddy bears and somber poems full of teen angst, lighting candles in her honor. And yet, nobody comes; nobody . . . cares."

"I care," I say defiantly.

Bones shrugs, looks at Dahlia.

Dahlia shrugs, looks at Bones.

"If you care so much," Dahlia says with steel in her voice, "then maybe we should do you a favor and let you join her."

The air is suddenly chill.

"Why would you even *say* such a thing, Dahlia?" I say.

Bones, who's been sitting on the headstone, slides off like ice cream melting from a cone. "Maybe she's right, Maddy. I mean, who would miss you, besides Hazel, that is."

Dahlia walks to his side and says, "Yeah, you've got no boyfriend, don't belong to any clubs, and if one more person in Ms. Haskins' Home Ec class were to die, well, what's the big deal? They'd say, 'It was only Maddy; it's not like she'll be missed.'"

Bones is laughing, the sound crisp and creepy. "Yeah, once Hazel got over it, no one would ever think twice."

My skin is alive with blood, my throat flushed through and through. And I know the fresh rubbing of Missy's grave is already ruined as I clench down, down around its middle. And I hate them, and I fear them; not because they're creepy or ugly or mean or stupid or bullies, but because . . . they're . . . right.

Who would miss me? Okay, Hazel, sure. Dad, of course. But . . . then who? Scurvy? Seriously? For a week or two, maybe, until some other morose teenager came along trading him apples to do grave rubbings (maybe even *my* grave rubbing), and then I'd be old news. Ms. Haskins? Mrs. Witherspoon? And . . . who else? Nobody. Five people, a single handful, and three of them would only miss me out of pity. Only Dad and Hazel would really care.

But the worst part is, these creeps know it.

And now Bones and Dahlia are slinking forward, one to the left, one to the right, and the threat is closer. Not just the words they're saying, which . . . they can't really be serious, right? They're kidding, pulling my leg.

They must have heard Hazel and me whispering about the Curse of Third Period Home Ec this morning. When they stumbled across me lurking in the graveyard after dark, well, they'd pretty much get drummed out of the Ugly Bullies for Life Club if they passed up that opportunity, right?

Behind me, a twig snaps.

As I turn to see who snapped it, a voice says, "Leave her alone." Not loudly; it's barely above a whisper, and it's over before I see Dane Fields standing to my right.

His eyes are either black or gray; it's hard to tell with the shadow from his hood covering them. His pale, prominent cheekbones make his face more angular than soft. On his size-11 feet are beat-up black sneakers with knots in the laces. His grimy gray cords are either so out of style they're cool again or so newly stylish they're hip; either way, they've been part of his uniform since he transferred here this year.

To Dane's left stands his girlfriend, Chloe Kildare, who's an inch shorter than Dane and twice as thick.

Bones is still walking forward, though slowly now.

"You heard him," Chloe says. "Scram!"

I give Chloe a good once-over, since even though she seems to be protecting me, she's not even looking at me. She's dressed all in black, which is her way; big black slacks, big black boots, big black jacket, death metal T-shirt with a touch of blood red, black lipstick, black hair like a helmet around her death white face.

"Says whom?" Dahlia says, though I notice she's stopped now, too.

"Says *who*," Dane says through the thin slit between his pale, gray lips, and I smirk hearing a tough guy correct someone's grammar. Then I speedily wipe off the smirk before Bones or Dahlia can see and hate me even more. "And *we* said, that's *who*."

Bones and Dahlia look at each other and laugh. No, that's not quite right. *Cackle* is more like it. That's what they do; cackle. A cackle fit for a graveyard; fit for a witch, or a ghost, or a girl who takes a class that's been cursed.

Bones and Dahlia swiftly go from cackling to growling, literally, their lips peeling away from their teeth, their teeth gnashing like animals', and I can feel Dane and Chloe creep forward menacingly before one of them says, "Beat it, losers."

More cackling, more growling, as Bones finally

crooks a long, candle-waxy finger and looks at Dahlia and they disappear into the shadowy bushes just off the sidewalk. In the darkness I can see their horrible yellow eyes aglow as they make a hasty, if unwilling, retreat through the dense shrubs lining the outer cemetery.

I wait until I'm sure they're gone before I turn to Dane. "Thank you, guys. I don't know what happened. I was just—"

"Better run home to Daddy"—Chloe picks up my pad and hands it to me—"before you piss somebody else off."

"B-b-but that's just it." I grab my pad from her. "I *didn't* piss anybody off. I was just sitting here doing a grave rubbing, minding my own business, when those two showed up."

Chloe looks over at Dane, who's hovering around Missy Cunningham's grave. "I suggest you take up another hobby then, Maddy. I don't think the graveyard's . . . *safe* . . . for you anymore."

4
A (Way!) Decent Proposal

"Oooomph," I say for the second time that day, dashing out of the graveyard with my satchel clutched in both hands, looking behind me to see if any of the creeps from the cemetery are lurking behind.

They're not.

A deep, sultry voice oozes, "We've *got* to stop bumping into each other like this."

I look up, exasperated, and say, "Stamp?"

It's half question, a third statement, a fourth shock, a fifth shame, and a sixth frustration. (And a seventh *va-va-voom!*) He takes it all in stride and looks dazzling doing it with a cockeyed grin and that little Superman curl dangling just-so.

He helps me up off the curb where I've landed, sprawled amidst my crumpled sketch pad and assorted grave rubbing tools. He flips through a few of my previous rubbings. "That's quite a sunny little hobby you've got there, Maddy."

I snort and snatch things away like *he's* the one I'm pissed at instead of Bones and Dahlia. (Or is it Dane and Chloe? So many creeps, so little time.)

"Do you always go around running into girls after school?"

"Not always," he says, still bemused as we stand there awkwardly across from the cemetery gates.

I'm still waiting for four pale goons to come out and stalk me all the way up the hill home, but they never do. At least, not where I can see them.

"But I *do* like to take a good run after practice," he says. "And, by the way, *you* were the one who ran into me—*again*."

I take a breath and look him up and down. He's in clingy sweatpants and a white V-neck T-shirt, also cling-a-licious. "Hold up." I sigh. "You're *running*? After *football* practice? On *purpose*?"

"Yeah, it's a little something we athletes like to do. It's called 'staying in shape.' You should try it sometime; you might like it."

"Yeah, I run." I want to flex my (some have called) shapely calves or something to prove it. "Just not in the middle of the day when you could run into any old person standing innocently on the street."

"You weren't standing." He corrects me (adorably), that half smile plastered on his pale face with those apple cheeks. "You were basically *sprinting* out of that graveyard. I have to say, for someone who does grave rubbings, you sure seem to hate graveyards."

I edge farther and farther away from the cemetery gates and start stomping up the hill, if only to distance myself from the graveyard creeps.

He follows me, step for step, as we walk shoulder-to-shoulder up Pompano Lane.

"Sorry," I say, more quietly this time, less frantically. "I'm normally not such a klutz."

"Me either. You must have that effect on me."

Then he stops short, and I do the same, like we both know he said something too goofy, too sweet, too soon. Then we start walking again, stride for stride, as if it never happened. Although, of course, now the whole time, I'm thinking, *Did he just say what I think he said? That I had an . . . effect . . . on him? On him? The hottest new guy to enter school since Dane Fields, the last new hot guy to enter school? And is he still walking beside me? And am I still having some kind of an effect on him? And what kind of effect, exactly?*

The hill isn't very steep, or long for that matter, but it seems to take us forever to climb it—in a good way.

"Are you okay?" he finally asks as we approach Hazel's house a little farther up the hill. "I mean, not to brag or anything, but I pretty much sent you flying halfway across the street down there."

"I'm fine, and besides, I leapt part of the way just to protect your manhood."

"How kind."

I try to avoid looking at Hazel, who's waving frantically out the window of her den-slash-home-gym, where she's still astride her mechanical stair-climber.

"I don't want to get overconfident the next time I bump into a girl sprinting out of the graveyard and she only goes six feet instead of twelve."

"Let me get this straight," I say, if only to change the subject and keep his mind off of Hazel and her spazztastic performance in the window directly behind me. "You go to school all day, go to football practice right after school, and then . . . run . . . some more?"

He looks down earnestly and says quietly, as if suddenly he's entered a confessional, "It's a new school, Maddy. I'm the new kicker. I just want to make sure I'm good enough."

I snort and say authoritatively, as if I keep track of such things, "We were, like, ten and two last year, Stamp. I think you'll do just fine."

He laughs and corrects me, "That means ten wins and two losses, Maddy; that's practically undefeated."

I stand in front of my dad's county-issued station wagon, looking twice as stupid as I feel. "Oh, I thought it was losses first, wins second. So that's . . . *good* . . . then?"

He nods emphatically, a drop of sweat landing at our feet. "That's, like, *really* good."

There's an awkward silence as I sneak a peek inside our house to see Dad puttering around in the kitchen. He's got a frying pan on the stovetop and an open loaf of white bread. My stomach almost rumbles as I think, *Sweet. Grilled cheese night.*

As Stamp regards the drop of sweat at his feet, through the window I watch Hazel surprise Dad as she slips in the back door and practically jumps him in the kitchen. That little minx. She must have been so curious about why Stamp was walking me home from the graveyard that she literally *leapt* off her stair-climber, snuck through six of the neighbors' backyards (three of which have pretty big dogs and one of which I think has an electric fence), and let herself into our house just to get the scoop.

"Maddy?" Stamp is saying as I watch Hazel make shushing motions to Dad while they both peer, rather obviously, out the side of the bay window overlooking the lawn. Stamp sounds kind of impatient, like maybe he's been talking and I haven't been listening.

"Hmmmmm?" I say absently, moving directly in front of him so he can't see the two clowns in my kitchen currently playing the world's most obvious game of I spy.

"Did you hear what I just said?"

I frown and bite my lower lip. "No, I'm sorry. Did you . . . say . . . something?"

Looking exasperated, he says, "Yeah, actually, I said a *lot* of things. Like . . . that Aaron Franks is having a huge party tonight. And that, you know, if you weren't doing anything, that maybe you could show up and that way, you know, we'd both be there at the same time." Now it's his turn to frown and bite his lip.

"Wow, you really said all that? Just now? I can't believe I didn't hear any of that. Not a single word. And I'm usually a pretty good listener."

He nods and says something halfway between

sure and *yeah* that sounds a lot like "Shhh-yeah."

Suddenly I zero in on one word and ask, "Tonight?" Because I'm already wondering if Dad will have a late shift and how I'm going to get there and what color panties I'm going to wear (you know, just in case), and before I've resolved all those issues I see Stamp's sweaty, glistening bicep poking out of his T-shirt and think how nice that would be around my shoulders in less than six hours. And so I blurt, "Sure, why not?"

He looks way too relieved and like maybe he's about to say something terribly sweet, but then he must all of a sudden remember he's a guy, so all he says is "Cool." And, just like that, he simply turns around, waves over his shoulder, and chugs off down the hill. Like maybe we're best buds and I just told a fart joke and he realized he was late for something, and so that's that: gotta bolt.

I watch him go—well, a certain part of him go, anyway—until I can't see that perfectly shaped derriere anymore, and then I turn to find Dad and Hazel standing in the doorway, looking at me like I've sprouted horns and a bright red nose and it's Christmas Eve. "What? Can't a girl talk to the hottest guy in school and not get hassled for it?"

The hassling commences shortly, inside the door. Hazel and I take seats across from each other in the breakfast nook while Dad's finishing the grilled cheese sandwiches he started before Hazel snuck in a few minutes ago.

"Tell me how you just happen to bump into the new kid—the *hot* new kid—twice in one day," Hazel says, eyes wide like it's some kind of once-in-a-lifetime event on par with Halley's Comet or a solar eclipse.

"You mean you already bumped into this fellow once before, Maddy?" asks Dad, holding up his greasy plastic spatula like a reporter's notebook.

I shrug. "Yeah, I mean—"

"The first time was right after Home Ec," Hazel answers for me. While I'm kicking myself for telling her about the first Stamp collision, she says, "That one I can write off to coincidence. But twice? In one day? That requires a smidge more explanation."

"I *can't* explain it, Hazel; that's the thing. I was just strolling out of the graveyard after finishing a grave rubbing, and he was running home from football practice and—*bam*—we bumped into each other."

"He doesn't sound very coordinated, dear," Dad says as he flips the grilled cheese. "Are you sure this is someone you should really consider boyfriend material? I mean, what if he asks you to the Fall Formal and trips while you're making your grand entrance? You only get one of those, you know."

Dad's thick, black bifocals are slipping down his nose as the grease sizzles from the pan. He's faintly smiling, like maybe he's playing with me. When I open my mouth to defend Stamp, he merely winks and returns to making dinner.

The minute it's ready, Dad eats with gusto; he does everything with gusto. I watch in amazement as he makes quick work of his own sandwich before eyeing ours hungrily. Hazel, who avoids cheese at all costs (and eggs, apparently), is only nibbling her first half to be polite. (To me, she can say—and do—anything. To Dad, she's the picture of Miss Manners.)

When she catches him looking at her sandwich, she lies. "Mom's making meat loaf tonight, and I'd feel bad if I filled up over here. Would you like mine, Mr. Swift?"

"Oh," he says, nose crinkling with delight, "only if you *insist.*"

She slides it over and eyes me suspiciously as I make short work of dinner.

Upstairs, after I do the dishes—and Dad's god-awful greasy pan—Hazel interrogates me some more as we linger in my bedroom. "You're sure he didn't ask you out?" She sits cross-legged on my bed, toying with the tassels of an aqua blue throw pillow. "It looked like he asked you out. I mean, I can kind of read lips, and he definitely said the words 'you' and 'out' in the same sentence."

I laugh. "No, he didn't ask me out and, no, there's nothing to tell."

Now, I suppose I should feel bad for not squealing to Hazel about everything the minute it happens, because we're best friends, right? But we're not *that* kind of best friends. We're not frenemies or anything like that. It's just that, well, Hazel's used to being the pretty one, the popular one, the one with a boyfriend, the one who tramps off to Fall Formal every year while I take the pictures in the yard, eat a pizza in my sweats, and wait by the phone until she gets home so I can hear how much fun she had.

She doesn't do well when the spotlight shines on me, which it rarely does, but . . . still. Like when Mr. Humphries, our History teacher and the guy who runs the school elections every year, misunderstood us sophomore year and printed *my* name on the ballot for class secretary instead of Hazel's.

Now, a *true* best friend would have laughed it off and cheered me on because it's not like we were running for secretary of state or something, right? But not Hazel; she flat-out *demanded* Mr. Humphries print all new ballots and threatened to write a letter to the editor of the local paper called "Voter Fraud Dampens Barracuda Bay Class Elections" if he didn't.

He did, I bowed out, and . . . that was pretty much that.

So ever since then, the small things in life that *do* happen to go my way—an A+ on a term paper (especially when Hazel gets a B), a free video at Mega Movies, an extra $20 in my birthday card from Aunt Maggie in Texas, the hottest boy asking me out to a party Hazel doesn't even *know* about—I tend to keep all to myself. Hazel has enough good things in her own life; she doesn't need to horn in on mine.

And this party tonight? If Hazel heard about it? Please. She'd be there with bells on, making a scene, taking things over, bending Stamp's ear, and then it would no longer be *my* little thing but Hazel's Big Show—and we'd all be the audience. No, thanks; not this time; not tonight. *Not this one night.*

I mean, you don't understand; things like this

don't happen. Not. To. Me. I'm the girl hot new guys jump over to bump into *other* girls on their first day of school. I'm the girl guys ask to a party just so I'll bring Hazel along. I'm the girl who misses bumping into the hot new guy a second time by a millisecond and then watches, helplessly, as the girl he *did* bump into becomes his hot new girlfriend for the rest of junior year.

But for some reason, today of all days, *I* was the one who got to bump into him; not once, but twice. *I* was the one who got to walk up the hill with him, flirt a little, and get asked to a party.

Soon enough he'll realize I'm not the kind of girl he should date, that I'm not hot enough or popular enough or easy enough or sexy enough. But for now, for this one night, for this moment, Stamp just doesn't know that yet.

For whatever reason—the peach scarf belt, the sparkling conversation, the bending of time to make this my lucky day—he thinks good old Maddy Swift is good enough to invite to a party, and if that's all I've got before he finds out differently, well, I'll be damned if I'm going to waste the time turning it into the Hazel Hour.

Several thousand questions later, she shakes her

head, disbelieving, as I follow her down the stairs. Dad is puttering around the kitchen, eating from an open pint of ice cream with a clean spoon, as we enter the foyer. He smiles, caught.

"What'd I tell you about that after-dinner snacking, Mr. Swift?" Hazel says, patting his tiny potbelly.

He says, in his own defense, "But it's reduced fat, dear."

She frowns teasingly, hijacks the scoop, and eats the bite of ice cream. (Hey, as a strict vegetarian, she's definitely got ice cream on her list.)

He pats her on the shoulder, steals his spoon back, and resumes snacking, fat and Hazel be damned.

We leave Dad to his dessert and I shoo Hazel out the front door. She waves over her shoulder, her thick red pigtails bouncing as she walks down the hill toward her house. It's a nearly nightly event, but who's complaining?

I slip back inside and see Dad's made us two bowls of ice cream. I have a few bites but am already wondering how I'm going to fit into that pleather skirt I'm planning to wear to Aaron's party, so I shove my serving over his way. He scoops it up greedily in three big bites and says, "So, Maddy, should I be as worried as Hazel is about your new beau?"

I blush. "Dad, seriously, he's *not* my boyfriend. We were just . . . talking . . . that's all."

"You know," he says, peering over his bifocals at me with those insightful green eyes, "having a boyfriend is one thing, but I've never seen you so giddy before. You know I love Hazel; she's one of the family. But if she were in my family, I might not be as forgiving."

"What do you mean, Dad?"

"It's just, Maddy, you're a good girl. You've always been a good girl. Hazel is a different animal altogether. I know her parents run a little looser ship over there, and I don't often remind you of it, dear, but when you turned sixteen, I only gave you three house rules, remember?"

Oh God, Dad's three house rules. How could I forget? He reminds me every other day or so. "Rule Number 1: no dating unless you've been formally introduced to the boy." I add, "Or girl, whatever," just to keep him on his toes.

He smiles, but only begrudgingly.

"Rule Number 2: my curfew is now and forever shall be 11 p.m. And Rule Number 3?" I sigh. "No sneaking out. Ever."

Dad smiles but adds forebodingly, "I love you, Maddy. That's why I want to protect you. If you were a coroner, if you saw the way the world treats people—so cruelly, day after day—you'd want these rules for your daughter, too. They're simple, really. And, of course, no need for me to remind you that the penalty for breaking any of these house rules is no talking to Hazel for 72 hours and no driving for a week."

I nod grimly. He's only caught me once, but it was brutal. Not the no-driving part so much, although when he says a week he means a full 7-day, 168-hour week. Not 6 days because I've learned my lesson or 167.5 hours because he's feeling generous, but one entire week. What was worse, believe it or not, was the no-talking-to-Hazel punishment. That was the longest 72 hours of my life.

I gulp a little, thinking ahead to breaking *all three house rules* in one single night. "Any particular reason you're reminding me of these rules tonight, Dad?"

He chuckles. "No, dear, other than the fact that you haven't heard a word I've said all night."

5
Raindrops Keep Falling on My Dead

D AD'S LAST-MINUTE warning echoes in my mind long after he's finally fallen asleep and I'm slipping into that snug little skirt that's been hanging in the back of my closet since, well, forever. Sure, I heard everything he said, and yet I'm still breaking all his rules.

Well, what would *you* do? (Yeah, that's what I thought.)

Even though I'm practically palpitating at the thought of Stamp at the party, I take it nice and slow, not wanting to get caught and lose my car or contact with Hazel for any extended period of time. I creep downstairs, hovering around Dad's bedroom door to make sure he's snoring. I'm so careful about this that even though he *is* snoring, and loudly, in a way that is almost un-fake-able, I tiptoe away and then sneak right back, just in case he's faking. He isn't.

Back upstairs I fold up a five-dollar bill (you know, in case there's some kind of cover charge) and slip it into a black cocktail purse I bought for last year's Fall Formal but never used (for reasons we don't need to go into here). I add my house keys, a compact, and some lipstick and slip the purse's long handle over my shoulder, messenger bag style. Then I slide open my well-oiled window (thanks to a can of WD-40 tucked under my bathroom sink behind a bag of cotton balls and a wall of Noxzema jars), and I climb stiffly down the old oak tree.

It's not something I do often, thanks to Dad's Three House Rules, but when your dad works the night shift and you've got a popular best friend like Hazel, well, let's just say I've found it's good to be prepared—just in case. Outside, the street is dark, solemn, and deserted, and the stiff breeze makes me happy I wore my black hair up in a simple ponytail.

It sucks that I lied to Dad, straight to his face. It sucks even more to be breaking his house rules behind his back, but when life sends you messages in the form of running into a six-foot-tall hunk twice in one day, it's best to start listening. (And better still to start acting.) Maybe Stamp is playing me, maybe this is all some big prank, but I don't think so. He seems sincere and friendly, and even if nothing at all happens tonight—not a single kiss or snuggle or peck on the cheek—at least I'll have something to tell Hazel tomorrow morning for a change.

I hug the curb, taking a left from Marlin Way onto Palm Street, where in the distance, another six blocks or so away, I can see Aaron's house high on the hill, overlooking Bluefish Bay and all lit up like a Christmas tree. I use it as a beacon, walking as the crow flies and taking shortcuts through backstreets and the occasional alley to save myself some time, not to mention the wear and tear on my white stockings.

The first jangling thrum of thunder sounds as I'm creeping through Mullet Manor, but by now I'm so fixated on the twinkling lights of Aaron's house that I can't be stopped. The road feels cool and slick beneath my sensible flats (thank God I didn't grab the heels I bought to go with the skirt). Whenever I feel like I've lost my way, I look up and the lights on the hill lead me ever onward.

The moon is still high, the cloud cover intermittently blocking out the huge silver orb, but by this point I'm too close to Aaron's house to turn back now. Only a few more blocks and I'll be at the foot of his hill.

The rain starts as I'm slinking through the back alley behind the vegetable stand. It starts slowly at first, little pebbles falling on my new white top that I hope will just go away. That happens in Florida: the sky can suddenly open up and dump an inch of rain in five minutes and then, just as rapidly, go back to being beautifully blue and scrumptiously dry.

It's clear this isn't that kind of storm as the rain goes from a sprinkle to a steady, fine drizzle. It's not splat-in-your-eye or knock-you-down heavy, but the drumming monotony is almost even *more* annoying. Even with the sensible ponytail, my hair goes from frizzy to split ends to drenched, my flats start picking up and putting down in toe-high puddles that get longer, and deeper, with every step.

The thunder is heavy and hard now, much too hard to be out in, but the first sign of lightning seems so far away I'm positive I'll be at the top of Aaron's hill, safe and dry, before it gets here. Wrong again. Thunderclap by rumble-boom, puddle by pond, the lightning keeps getting closer and closer.

Still, it's either keep going or turn back, and I'm

much closer to Aaron's house than my own if I just . . . keep . . . going, so that's what I do. The funny thing is I'm almost there, rounding the thickest part of Crescent Cove and within spitting distance of Aaron's street when the lights go out. All the way. I hear the thunder, see the lightning, and then— *zap*—no picture, no sound, no . . . nothing.

Now, I've lived in Florida all of my life, gone swimming in the rain, watched lightning from the bay window, and never flinched; heard it flash and sizzle close enough to make the hairs on my arms stand up, but I've never had it strike so . . . close . . . before.

I wake up a few minutes later, facedown in a puddle (gross), shake the muddy water off my chin, and sit up. The rain is a slight mist now, the Florida air still thick with humidity but barely a cloud in sight. The moon is high, and I look at my hands in the shimmering silver light: muddy. The sleeves of my blouse? Even muddier. I look down at my chest. Not only is it muddy, but it's completely see-through, straight through to my push-up and vital cushion bra, and I can only imagine myself showing up at Aaron's party in a wet T-shirt. (Okay, wet peasant blouse, but . . . still.)

My heart sinks. I grab the compact out of my

little black purse and open it to stare back at my pale, expressionless face, struggling not to cry. I look like death warmed over. I'm not kidding.

The mud is the least of it. My hair is limp, my makeup is obliterated, my lipstick is completely faded, there are big circles under my eyes, and is that? Is that . . . *really*? Why, yes it is—there is the slightest whiff of . . . smoke . . . coming from the top of my head. I groan, stand up, and straighten myself out. There's no way I can go to Aaron's party looking like the Little, Wet T-shirted Engine That Could.

I think of the party, the red cups, the beer, the lights, the house music, and that beautiful, glistening bicep attached to that beautiful, glistening Stamp, and I slowly turn for home.

I mean, what would *you* do? Run straight up the hill anyway, all wet and muddy, and shout Stamp's name over and over? Trust me, I'd love nothing better than to do just that, but desperate as I am, even I have (some) standards. By now it's late, I'm wet, I'm cold, I don't know how long I've been out, and I want to get home and sort things out before lightning strikes and I go down again.

That's the thing, though. The dark, brooding sky's not spewing lightning anymore; it's not even thundering. What's more, the moon was overhead when the storm started; now it's nearly halfway across the horizon. I must be imagining things, or maybe it's the cloud cover getting in the way.

Then I look up to Aaron's house on the hill and it's completely dark. Not dimly lit, like in a romantic way, but bleak, lights-out, everybody-go-home dark. Great. The party gets canceled, I walk for half an hour in the rain, and nobody bothers to tell me?

It's still raining as I head for home, and I'm kind of starting to wonder what that "hissing" sound on the top of my head is. It doesn't hurt at all, just sounds a little like fresh burger meat sizzling on a hot summertime grill.

I can tell I'm a little stiff. Okay, but who wouldn't be after a nighttime jaunt in a tsunami? I mean, lightning strikes nearby, you get knocked on your butt, you're gonna feel a little bad, right? It isn't until I get home and check my heart rate that I realize I'm not just stiff; I *am* a stiff.

6
You Might Be a Zombie If . . .

THE HOUSE IS quiet after my late-night sneak-out. Unfortunately, so is my entire chest cavity. That's right: no pulse, no heartbeat. By the time I look in my bedroom mirror to make sure I haven't scratched myself or broken an eye socket bone or something, I suddenly realize the reason rain was sizzling when it fell on my scalp: there's a huge black hole burned into the top of my head.

That's when it hits me: Lightning didn't strike *near me*; lightning struck *me*.

I bend down in front of my mirror to examine my scalp. The rainwater on my clothes is dripping steadily on my bedroom carpet, but—guess what?—priorities, people! Where the scalp should have been fish-belly white underneath my hair, it is scorched tough black. A smooth, almost perfectly round circle is sitting right there in the middle of the top of my head.

I reach my pale, pale hand toward it and, after a few false starts, touch it. It feels rough but solid, almost like the top of a quarter. Some hair around the burn hole has gotten singed. In fact, now that I'm inside and my bedroom window's shut tight, I get that first whiff of just-moved-your-arm-hair-too-close-to-the-Bunsen-burner-in-Science-class smell, but it isn't *too* bad. (I mean, not when compared to the pass-out-in-a-mud-puddle-wake-up-with-no-heartbeat thing.)

Then I look at my face. It's muddy, but what's worse than the mud streaking down my cheeks and plugging up my nose (eewwww) are the deep black smudges under my eyes. I mean, I wasn't down *that* long, was I? Not enough to look so . . . bad . . . all of a sudden.

I can't take staring in the mirror anymore, so I look at the digital clock on my nightstand instead. Wow, big mistake. It says 1:48 a.m. But that . . . that can't be right, can it? I mean, I only snuck out at 10:30. So let's do the mental math: 5 minutes up the street, another 15 or 20 minutes or so through back alleys and side roads, 25 minutes or so to make the trip back after the party got canceled, so at the latest it should be 11:30. *Maybe* midnight. Tops. But nearly 2 a.m.? I lean on the vanity, add everything up, and realize I wasn't facedown in that mud puddle for a few minutes; I was there for a few *hours*.

Suddenly everything changes. Seriously, how does one stay alive with her face down in a puddle for a couple of hours? So that means . . . I *have* to be dead, right? But here I am, back home, safe in my room, looking at the clock, the lights on, my feet on the ground . . . so how can I be dead and still standing? How can a dead girl walk home from a party she never got to, climb up a tree, slide open the window, climb inside, turn on all the lights in her bedroom, and touch the sizzle hole on the top of her head?

At first I think I must be—don't laugh—a ghost. I mean, how else do you explain getting up and walking away from a direct lightning strike in the middle of the night? But I can't pass through walls like a ghost would, and when I look in the mirror there I am, looking straight back. Sure, a little worse for wear but not exactly ghostly, if you know what I mean. So what *am* I?

How can I be dead—no heartbeat, no pulse—and *not* be a ghost?

What else *is* there?

Well, there's this: I'm not breathing, either.

Not that I do it all that often, but usually when I climb up the old oak tree outside of my window, leap from the top branch into my room, and slide the window shut, I'm out of breath. Not winded like I've just taken the Presidential Fitness Challenge in PE but, you know, definitely exerted. Now?

Nothing.

I didn't exactly realize the no-breathing thing on the way home because, seriously, the no-heartbeat thing had me kind of preoccupied, but now? It's becoming a pretty big deal. I mean, my lungs work but only when I think about it and actively suck in a breath.

I try it. Big breath in, big breath out, like the doctor makes you do every year for your end-of-summer physical. Great. Works fine. I even try whispering: "Testing, testing . . . one, two, three." Fine, okay; I may sound stupid, standing in my room at nearly two in the morning, every light on, me still dripping wet, counting to three, but at least I know

I can still talk.

Then I do a little experiment: I stand in front of the digital clock, wait until it magically turns over to 1:52 a.m., and hold my breath. That's right: plug my muddy nose, purse my lips tight, make a puffer fish face, and . . . just . . . wait.

1:53

Nothing.

1:54

Nil.

1:56

Nada.

2:00

Still nothing. After a solid 8 minutes (I would go all the way to 10 but I'm starting to get a little bored), I finally open my mouth and—nothing. No big exhale, no big inhale; I don't feel lightheaded, not short of breath, not . . . anything.

Maybe I should be calling 911 or something. You think? Because it's been, what, 15, maybe even 20 minutes since I got home. (Not to mention the two-plus hours I spent in a mud puddle.) What if I'm in shock? Or hallucinating? What if I *don't* report what happened and I lie down, go to sleep . . . and never wake up again?

But what do you say on a call like that? "Yes, Officer, uhhm, listen, I know you're going to think this is a prank and it may sound a little crazy, but I've been dead for a few hours now and I'd *really* like to talk to someone about it. Is there, perchance, a grief officer standing nearby? Or maybe a lightning specialist on call? Perhaps a voodoo priestess or witch doctor on retainer? Or maybe even someone familiar with Ouija boards? What's that? No, actually, I *don't* need the number for Psych Services, thanks very much; I need someone to come out and—hello?"

As I pace my bedroom, shaking my fingers out as if moving my body will somehow kick-start my heart, I feel a shiver pass through me. It isn't quite a shiver, though; not exactly. It's more like someone has turned the thermostat down—inside my body; like I've gone from 98.6 degrees to 68.9 in zero seconds flat.

What.

The.

Hell?

Naturally, I go online. I start by Googling the keyword "lightning," hoping some site, somewhere, will explain, well . . . something. You know, like maybe there's a blog out there somewhere called www.youarenotdeadMaddy.com that will list all the symptoms of a lightning strike with the final diagnosis being "Have some warm milk, Maddy, get some sleep, and in the morning your heartbeat and lung capacity will return, and by the time you pick up Hazel for school, you'll forget this whole thing ever happened." (Okay, maybe not *that* personal, but . . . still.)

Believe it or not, I do *not* find such a site.

I *do* learn a few nifty things about lightning, though.

Case in point: Did you know that the typical lightning bolt contains over 1 million volts of electricity? That some can even have up to *30 million volts*? Now, on the other end of the spectrum, did you know it only takes about 5,000 volts in those little Vaseline-covered defibrillator paddles for a doctor to bring you back to life in the ER?

So, if only a few thousand volts can save a life, why wouldn't one million—let alone 30 million—give you . . . the afterlife? I mean, could *that* explain why I've got no heartbeat but am still, technically anyway, alive?

But what creature of the undead has no pulse?

Can lie facedown in a puddle for two hours?

Doesn't need to breathe?

I know vampires *have* to have a pulse because, let's face it, blood is their god.

And werewolves, well, you *always* see them breathing heavily after chasing some mere mortal down and snorting out globs of phlegm and drool when they attack, so they *must* have some pretty decent undead lung capacity.

Ghosts? Been there. Not that.

Mummy? No Egyptian curses or toilet paper wrapped around my legs.

Frankenstein? No mad doctor anywhere around that I can see.

There is only one remaining possibility, so with trembling hands I Google "what are the physical traits of a zombie?" and, once I get past all the *Night of the Living Dead* links, I discover a helpful little site called www.youmightbeazombieif.blogspot.com.

Amazingly, there's a quiz called "You Might Be a Zombie If . . ." and, unbelievably, I actually take this quiz . . . with a totally straight face and my tongue out, as if my very life—*Afterlife?*—depends on it.

Here's what I come up with:

QUESTION: HAVE YOU RECENTLY
EXPERIENCED AN ELECTRICAL ANOMALY,
SUCH AS SLAMMING INTO A POWER LINE,
BEING TASERED BY THE COPS (WHILE
STANDING IN A PUDDLE), SPENDING THE
NIGHT AT A POWER PLANT, GETTING STRUCK
BY LIGHTNING, ETC.?

ANSWER: YES. *And thank you for using "anomoly" in context.*

QUESTION: HAVE YOU RECENTLY LOST
CONSCIOUSNESS FOR AN EXTENDED PERIOD OF
TIME ONLY TO AWAKE FEELING . . . STRANGE?

ANSWER: *I know I shouldn't answer a question with another question, but . . . does lying facedown in a mud puddle for two straight hours and waking up with no pulse count?* YES.

QUESTION: IS YOUR HEART CURRENTLY BEATING?

ANSWER: NO. *Seriously, not even a little.*

QUESTION: HAVE YOU EXPERIENCED ANY
SHORTNESS OF BREATH RECENTLY?

ANSWER: *Does no breath count as shortness of breath? If so . . .* YES. *And I'm still experiencing it.*

QUESTION: ARE YOU EXPERIENCING COLD FLASHES?

ANSWER: YES. *And they're actually getting colder.*

QUESTION: HAVE YOU BEEN ABLE TO SLEEP SINCE THE ELECTRICAL ANOMALY?

ANSWER: NO. *And it's the middle of the night and I'm not even tired; not even a little.*

QUESTION: DO YOU HAVE AN INEXPLICABLE, SUDDEN, AND OVERWHELMING DESIRE TO EAT . . . BRAINS?

ANSWER: *Uhhm, not until this very minute, but . . . now that you mention it . . . as a matter of fact . . .* YES. I. DO.

After I answer all the questions and hit enter on the final page, the screen goes blank. At first I figure, *Great, no heartbeat, no breathing . . . now no electricity. What next? A sinkhole's going to swallow up the entire house?* But every light in my bedroom is still on, the air-conditioning is still blowing, and my computer is still humming, so *that's* not it.

Then red spills across the monitor and the following message pops up:

WARNING:

Your answers suggest that you MAY be a zombie. New zombies MUST ingest fresh brains within 48 hours of reanimation or risk returning to the dead . . . forever.

If you do not wish to remain a zombie, skip this step. If you still have the will to live, sorry, <u>YOU MUST EAT BRAINS.</u>

7
Brains on Aisle 9

YOU KNOW, SURPRISINGLY, they don't sell a lot of brains in the local 24-hour grocery store around the corner from my house. And, believe it or not, they don't really like it when you ask about them. At least, not the sleepy college kid working the only open cash register the night I become a zombie.

Standing at the counter in my high ponytail, freshly laundered yoga pants, hoodie, and flip-flops, I try to look him in the eye. "Hi, yeah, listen, uh . . . Tad? Tad, I'm looking for, well, see, my, uhhm . . . grandfather . . . is coming into town this weekend, and he really likes, well, believe it or not, he *loves* brains. Don't look at me like that. I guess they ate them on the farm when he was growing up or something, but . . . do you know where I could find any?"

"Tad," or so says the name tag on his chest, looks past me, around me, out into the parking lot, and everywhere *but* at me before finally saying, "Very funny." Then he stares at me, as if to say, without words, "I'm too smart to be punk'd. Even if it is two in the morning and there's not another soul around for miles."

"It's not a prank, Tad. Seriously. I looked all over the meat department, found tubs of chicken livers, something called 'chitterlings'—not sure I want to go there—even a big, gray cow's tongue, but . . . no brains. So . . . do you know where I could find them? I mean, I'm asking as a customer"—here I hold up the insanely fat roll of $20 bills Dad keeps in a cookie jar in the kitchen in case of an emergency (which, I think you'll agree, this is)—"so I'm really *not* trying to prank you."

He sighs, reaches for a curvy microphone next to his cash register, pushes a button at the base, and says, "Harvey, I'm sending a live one back to the butcher for a few pounds of, get this . . . *brains.* Try to meet her there? We don't want her wandering around the store scaring off all the other customers." He snickers, but I don't care.

Visions of conking out halfway up the grocery

store aisle make me brave enough to storm back to the butcher's section and demand. My. Brains.

Harvey is waiting for me, a quizzical look on his sleepy face and a hairy wrist extended, his big silver watch showing past his bloody butcher's coat. "You know what time it is, missy?"

"It's 2:27 a.m.," I say, eyeing the old-school black-and-white clock above his head.

Harvey looks up and scratches at his hairnet. "Oh yeah, well, I shouldn't be on shift yet, but we've got a big shipment of rump roasts coming in a few hours, and who's gonna turn down a little overtime these days, right?"

"Sure," I say uneasily, having never worked a day in my life, let alone qualified for overtime. "Why not?"

He looks me up and down, frowning. "Brains? You sure? Lot of fat in brains."

Right when I'm about to tell him I'm a size 2, thank you very much, he holds up his hands and explains.

"Not that I'm saying you need to count calories or anything. Far from it. I know how you girls are these days. Well, here's the thing: I can't give you brains." Harvey must see my face fall to the dirty linoleum floor because he promptly adds, "Not *cow's* brains, anyway, on account of mad cow disease and all. And I can't give you pork brains, on account of swine flu. But . . . it just so happens the lamb hasn't been moving much lately so I can do lamb's brains, fresh as of two days ago. How many pounds?"

"Pounds?" I hesitate. The website didn't say how much brains—or even how many—I should eat, only that I should eat them in 48 hours OR ELSE. Why doesn't anyone pay attention to details anymore? Would it be so hard to add a simple line like, *BTW, Maddy, 3 pounds of brains per week is plenty*?

Seriously, am I the first new zombie ever to *ask*?

"Yeah, honey," Harvey is saying as I fume at the www.youmightbeazombieif.blogspot.com webmaster. "This is a deli right here; we weigh things by the pound."

"Well, how many pounds of lamb's brains can I get?" (Introducing item number one on the list of things I never thought I'd hear myself ask a grown man at 2:27 a.m.)

He rolls his eyes. "As many pounds as you need, darlin', but I gotta hear a number before I can start filling the order."

"Ten pounds," I blurt, half expecting the Butcher Police to come out from behind the gurgling lobster tank and bust me for brain abuse.

But no, old Harvey merely scratches his hairnet again like I haven't just asked for 10 pounds of mushy cerebrum meat and whistles softly around a soggy toothpick. "Ten pounds it is." He says it without judgment, disappearing into the back room through a series of five dingy plastic straps that hang from the top of the metal doorframe to the red-tiled floor.

I pace nervously in front of the steaks and cold cuts, chicken thighs, and pork loins while Harvey fills my order. Something by The Beatles is playing over the sound system; something instrumental and lame, but I can't quite figure out what it is. For a song that was most likely written (on rock tablets) the year my dad was born, it's surprisingly catchy. Lame, but still pretty catchy just the same.

I'm still trying to figure it out when someone says from behind me, "'The Fool on the Hill.'"

"Huh?" I turn around to find none other than Chloe Kildare staring back at me, black hair, black eye shadow, black eyeliner, black lipstick, black mole, black eyes, and all. She smiles, her pierced gray tongue flickering behind yellowish teeth.

"'The Fool on the Hill,'" she says. "That's The Beatles song you're trying to figure out."

"That's it!" I say it a little too loudly for the

graveyard-in-aisle-9 setting.

Chloe frowns, looks down the empty aisles to our left and right, and says, "What are *you* doing here?"

"What are *you* doing here?" I reply.

In case you haven't connected the dots by now, Chloe is Barracuda Bay High School's resident Goth Princess, so I guess it's really no stretch at all to find her lurking the aisles of an all-night grocery store at this hour.

I think of the last time I saw her, back in the graveyard after school, standing beside me and backing down Bones and Dahlia with little more than a finger point. Was she following me then? Is she following me now? And where is her boyfriend, lover, and/or constant companion, Dane? (Even waiting for 10 pounds of brains at 2:27 a.m., you hardly ever see one without the other.)

I surreptitiously peer into her little green plastic Greenbriers Grocers basket and see about what you'd expect a gaudy Goth poser like Chloe to be buying: cheap white makeup, cheap black lipstick, cheap black nail polish.

Suddenly Chloe looks down a side aisle, rolls her eyes, and sighs. "Hey, Dane, did you find them yet?"

Dane Fields, resident Goth Prince to Chloe's

Goth Princess, tosses some cheap black candles and a box of old-school wooden matches into her basket. "Yeah, just like you said, in aisle 6. Hey, Maddy, what are *you* doing here?"

"Funny," Chloe says as I shuffle my feet and smile up at Dane, "I just asked her the same thing. Still waiting on an answer, in fact."

I peer over my shoulder, hoping Harvey will take his time with that 10-pounds-of-brains order of minc. I inch slowly . . . *very* slowly . . . away from the deli and reach for the first thing on the nearest shelf. "Oh, nothing, you guys; you know, I just looked in my pantry and realized that I needed some"—only now do I look at what I've grabbed: a fresh can of athlete's foot spray (seriously?)—"of this here, and so I ran right out to . . . get . . . some?"

"How . . . domestic . . . of you," Chloe says, obviously not buying it for a second.

I'll give her this much: Chloe gives good sneer. She's tall to start with, but in her grubby black army boots and fishnet stockings, she's nearly as tall as Dane and pretty much towers over me. I try to read her face to gauge whether she's still mad after having to save my butt in the cemetery.

Chloe always looks mad, but she doesn't really

look any madder than usual, and from the way Dane is kind of puppy dog eyeballing me whenever Chloe isn't looking (or am I imagining things?), it doesn't look like he's all that bothered to see me, either.

Dane nudges her with a bony elbow and grabs a can of antifungal itch spray for himself, tossing it in the basket and looking at me. "I get that all the time, Maddy. You must have good taste; this stuff works really great."

If there is a polar opposite to Stamp Crosby's macho, rugged, handsome, frat-boy, varsity-stud, house-party, black-haired, brown-eyed look, then Dane Fields, with his pale skin, bony hips, long fingers, short blond hair, black jeans, white T-shirts, and ever present black hoodie is definitely it.

Which is why, I suppose, I've been secretly crushing on him (sssshhhhh) for months now; ever since he showed up for the first day of our junior year (with Chloe, unfortunately), all tall and moody and gray and mysterious and never once giving me the time of day. (Except, you know, when two creeps threaten me with bodily harm in creepy graveyards after dark.)

As the conversation, or lack thereof, grows awkward, I take one step farther away from the butcher's counter, kind of hide my can of athlete's foot spray behind my back, and say, "Listen, you guys, about earlier, you know, back in the graveyard—"

"You need to be more careful," Chloe snaps, cutting me off, as if she's been waiting to lecture me ever since. "Who sits in a graveyard rubbing head-stones after dark, anyway?"

"I like it," I say, a tad defensively. "It relaxes me and, besides, I've never had trouble before."

Chloe taps her left army boot against her right.

Dane explains, "What Chloe means is that, well, Bones and Dahlia are creeps, is all. So you should probably stay away from them."

I chuckle, but neither Goth is amused. "That's kind of hard, you guys. I mean, there are only, like, 600 kids going to Barracuda Bay High in the first place. What am I supposed to do? Get home-schooled until I graduate?"

Neither Goth answers. At least, not right away. We kind of shuffle our feet until Dane clears his throat and says, "Aren't you afraid of the Curse of Third Period Home Ec?"

I snort, out loud, all over them. "Not you guys, too?"

"I'm serious, Maddy. You're in that class; you know what's going on. I don't know how you can think three girls dying in one class—in three months—isn't enough to keep you out of a graveyard after dark."

"For starters, Dane, the Curse is BS. For another thing, all three girls died accidentally, separately, and nowhere near a graveyard. That's like me asking, 'Aren't you guys afraid of shopping in the grocery store after midnight?' Seriously."

"He's just saying, Maddy, there's a time to be reckless and a time to be careful," Chloe says. "With so many of our classmates dying, I think, well, now is the time to be careful."

I snort again. "Okay, well, I'll start being careful when you do."

Chloe opens her mouth to say something, but Dane stops her. They stand like that, lecture over, the sound of the flickering lights overhead punctuating the awkward silence.

Finally, I shrug. It's 2:27 a.m., I have no heartbeat, I can't breathe, and this is all getting a little too surreal for me. I figure I can ditch out on the brains—this was a stupid idea anyway—go home, fall asleep, wake up, and this will all be a bad dream.

And if not? Well, according to the zombie website (which, let's face it, could be run by a 5-year-old in Timbuktu using his mommy's computer and a stack of 20-year-old comic books as source material), I'd still have another 24 hours to come back to the store and pick up my order.

Inching away, I hold up my athlete's foot spray and wave it in the air so they can both see it, when out of nowhere a voice booms from behind me: "Here's your 10 pounds of brains, miss." In the very same breath, Harvey the butcher calls out, "Chloe! Dane! Back again?"

I turn to Harvey and say, "You *know* her?" just as Chloe turns to Harvey and says, "You know *her*?"

He carelessly hands me over three packages of heavily taped butcher paper that feel, well, exactly how you think 10 pounds of fresh lamb brains might feel. "Sure, I know her," Harvey says to me first. "She's the only other person in this town who puts in an order of brains that big before sunrise."

Chloe and I look at each other and, amazingly, she does not look sarcastic, rude, snide, crude, mean, salty, sassy, or even snarky, for that matter. "Hmmm." She eventually nudges Dane as she eyes my three bags of brains suspiciously. "Athlete's foot, huh?"

8
"Maddy, Do You Know?"

I'M HALFWAY ACROSS the parking lot when I hear footsteps behind me. Next to the pay phone, I look over my shoulder and see Dane and Chloe walking my way. I turn around, my Greenbriers Grocers bag held up defensively, but they just laugh and hold their hands up.

Dane says, "Maddy, do you know?"

"Know what?"

"Know what you are?" Chloe asks.

"A . . . high school junior? A . . . Capricorn? A . . . Geico safe driver? I'm all those things."

Dane chuckles while Chloe fumes. Dane takes a step forward, and I lower my bag. His eyes are gentle as he takes down his ever present black hood.

Instantly I see the dark circles under the eyes; then I see the pale skin. He takes off his hoodie and hands it to Chloe, who takes it without comment.

I stare at the ratty white T-shirt he's been hiding. "What *is* this?" I ask, trying to sound brave and flip and, I'm sure, merely coming off as too loud and annoying. "Strip grocery shopping? If it is, I have to tell you, I've got on 16 pairs of underwear, so you're going to lose big-time—"

He reaches out a hand, and I stop joking. Gently, he touches my bare arm. I don't know whose arm is colder: his or mine. (And I didn't think anybody's arm could get colder than mine.) He opens my stiff fist carefully until it's fingers out, palm down; then he guides my hand toward the center of his chest. I try to pull back, but for a skinny, pale, Goth boy, Dane is actually pretty strong. My body follows where my hands go, my sneakers squeak-squeaking on the concrete as he guides me toward him with some superpower tractor beam or something.

Finally he has my hand flat against his rock-hard chest, right over where his heart is. Or, at least, where it *should* be. "Feel that?"

"Feel what?"

He smiles, leaving my hand there even as I try

desperately to wrench it away, to avoid hearing what he's about to tell me, to avoid hearing . . . the truth.

"Exactly." He sighs. "No heartbeat." Finally he lets my hand down and, before I can slap his away, reaches for the precise spot above my sports bra and shirt where my own heart should be felt beating. I struggle to get away, but he follows me, back, back, his hand square over my dead, lifeless heart.

After a few minutes, he asks, "So, do you know . . . *what* . . . you are?"

I finally shove his hand off and stumble back a safe distance.

Chloe steps up. "You have to know, Maddy. Why else would a preppy girl like you be out so late at night buying brains at Greenbriers Grocers?"

"I-I-I'll tell you what I told the cashier."

"Yeah, yeah, your grandpa's coming into town, yadda yadda. That's bull, Maddy, and you know it. What's more, Dane and I know it. You're a zombie, Maddy, just like . . . us."

I open my mouth to protest, to yell, to holler, to deny, to . . . cry, but don't do any of those things. Instead I simply say, "How'd you know?"

Dane puts his hand back over his heart. "You can't fake a heartbeat, Maddy." He slips back into his hoodie. "Come on, we'll give you a ride home."

"Really," I say, backing away, "it's not very far and I'll be just—"

Chloe steps toward me. "We weren't asking."

I gulp and hold my bag-o-brains closer to my chest as I stumble along between them, Dane in the front, Chloe right behind me.

Dane leads us to a beat-up truck with primer splatters all over it. With an embarrassed smile, he says, "Your chariot awaits, madam."

Chloe slugs him on the arm and shoves me inside before climbing in next to me. Dane swiftly rounds the corner and slides into the driver's seat so I'm safely wedged between them.

"First things first," he says, strapping me in. "We need to get those brains on ice. Secondly, you need a copy of *The Guide*. Lastly, you need to meet the Elders, stat."

"What's the—?"

Chloe interrupts me with an elbow jab to the side. "We'll explain on the way."

9
Zombies 1 and 2

WE RIDE IN silence the whole way to their place. There is no more talk of zombie this or *Guide* that, or brains that or Elders this or, for that matter, the Curse of Third Period Home Ec. In fact, the mood in Dane's pickup grows slowly more somber the closer we get to the wrong side of town. Finally, Dane pulls the truck into the Mangrove Manor trailer park.

The truck trundles down the rutted road until we pull up in front of Trailer 17, a green-on-green number with a precariously leaning carport.

"Home sweet home," Chloe says, getting out and beckoning me to join her.

I stay put, clinging to my brain bag. "I really

need to get home, you guys. My dad will be expecting me, and—"

Dane shuts the engine off. "Maddy, listen, no one's going to hurt you. We're your friends. In fact, right now, in your . . . situation . . . we're the only friends you've got. There's a lot you need to know and not a lot of time to know it in. Frankly, even if we *wanted* to let you go now, we can't. There are things that need to be taken care of. Right now. That little zombie website you probably visited? The one that told you to eat brains right away? Well, that's only the beginning. We have a lot to do and not a lot of time."

I sit there, still nestled safely beneath my seat belt, and say, "If this is the Afterlife, then don't I have all the time in the world?"

Chloe laughs, leaning against the truck impatiently. "Oh sure, you've got forever to figure all this out. And it will take some time, trust us. But for now, for *right* now, it's our duty to get you checked out, report you to the Elders, and get you a copy of *The Guide,* or we're all in lots of trouble."

"Trouble?" I finally slide out of the truck. "What kind of trouble?"

"The permanent kind," Chloe says in a tone that

leaves no room for argument or, for that matter, any further questions. She tromps up the rusted steps leading to the front door and swings it open without knocking. I follow slowly, expecting a house of horrors inside. You know, skull candleholders buried in dripped black candle wax, dark red walls, black curtains over the sink, a goat chained to the corner for their next sacrifice—that kind of thing.

Instead, I find a spotless living room with (color me surprised) cherry hardwood floors, eggshell painted walls, and moderately sophisticated black-and-white wall art. A funky retro lamp featuring half a dozen arms is in one corner facing the door; a fake (but a pretty good fake) potted plant is in the other; and in between is a wicker love seat with a matching coffee table and two side chairs. It's kind of dorm chic meets runaway classy.

As I follow Chloe into the trailer, Dane tags along right behind me. With a gentle hand, he pries my 10 pounds of brains from me and walks into a small but clean kitchen. He pulls one of those Igloo Playmate lunch coolers from under the sink, dumps the ice tray from the freezer inside, and puts the brains on top before closing the cooler and setting it on top of a table for four.

There are only three chairs, and he pats an empty one. "Come here, Maddy." His gentle voice is deep and dark and three shades of, dare I say, sexy? "We have a few things to sort out before we get going."

I try to think of what he means by "get going" and have no idea. All I know is that I'm dead but not dead, that I'm a zombie but not alone. There are other zombies in this town, and should I be so surprised they're Dane and Chloe?

"First, an introduction is in order," Chloe says, pointing to herself. "I'm Zombie Number 1. Dane is Zombie Number 2 . . ." Her voice trails off, and they both look at me expectantly.

"I guess that makes me"—I swallow, twice, before finishing—"Zombie Number 3?"

Chloe smiles proudly, like I've just learned to spell my name in red crayon.

Dane explains in a conspiratorial whisper, "She's only Zombie Number 1 because she's the oldest." Then he slides out his chair and asks, "How'd it happen? I mean, I'm assuming it was tonight's lightning strike, but what were you doing out in it?"

"Jogging." I'm tempted to tell him more, to brag about Stamp and how the hottest new guy in school asked me to the hottest party of the week and how

I stupidly decided to walk there—in the rain, with thunder rolling in and lightning not too far behind—but something holds me back.

Chloe eyes me dubiously. "Jogging? In a thunderstorm? Good thinking, Maddy."

"Hey"—I laugh, trying to keep the lie in play—"it seemed like a good idea at the time."

But Dane's not smiling, not really. Not that he's a smiley type of guy in the first place, but now his thin lips are straight and set and he's looking at me very, very carefully. He opens his mouth to add something, or maybe even *ask* something, then pauses. His eyes are deep and dark and probing, like maybe he knows I'm leaving something—okay, a lot of somethings—out. Then he snaps out of it, blinks twice, and asks, "So, how'd it *feel?*"

I sit across from him. "I dunno, I was passed out for a couple of hours afterward, so . . ."

"The Awakening," he whispers almost reverently, like a geek sitting in the front row when the new *Star Wars* trailer comes on the screen.

"I'm sorry?"

"That was the Awakening," he explains, louder this time. "We all go through it. The time frame is different for everybody. For some of us it only lasts a few minutes; for you it was a few hours; some of us, like Chloe here, can lie there for days. That's why so many of us wake up in graves. If the Awakening lasts longer than a day or two, well, most folks assume you're dead. They just don't assume you're going to wake up."

"I don't understand. I thought zombies bit each other and you caught some virus in your blood and—"

"Bull," Chloe says. "Hollywood bull. You *can* bite someone and make them a zombie, but it's not what's in our blood that turns them. After all, you know by now your blood's no longer pumping. It's electricity; *that's* what turns them."

"It's why zombies can only date other zombies," Dane says, his voice steadily rising as he looks me in the eyes.

"That's crazy, though," I practically shout back, thinking of Stamp, of the way he looked embarrassed asking me to the party this afternoon, of how relieved he looked when I said yes, of his chocolate chip eyes and sporty bicep and how good it was going to feel around my warm, soft, undead shoulder. And how all of that is gone now, forever, and now these two are the ones to tell me all about it. And is it just me, or is Dane actually *happy* to tell me about it?

"*Is* it so crazy?" Chloe asks.

"Think about it." Dane's sitting up in his chair. "You're getting all hot and heavy with some Normal guy, you forget yourself in the heat of the moment, go to give him a little love tap on the neck, bite a little harder than you meant to, and—*zap*—just like that, meet Zombie Number 4. Is that what you *really* want for someone you supposedly care about?"

When I don't answer right away, he adds, "And let's say this Normal is one of those lucky zombies whose Awakening only lasts a minute or two, or maybe an hour. He goes home, he doesn't know what he is yet, and he's sitting there at the dinner table; instead of steak and potatoes he decides, in a weak moment, to munch on Mom and Dad. Meet Zombies Number 5 and 6. And let's say the neighbors stop by with a housewarming gift right then. Meet Zombies Number 7 and 8. And they go home and bite two friends, and they go home and bite two friends. It's how whole towns get infested, Maddy."

"B-b-but that's not fair. I'd be careful. I wouldn't want this for . . . anybody."

Dane waves a hand dismissively. "It doesn't matter if it's fair or not." He taps a thick, green book nestled between the salt and pepper shakers on the table. "The Council won't allow it. You're a zombie now, Maddy. Part of a very, very select group. We have rules, procedures, protocols, laws. Law Number 1, Maddy, is that zombies don't date Normals. Period. End of story. I'm . . . sorry."

"You don't *sound* very sorry," I snap.

"Maybe not, but I really am. I know it's going to be hard, that you'll have lots of questions. That's why we're here. We're your chaperones, Maddy. Your guides to the Afterlife." When I don't respond right away, he sighs and drums a little ditty on the big green book cover. "Did you tell her yet?" he asks Chloe, his voice low, eyes on me.

"Tell me what?"

Chloe shakes her head.

He frowns, then smiles. "No worries. We can tell her tonight; give her something to do on the long trip."

"Tonight? What trip? I've got to get home, you guys. I don't know about you two, but I've got a dad who doesn't know I'm a zombie, and school tomorrow, and—"

"Don't worry." Dane puts an ice cube hand on my Frigidaire wrist. "We have to go at night anyway; the Elders prefer it that way."

"Elders?"

He and Chloe grin.

"It's all in here," Dane says, sliding the big green book across the table. I glance briefly at the title: *The Guide to the Proper Care and Feeding of Zombies, 24th Edition.*

Oh, great. Even when you're dead, you get homework.

10
The Proper Care and Feeding of Zombies

"**I**'VE GOT A vocabulary test in second period," I complain as Dane cruises past the city limits at precisely 3:07 a.m.

Chloe rests her head against her seat. "Relax, Maddy, you're going to be back in plenty of time to make second period. Besides, let's say you miss the test; let's say you fail the class. Heck, let's say you fail your entire junior year. Girl, you've got the rest of eternity to take your junior year over—and over and over." She says it with a smile, like maybe that's what she's been doing for the last, oh, I dunno, 300 years or so.

"But I need to get some sleep if I'm going to do well."

Dane laughs, and they give each other another

one of their superior "inside joke" glances. "You wanna tell her, or should I?"

"You've got a better bedside manner," she says, and it's the first time I've agreed with her all night.

He sighs. "Maddy, I don't know if you'll think this is good news or bad, but . . . zombies don't sleep."

"Much?" I ask hopefully. "You mean, zombies don't sleep . . . *much*? Like Benjamin Franklin? Or Einstein? I hear they only slept four hours a night."

Dane is already shaking his head. "Zombies don't need *any* sleep, Maddy. Ever."

I look out the window, at the endless miles of dark road stretching out before us. "So what am I supposed to do all night?"

Dane shrugs.

"Well, you can catch up on your reading, for one thing," Chloe says, tapping *The Guide* in my lap. "I'd start with that."

After that the truck cab goes silent and I look at the book. Although it's dark in here, I can see the title on the cover as clearly as if the dome light were on: *The Guide to the Proper Care and Feeding of Zombies, 24th Edition*. I open it, flip to a random page, and read this:

> *Zombies in the first stage of the Assimila-*
> *tion (weeks 1 and 2 after their Awakening) can*
> *expect to feel the following: a gradual stiffening*
> *of their limbs as muscles solidify and harden,*
> *a yellowing of the teeth as oxidation ceases at*
> *the gum line, and shadowing under the eyes as*
> *blood flow to this region stops completely. . . .*

Sweet. Can't wait for the whole stiff-limb, yellow-teeth, shadow-under-the-eyes phase to kick in. I'll really be beating the guys off with a stick then.

I flip through some more pages and read this:

> *The zombie laws prohibit telling any*
> *Normal (i.e. a mortal human being) about*
> *said zombie-ism. Zombies are expected to*
> *"pass" among the general Normal population*
> *without incident, and those refusing to do so*
> *will be harshly penalized by the Sentinels. . . .*

Awesome. Even in death you still have to play by the rules. What, is there zombie detention?

Next I turn to page 74 and find this little nugget:

New zombies are expected to report to the Council of Elders within the first 24 hours of crossing over from the Normal world. Those who fail to do so will face serious repercussions from the Sentinels and potential exile to the post-zombie world. . . .

The *post-zombie world*? What's that? The Island of the Pale, Stiff, and Yellow-Teethed? A prison camp for bad zombies? I look up to ask Dane, but his face is serious and focused on the road. I go to ask Chloe, but the permanent scowl on her Goth face makes me think twice. Finally, I start at the beginning and read *The Guide* until I can't take it anymore.

"How far now?" I ask an hour or so later, holding *The Guide* tightly against my chest and rubbing my eyes.

"Not much farther," Dane says, "but the ceremony takes awhile." He eyes *The Guide* in my hands. "You read about it?"

"The Assimilation Ceremony for the Newly Animated? I read about it; sounds pretty official."

"It's basically to make sure you understand your rights and responsibilities as a member of the zombie race," Dane says. With a straight face. Like this is all really happening. Right now. To me.

I sigh. "I thought being dead would be . . . easier."

They both snicker.

"Being dead is easy," Dane says. "Being *undead* is what's so hard."

Finally Dane pulls off the interstate, makes a few sharp turns at the next three intersections, and has us pointed down a lonely strip of dirt road in the middle of nowhere. I have no idea where we are, but Dane seems unfazed by the rocky road and lack of visibility. There are no street signs this deep in the middle of the state, no road markers, not even streetlamps.

"How do you know where you're going?" I nervously bite my lip.

"Every zombie has to visit the Council of Elders before they're official," Chloe says. "I made the trip; Dane's made the trip. It's not hard to remember."

"I meant, how can you *see* out here?"

They look at me.

"Maddy," Dane says calmly, "we're only using the headlights for the protection of others. We could see this road—*you* could see this road—without the headlights."

To prove it, Dane turns them off. I open my mouth to scream, but Dane is actually right. I gasp.

Even without the lights, everything—the outline of the dirt road in front of us, where the line of trees ends, even how tall they are—looks crystal clear.

"Why is it yellow?" I ask, blinking rapidly as if the yellow "zombie vision" might suddenly clear up or go away.

"Nobody knows," Chloe says. "Something to do with the color spectrum is our best guess. The point is, zombies have excellent senses. Without your heartbeat and your lungs to drown them out, your other senses come more sharply into focus. We can smell for miles, see in the dark, and hear a mosquito fart two towns away."

"Lovely," I say as Dane flicks the lights back on. Moments later a large, rectangular building suddenly appears out of the dense brush cover.

"Here we are," Dane says, a tad unnecessarily. He sees me hugging *The Guide* and gently pries it from my hands. "They'll give you your own," he whispers, looking around suspiciously. "I'm not supposed to show it to anyone." As if to prove it, he hides it in the glove box.

I'm about to ask him why he's whispering when I suddenly find out. From nowhere, four armed guards approach the truck. They are not very old, our age, mostly, maybe a tad older, and dressed in solid blue uniforms, blue ball caps, black boots. Very official-looking, very grim, very . . . menacing; like Bones in boot camp.

"Sentinels," Chloe says as she rolls down the passenger side window. "They protect the Elders and enforce zombie law."

"Identification," says the Sentinel at the driver's side door.

Dane pulls out a laminated card with his picture and a number on it.

Chloe hands hers over as well.

The Sentinel looks at them both, then glares at me.

"She's new," Dane explains. "We're here for her Assimilation Ceremony. We called a few hours ago."

"How long?" the Sentinel asks me. His face seems carved of granite, his navy blue jumper hiding (but not very well) thick muscles and broad shoulders. "How? *Long?*" he says again, yellow teeth and thin lips spitting out the words one at a time.

Dane nudges me. "He wants to know how long you've been a zombie."

"L-l-last night," I stammer.

The Sentinel looks angry and about to shout out something else when Chloe says, apologetically, "We only spotted her this morning, when she showed up at the local grocer's looking for brains. We got here as fast as we could."

It sounds so odd to hear Chloe—surly, angry, bully Chloe—sound so meek as she talks to the Sentinel. She seems almost afraid to look him in the eye. Almost.

He looks from Dane to me, past Chloe, and out her window to where two more of his Sentinel friends stand. "Proceed to the main hall," he says in his croaky youngish but oldish zombie voice. "We'll alert the Elders you're on your way." The Sentinel slings his rifle back on his shoulder and salutes us.

We drive on. A few seconds later, I say, "I thought I read somewhere in *The Guide* how bullets can't kill us."

"The rifles aren't for us," Dane says. "They're for the Normals. You know, in case they wander onto the property or threaten to out us."

Dane puts the truck in park at the main hall, a low, slender, almost tubelike building in the center of the Council of Elders compound. The whole place has a community college campus feel to it.

When I mention that to Chloe, she nods. "It used to be a college until the Council of Elders bought it."

I'm about to ask how zombies make money or, for that matter, how they convince the state of Florida to sell them an entire college, but I figure I'd better prioritize my questions for now. Like Chloe says, I've got nothing but time.

More Sentinels guard the front door to the main hall, only now they've holstered their guns and stand at the ready with what look like phasers from that old *Star Trek* show.

"Stun guns," Dane whispers, following my gaze, "like the cops use."

"Wouldn't the rifles work better?" I whisper back.

"Not on us. The rule is if electricity brings us back to life, electricity can kill us again."

"So *that's* how zombies die?" I ask as Chloe opens her door.

"That," she says, leaning back in, "and physically removing the brain from the skull. Trust me, the stun guns are a lot less messy."

As I slide out, Dane taps his temple. "The brain's the power generator for the body. Take it out, no more power. No more zombie. No more life."

"Good to know." I smile, easing past him.

Four Sentinels flank me on the way into the main hall, two on each side. Chloe and Dane are stopped at the main door and told to wait outside. I look back at them helplessly, like a kindergartner being dropped off at her classroom on the first day of school.

The main hall is actually a gym, complete with accordion bleachers folded up and pushed against one wall and basketball hoops yanked up to the very high ceiling. The light is sufficient but not as bright as any I've seen in a gym before, where usually the rows and rows of ceiling lights are so bright you can see a wart or blackhead from all the way across the auditorium. I look up and see why; every other bulb has been left out of the dozen or so fixtures hanging high overhead.

The Sentinels guide me to a single chair directly in front of two fold-out picnic tables shoved together. Seated at the tables and facing me are six Hollywood movie-looking zombies. I try to keep from gasping and barely—just barely—manage. But it's hard.

One of the Sentinels, seeming to sense this, gives me a compassionate wink. "Just look at their ties," he whispers as he hands me my own copy of *The Guide to the Proper Care and Feeding of Zombies, 24th Edition.* "It makes it . . . easier."

I swallow and do as I'm told. Or, at least, I try to. They're all dressed in suits—gray suits, mostly; a few black—and stiff, white shirts. A tie dangles loosely around each fat-free neck. It's too hard not to stare at those old, skeletal faces.

These are your real zombies, your true immortals. Some of them have to be centuries old. One has no hair. I mean, he barely has skin. His eyes are deep and dark, his lips pulled permanently away from his teeth so that you can see the gray gums and large, yellow teeth and the dozens of wide spaces between. Another only has tufts of soft, white hair sticking up at all angles from his rawhide skull covering. Two more have wigs.

I look at the Elder in the middle and smile.

He clears his throat. "State your name, zombie."

11
The Zombie Pledge

I WINCE, NOT ONLY at his dagger-sharp voice but at being called a zombie by a true zombie. "Madison Emily Swift, sir."

Behind each Elder stands a Sentinel, erect as a two-by-four and ever wary, like we're at some fancy restaurant and each Elder has his very own personal butler. The Sentinel behind the Elder who asked my name types the answer into a laptop no bigger than most cell phones. The Elders may look last century, but at least their technology is cutting-edge.

"How long?" asks the Elder in the middle, who must be the ringleader.

"I turned last night, sir. I didn't, well, I didn't know about any of . . . *this* . . . until my zombie friends explained everything to me. We got here as soon as we could."

"Ignorance is no excuse," the Elder on the end says, wheezing.

"I know that now, sir."

He nods, satisfied. So does the Elder in the middle of the table, licking his lips with a dry, dead tongue.

Though every muscle of my head and neck wants me to look away, I look straight ahead and smile back.

With a voice as dry as crackling paper, the main Elder asks, "How much did your friends tell you, Madison Emily Swift?"

"Just, well, that there are rules, laws I must abide by. And those rules and laws are in *this* book." I hold up my own personal copy of *The Guide to the Proper Care and Feeding of Zombies, 24th Edition.*

He croaks, "Laws are all we have, Madison Emily Swift."

His fellow Elders murmur, a few of them nodding so severely I think some heads are going to roll, literally.

"Laws, Ms. Swift, are all that separate us from the Zerkers."

I raise my hand, and the main Elder smiles. Or, I think it's a smile; either that or his jaw shifted. (I hope he'll be all right.) "What are . . . Zerkers?" I ask.

There's a slight change in the room; the Sentinels behind each Elder stiffen, the Elders themselves seem to puff up slightly and, finally, the main Elder says, "The Zerkers are the worst of the zombies, Ms. Swift. That's why we don't even call them zombies. Zombies can talk, reason, drive, think, communicate, read that book you're holding, and . . . care. Zerkers *care* about only one thing: brains. About feeding their insatiable need for electricity. Read *The Guide*, Ms. Swift; read *The Guide* and you will know all you need to know about the Zerkers and how it is every zombie's duty to wipe them out, one by one."

I nod, clutching *The Guide* for good measure.

The Council nods, too, and one of them, the one with the powder gray wig, says, "Stand, now, and repeat after us."

I stand, tempted to put my hand over my heart, but I scan the gym and there is no flag in sight. Instead I kind of hug *The Guide to the Proper Care and Feeding of Zombies, 24th Edition* like a Bible to my heart as the main Elder says, "I, Madison Emily Swift . . ."

Slowly the others join him until the voices, old and creaky and wheezy as they are, sound like one, and I repeat them after each pause.

"I, Madison Emily Swift . . ."

"Do hereby solemnly swear . . ."

"To uphold the zombie laws and regulations as published in *The Guide* . . ."

"To the best of my ability . . ."

Then comes the final line: "Under penalty of death."

"Under . . . penalty . . . of *death*?"

The Council of Elders stands, with a little (okay, a *lot* of) help from the Sentinels behind them. With veiny hands that look more like Halloween party props, they manage a bony, mostly silent golf clap as I bow.

The four Sentinels who brought me in lead me gently back outside. I turn back around before we exit through the double gym doors. The Elders are still staring at me, smiling with their skeletal jaws, some of them still clapping until, at last, their Sentinels guide them slowly, very slowly, away from the table.

12
Ambushed

"WHAT'S A ZERKER?" I ask when we're nearly home. Beyond the dusty windshield of Dane's truck, the sun begins to rise.

Dane and Chloe share one of their "how could she be so stupid?" glances.

Dane says, "Didn't the Council explain Zerkers to you?"

"Of course they did," I say, "but obviously not well enough. I thought I'd eat some brains, hang out with you guys, get used to being celibate for the rest of my life, and that would be that. Now I find out there are these Zerker characters that aren't like regular zombies. That we're supposed to hunt them down and eliminate them. What's up with that?"

"They're not just 'not like' regular zombies, Maddy," Dane explains gravely as he signals to turn off the interstate and onto Marlin Way, the main road into Barracuda Bay. "They're not zombies, period."

"Well, what makes a regular zombie a regular zombie then?"

Dane looks at Chloe.

Chloe rubs her eyes. "The same thing that makes a kid get to school on time, or follow the rules, or not drown live kittens: a conscience. Regular zombies are like regular people, only dead, reanimated regular people. Zerkers have no conscience; they don't read *The Guide*; they don't visit the Elders, register with the Book of the Dead, or follow the rules."

"Why not?"

Dane says, "The thing about Zerkers is, they aren't personally reanimated; they're turned."

"Huh?"

"Take you, for example," Dane says. "You wake up yesterday morning, all was right with the world. You go to school, eat your lunch, gossip with Hazel; you're the All-American Girl. But for whatever reason you *stupidly* decide to go jogging in a thunderstorm and, zap, you're struck by lightning. That's Reanimation in the First Degree. You, personally, received a pure dose of millions of volts of electricity and went from being alive to being undead. However it happened to us—to you, to me, to Chloe—we were all three Reanimated in the First Degree."

"Zerkers," says Chloe, "aren't born; they're made. In other words, some zombie who was Reanimated in the First Degree turned them. So they're not born of pure energy; they're Reanimated in the *Second* Degree."

"Sort of like when a vampire turns one of us, and we're never as strong as he is, or powerful, or—?"

"Not quite," Dane says with a sour expression. "For one, there are no vampires. What are you, crazy? That's pure fiction. Second, Zerkers are usually more powerful than we are because rather than ordering animal brains from Harvey at the all-night deli, they get them straight from the source."

"What, like, the cattle processing plant?"

"More like some poor soul's skull," Chloe says. "Zerkers rob fresh graves; they dig up the dead; and, when they're feeling *really* destructive, they feed on the living, too."

"You mean, Zerkers kill . . . people? Like, real, live . . . human people?"

"Not just human people, Maddy." Chloe rubs

the spot between her eyes right above her nose. "Zerkers like to stalk people; they actually *enjoy* killing people. They pick somebody close to them, say, a neighbor, or a cashier at their favorite grocery store—"

"Or someone in their Home Ec class," Dane says pointedly, but I'm too overwhelmed, too shocked, to process that particular scenario.

"Or someone in Home Ec class," Chloe continues. "And they'll toy with them for awhile, you know, like a cat with a mouse. Stalk them for a few days, bump into them in class, pop in on them in the graveyard—any of this sounding familiar yet? Anyway, they basically try to scare the pants off of them, and then when this person—or student—can't take it anymore, when their brain is literally frazzled, the Zerker strikes, chomp, and . . . good-bye, brain."

Dane takes over. "They say the hunt, the chase—all that fear—makes the brain more electrified so that when they finally crack open their victim's skull and scoop it out, the brain is twice as powerful as if they'd snuck up on somebody and conked them over the head."

Suddenly I'm thinking of Hazel, of all those empty seats in Home Ec, of the Curse—and who might *really* be behind it. "Who would *do* such a thing?" I ask, not really expecting an answer.

Dane slams on the brakes and the truck fishtails, the end swinging around to the left as we dig into a slide in the middle of the road. I look to see what made Dane brake, only to see Bones and Dahlia standing in the middle of the road.

"Who would *do* such a thing?" Chloe says, flinging open her passenger side door and leaping into the road before the truck has even stopped moving. "You're looking at 'em."

"Fancy meeting you three here." Bones cackles, rubbing his large, pale hands together like he's getting ready to dig into an all-you-can-eat brains buffet.

Beside him, Dahlia looks petite but powerful in her all-black outfit and higher-than-normal heels. Under the waning moonlight, their skin is almost porcelain white, the hollows under their eyes deep pools of sadness, fear, and death.

"What do you want, Bones?" Dane says, rising from the truck almost casually and standing shoulder-to-shoulder with Chloe. There's a relaxed but practiced manner to their movements, like maybe they've done this before. I join them on the road, hanging slightly back, just in case.

Bones takes a step toward me. "Why, what we've

wanted all along, Dane. Her, of course."

Chloe steps in front of me while Dane moves to my side. "Nice try," Chloe says. "She's already been assimilated, Bones. You're too late, as usual."

"Assimilated," Dahlia says, as if she's uttering a curse word. "Like *that* matters."

"Maybe it doesn't matter to you Zerkers," Dane shouts, "but it matters to us zombies."

"Please." Bones stands his ground, his white track suit shiny and his eyes grim under his soft white ski cap. "Let the Elders make their rules and we'll make ours. You're in Barracuda Bay now, Dane. The Elders can't help you here."

"Maybe the Elders can't, Bones, but the Sentinels sure can."

Bones and Dahlia laugh.

"The Sentinels." Bones mocks. "The Keystone Cops is more like it; they couldn't catch a Zerker with two hands tied behind his back."

"Or *her* back," Dahlia says indignantly.

"Too right," says Bones distractedly. "Too right. Besides, we're through playing nice. Give us the girl, or the Truce is off."

"What Truce?" Dane says, spittle flying from his mouth as he steps forward threateningly. "You think we're blind, Bones? You think we don't know what's been going on around here?"

Bones opens his mouth, and a scary smile spreads across his stiff, white face. "Why, whatever do you mean?"

"The *students*, Bones," Chloe says. Then she starts ticking them off one by one, as if she's crawled inside my head and onto my bedroom wall and is reading them off my very own grave rubbings. "Amy Jaspers. Sally Kellogg. And now Missy Cunningham. Are you guys *that* stupid? It's not bad enough you go cracking skulls in Barracuda Bay High School, but you have to pick them all from the same class? You didn't think anybody would notice?"

Dahlia smiles, giving nothing—and everything—away. "So what if we did crack a few skulls, Chloe? Like we told your little friend there, they were girls nobody would miss. I mean, it's not like they were popular or anything. And even if they were, what are *you* going to do about it?"

Chloe takes a step toward Bones. "Maybe we can't do anything about it on our own, but the Elders sure can—"

Bones shouts, "Enough with the Elders. So what if we broke the Truce? So what if a few local girls have a few . . . accidents? Nobody's putting two and two together; nobody's come asking questions, and the Elders couldn't care less. We want the girl, Dane, and we want her now. If you don't hand her over right now, there *will* be consequences."

"Not happening, Bones," Chloe shouts just as loudly. "And if you break the Truce again, know this: there *will* be consequences."

Bones and Dahlia look at each other and shrug.

"Don't say we didn't warn you, zombies," Bones says as he retreats back into the woods near the side of the road.

"Just remember, Maddy," Dahlia whispers forcefully before following Bones. "They can't protect you all the time. Sooner or later, you're going to have to face us alone. And *then* whose empty stool will Hazel be staring at in Home Ec?"

13

Cloudy with a Chance of Gray Matter

WE'RE ALL STILL silent when Dane pulls the truck onto Pompano Lane. A few houses before ours, I say, "Here's fine," and he stops; no arguing, no fussing, just applies the brakes.

I move to my left to get out of the passenger side, but Chloe is showing no signs of moving anytime soon. Although I have all of eternity stretching out in front of me, I'm still pretty impatient to get out of this truck once and for all tonight.

Dane sighs and slides out of the driver's seat. He extends a hand to help me out, and I take it, feeling once again how cold it is.

"Is mine that cold, too?" I ask self-consciously.

He nods slowly, almost like he's embarrassed to

admit it. "Here's the thing I've found, though," he whispers. "If I'm going to meet someone new, and I know it ahead of time, I rub my hands together for a few minutes first or, if that's going to be too obvious, I'll sit on them; that way at least they warm up enough not to raise suspicions."

"Thanks for the tip," I say sincerely.

Then there's this awkward little moment when we're both still standing there, with no reason to be and nothing to say. The sky is turning a kind of amber as the veil of darkness lifts and the blue of morning takes its place.

It's quite beautiful, actually, and the stark light causes dramatic shadows to form under Dane's prominent cheekbones. They're so beautiful I want to touch them, and I almost reach out a hand to, but then . . . I don't.

And just like that, the moment is over. He climbs into the truck and slides away without a sound.

I watch them drive off and then hear a quick blurt of brakes followed by a low whirr of reverse as the truck swings back into view. Dane backs up, slows to a stop, and holds out the little cooler through the window.

"Don't forget your brains." He smiles before

driving off again.

As I round the corner, I'm crossing my fingers that Dad will have been called out on an early run and his car won't be there and, and . . . there it is, snug and sound. At least when I get in he's in the shower, singing some old '80s pop song at the top of his lungs, which gives me time to unload the brains, empty the cooler, hide it in the garage, and prepare to be totally, thoroughly disgusted.

The brains are cold (thanks for all that ice, Dane) and big, much bigger than I'd imagined them to be. Harvey has sliced them up nice and thick. I cut off what looks like a pound of brains onto a paper plate. Then I look at it and think, *Okay, no.*

I mean, not that I won't eat the brains—because I have to, right? But . . . brain accessories, please? I know I'm not supposed to cook them; I get that part, but *The Guide* doesn't say anything about *not* using spices or herbs.

So naturally I dash on a little light soy sauce for good measure, throw on some things I find in the spice cabinet over the stove: oregano, thyme, salt, pepper from a grinder—you know, all the Food Channel basics. There's some crushed garlic in the fridge, a little relish to go on top of that, some olives, and a tube of sesame seeds, until, finally, it looks like the poor little pound of brains is wearing a spice helmet.

So I stop and even scrape off a few of the dozen or so garlic mounds, swirl the seasonings around, and . . . *chomp*. Now, here's the thing about brains: they're chewy. And not like fun, sweet, enjoyably chipper bubble gum chewy, either.

Like, gristle chewy; plastic-straw chewy; piece-of-shell-in-your-crab-salad chewy; shoelace-tip chewy (not that I would know, but still, you catch my drift).

And as for the taste? Kind of earthy; you know, like liver pâté or dark meat when you're having seconds of Thanksgiving turkey and it's all that's left because your stupid uncle Harvey is a pig and the hostess, your aunt Harriet, is too cheap to buy a bird big enough for eight people.

Now, the brain's an organ, right? So why *shouldn't* it be chewy? Still, chewy or not, once I start chewing, I can't stop; I mean, suddenly I realize I haven't eaten any human food since my grilled cheese sandwich the night before and I. Am. Famished.

Chewy as they are, I know my suspicions about becoming a zombie are correct when I gobble them up, whole, without retching even once. (This from a girl who gags when she even *drives by* a raw bar.)

If zombies need brains to keep going, then it's official: I. Am. A. Zombie.

Heartbeat or no, I've never felt so . . . *alive* . . . before. The brains, they are . . . intoxicating, electrifying, rejuvenating. I feel like I've inhaled 15 Red Bulls at one shot—without the after-crash. Or like the runner's high I get sometimes—without the running.

It goes down a lot—a *lot*—faster than I thought it would. Believe it or not, I'm so ravenous for the gray matter, I grab the first bag of brains, lop off a second pound, and eat it straight up. No chaser—not a single spice. No garlic cloves, no salt, not even a little pepper or soy sauce to cut the chewy, musky, organ-y taste. No fork or knife, either; just standing right there over the sink, gnawing on these little gray brains, chomping away caveman style like those guys who enter the all-you-can-eat buffalo wing contests on TV.

Halfway through my over-the-sink cerebrum pig-out, I hear some kind of animal sounds, like a distant groaning. No, not quite groaning—more like growling. That's it! Like a German shepherd when you get between him and his bowl.

Then I realize it's no animal. It's *me* doing all

that growling.

I try to picture myself there at the sink, 17-year-old girl in her flip-flops and yoga pants, a high ponytail to cover the half-dollar-sized black mole in the middle of her head, brain juice oozing down her forearms toward her rolled-up hoodie sleeves as she chomps, chews, gnashes, gnaws on a pound of brains straight from the butcher bag, growling like some dog with a bone.

Sexy, huh?

I swallow, quickly, and wash my hands all the way up to and past the elbows, *Grey's Anatomy* style. I dry them off with a dishrag and am tossing out my second paper plate of the morning when I realize, well . . . that won't do.

What if Dad comes out of his shower and sees the full trash and wants to recycle, and as he's sorting the trash finds brains all over the paper plate?

So I groan and empty the trash, lugging it out to the curb while looking around to see if maybe the neighbors can somehow see through the can and spot the brain crumbs drying as we speak. Nope. So far, so good.

I go back inside and hear Dad whistling in his room. Okay, coast's clear, for now. I risk a quick shower, skipping washing my hair, and then grab my usual school uniform: khaki slacks, white blouse, high collar, black flats, a pomegranate scarf around the waist for color.

And boom, I'm back in 10 minutes or less and there's Dad, standing in the kitchen looking clean and dapper, with his thinning hair combed back, his powder blue boxer shorts and starched white undershirt hiding beneath his frazzled green terry cloth robe, which never quite fits all the way around his bulging belly.

He's chewing and swirling a morsel around in a little plate of soy sauce. Around a full mouth of something, he says, "You know, I've never been a big fan of sushi for breakfast, but I have to say, this raw fish you brought home from the deli is really great. What is it? Tuna? Whitefish?"

I look at the "it" he's talking about and, of course, I've left the half-empty bag of thickly sliced brains out on the countertop and the soy sauce and sesame seeds nearby. Wouldn't you know it? Dad has confused a pound of leftover lamb's brains for his morning serving of sushi. (Hmm, doesn't say much about his coroner's training, now, does it?)

He's already got the second bite wedged in his

mouth and is soy saucing up a third, so it's too late for me to tell him what they are now. Instead, I kind of putter behind him, bag up what's left of the brains, and stow them in the freezer.

"I'm glad you like it, Dad, but I was saving that . . . uhhm, sushi . . . for a special occasion."

He swallows his last bite of brain sushi. "Well, dear, I hope it's not *too* special." He takes out one of the business cards from his wallet and picks the brains out of his teeth. "I don't think sushi's supposed to be quite *that* hard to chew."

As he teeters back into his bedroom to start dressing for the day, I look in the foyer mirror and flinch at the pale, dead face staring back. Then I remember the burn hole in the middle of my head and let down my greasy ponytail while scouring the hallway closet for something suitable to cover my head with.

I find an old beret Dad gave me after he found out I watched all of the *Pink Panther* movies on cable one night. I slip it on and stare at my reflection. Not bad. Not good, by any stretch, just not . . . bad.

Kind of edgy, a little out there, but . . . definitely something Hazel would approve of. Then I grab my keys and stomp out the door, ready to face Day Number 1 as Zombie Number 3.

Part 2
The Dead and the Near Dead

14
Maddy Gets a Makeover

"CAN YOU HELP me?" I ask, showing up at Hazel's door 15 minutes before we usually leave for school.

She takes one look at my face and says, "Jesus, what *happened* to you? And where the *hell* did you get that god-*awful* beret?"

I clutch the beret tightly and say, "It was in the back of my closet. I thought, you know, it would detract from my face." In reality, of course, I need it to cover the lightning hole in my head (but that info's strictly on a need-to-know basis).

"It's not working," Hazel says, dragging me toward her room.

We wave to Hazel's parents as they argue over

the last piece of toast in the kitchen.

"Hey, Maddy," they shout before just as enthusiastically going back to arguing.

Hazel's mom pauses from the argument as we disappear up the stairs. "Nice beret," she calls.

"Bon appétit," Hazel's dad says.

Upstairs I sit at Hazel's vanity (yes, not only is Hazel the one girl on the planet with an actual vanity in her room; she actually uses it regularly). Staring at my pale face in the mirror, I say with panic in my voice, "I tried doing something myself, Hazel, but then I gave up, wiped it off, and came over here."

"Well"—Hazel pats my shoulder and then opens up a tackle box full of makeup on either side of the vanity mirror—"you've come to the right place."

"I just—"

She stands there, hands on hips, gawking at me staring at myself in the mirror. "What . . . is . . . going on here? Are you sick? You didn't look this bad when I saw you last night. What gives?"

(I nearly gasp. Was it really only last night? With all that's happened, it feels like a lifetime ago that I stood in my driveway waving Hazel off yesterday.)

She pinches my cheek and yanks her hand away

as if she's touched a hot iron. "Yikes, Maddy, you're cold. I mean, *ice*-cold. Are you sure you feel up to school today?"

"I feel fine, Hazel. I just, I dunno, maybe I'm allergic to my new face cream or something. Can you just make me look less . . . less . . ."

"Dead?" She smirks.

I avoid her eyes and nod as she gets to work. I watch in amazement as she brings color to my cheeks, shades over the dark circles under my eyes, and fills out my thinning lips with color, but not too much. I'm so dumbfounded by the before-and-after transformation that I don't even protest as she goes to take off my beret. That is, until I hear a gasp and look away from my reflection to see hers in the mirror. She's staring at the top of my head. My spot!

"What is *this*?"

I stand abruptly, grabbing a fresh barrette off her vanity and working speedily to cover the spot back up. "Nothing, just . . . I don't know, actually. I woke up this morning and . . . there it was; I must have fallen out of bed and hit my head on the nightstand or something. If I did, I don't remember."

She cocks her head in that "I don't believe you" way. "I think you'd remember hitting your head *that* hard, Maddy. I mean, you have a huge, black bruise on the top of your head. I touched it. It's not even a bruise; it's like a . . . scab."

"It doesn't hurt." At least *that's* not a lie.

She makes her "just saw a spider" face. "It sure *looks* like it hurts. It hurts me to look at it; I can tell you that much."

"That's why I covered it up," I say, not addressing her insensitive dig.

We're getting late for school now, and she follows me back down the stairs. Her parents have gone off to work, leaving the kitchen a mess, but Hazel barely looks at it as we traipse out the door. She gets in my passenger seat and, before she can protest, I yank on the steering wheel and turn back toward my house.

"Hey," she shouts, "you're going the wrong way."

"I forgot something." I'm scoping the driveway for signs of Stamp. I've been thinking, you know, when I didn't show up at the party last night, he'd at least come looking for me this morning. I mean, it's the gentlemanly thing to do, is it not? Make sure the girl you asked to Aaron's party who never showed up is still alive? (Or undead, whatevs.)

Unless, of course, he asked every girl he bumped into yesterday to the party and can't keep track of them all by the next morning. *Is that it, Stamp? Are you a serial-bumper-turned-party-inviter?* (Please, oh please, don't let him be a jerk. Not after the night I've had; the night I'm still having.) I cruise by the empty driveway, see nothing there, not even Dad's coroner's wagon, and swiftly step on the gas.

"I thought you said you forgot something," Hazel says as we speed toward school.

I shrug, cursing her stupid photographic memory. "I just suddenly remembered I didn't forget."

"Okay"—she turns in her seat to face me— "what's the deal with you? I leave your house last night, you're Maddy. Young, pretty, warm skin, *tan* skin. You show up on my doorstep this morning, and everything—I mean *everything*—has changed. Suddenly your skin is white, your body's cold, you look like death warmed over, with enormous circles under your eyes, you've got a huge black . . . hole, scab, circle thingy in the middle of your head, you're wearing a beret, for Pete's sake, and now you say you're remembering not forgetting things you thought you forgot in the first place. So . . . what gives?"

"Hazel, I don't know. The spot, the skin, the cold—the beret—I can't explain it."

"You're lying to me." She sits back in a huff, arms

folded, as we inch up the long line toward the junior/ senior parking lot. "You're hiding something."

"I'm not."

"You are, Maddy. It started yesterday with this Stamp character. I mean, first you bump into him in the halls; next thing I know you're walking back from the cemetery with him, and you tell me last night nothing happened? Then today you show up like this? Something's not adding up, Maddy."

"Hazel, honestly, I'm not—"

"You remember what I said to you 11 years ago when I made you my best friend?"

"How could I forget?" I sigh, miserably, staring at the steering wheel since we're only going less than zero miles per hour.

"What'd I say to you, Maddy?"

"You said if I ever lied to you, if I ever hid anything from you, we wouldn't be friends anymore."

"That's right, Maddy. I don't take this friendship crap lightly; you know that about me. I don't know if you caught some virus you don't want anybody to know about, if you're pregnant or hung over or strung out or dying or what, but if you can't tell your best friend about it, well, then maybe you're not best friend material after all."

We're parked now, but I have the feeling that, even if we were still three blocks from school, Hazel would have stomped off and slammed the door on me, if only to have the final word, like she does right now. I sit there alone in my car, engine ticking, second bell ringing, kids streaming past, alone, and burst into tears.

Only . . . no tears. No water, no snot, no . . . nothing.

"Oh, great," I say to I-don't-know-who. "Now I can't even *cry.*"

15
Reversal of Fortune

NOT SURPRISINGLY, HAZEL gives me the cold shoulder later that morning in Home Ec. I mean, we're supposed to be writing down recipes for our end-of-semester five-course-meal project, but basically she's just texting her other friends while I flip listlessly through a couple of the ancient recipe books from Ms. Haskins' library. (Although, if I had any other friends, I guess I'd be doing the same.)

This happens to us every so often. Maybe two, three times a year. I mean, girls, back me up here: that's normal, right? You spend 99 percent of your time with the same person every day and, odds are, you're going to snap eventually.

Usually I can joke her out of anything, but today

Rusty Fischer

I'm not in the joking mood, so I figure I'll annoy her to death. (Sorry, bad joke, wrong class, wrong day, wrong lifetime.)

"Hey, Hazel," I say in a singsong voice as she focuses on her jeweled pink cell phone. "What do you think about possibly preparing roasted turkey with sage and sausage stuffing for our end-of-the-year project?"

Nothing; she doesn't even look up from her phone. I smile to myself and ask, "Hey, Hazel, what do you think about possibly preparing roast pork and sauerkraut for our end-of-the-year project?"

With each question, my voice grows less sing-songy and more passive-aggressive, until toward the end there I'm practically shouting as I turn the recipe book pages. "Hey, Hazel, what do you think about possibly preparing pheasant under glass with roasted parsnips for our end-of-the-year project?"

It goes on like that, ad infinitum, well, until even I can't take it anymore. Finally, I practically scream one last suggestion. "Hey, Hazel, what do you think about possibly preparing a big, fat, heaping dish of 'kiss my ass; I'd never lie to you' with a side order of 'go to hell; I haven't done anything wrong' for our end-of-the-year project? Hmm, how's that sounding to ya?"

Without so much as a glance in my direction,

Hazel stands up, pockets her phone, grabs her bag, walks to the back of the room, and asks Ms. Haskins for a pass during the last 15 minutes of class.

She never returns.

Not long after she's gone, Ms. Haskins walks over to me. Her voice all concerned-like, she says, "Maddy, are you . . . *okay?*"

Her tone is only vaguely teacherly; it's like she's talking to a friend at a bar or restaurant or something. With her husky, breathy voice, she sounds at least five years younger—and ten shades cooler.

I'm all ready to lie, to perk up, get chipper, and blow her away with some great, enthusiastic, pom-pom, "ooh-rah" BS, but there's something about the authentic concern in her eyes, so I kind of sigh, deflate from the shoulders on down, and say, honestly, "I don't *know*, Ms. Haskins." I wasn't going to, but something about an adult taking an interest in me at this very vulnerable minute crumbles my resolve.

She sits atop Hazel's empty stool. "Did you catch something from Hazel?"

I don't know what to do with that. Either my brain isn't working right, or the question is so ridiculous my overworked system can't handle it right now.

Ms. Haskins clears her throat. "Well, she just asked me for a pass, saying she wasn't feeling well, and I couldn't help but notice that, well, you don't look so hot yourself . . ."

I shake my head. "It's not Hazel, Ms. Haskins. I just . . . woke up like this."

No one's quite saying what "this" is yet, but it's obviously something, what with all the stares in the hall and now Ms. Haskins' worried face. If I thought I could become a zombie overnight and put on some makeup and go to school the next day and no one would notice, well, I guess I've got another think coming.

"I'm trying to be tactful here, Maddy, but you don't look . . . how should I say this? I guess I'll say it: you don't look well. At all. Is there anyone who can drive you home?"

"Drive me home? Right now? We still have four periods left. I mean, if I leave now I'll miss Art."

Ms. Haskins doesn't answer, but I figure if a *teacher* is telling you to go home, there's a reason for it.

"Is it *that* bad?" I say, looking down at her $200 shoes.

Again, she doesn't say anything, just keeps looking at me until I brave her sorrowful expression and look back. She finally nods, biting her lip, and hands me an office pass so I can go check out.

I thank her, embarrassed, thoroughly, and get up to walk out. I'm watching Ms. Haskins walk back to her desk, wanting her to turn around so I can thank her again, to let her know I appreciate her honesty, when I spot Bones and Dahlia lounging in their own little corner of the room.

I've seen hundreds of stares this morning, but this is a first: smiles. Bones and Dahlia are *smiling* as I catch their eyes. I shiver. What with their pale skin, pronounced cheekbones, and those spooky yellow eyes, it's not a good look on them.

And suddenly I remember their threat: "Sooner or later, you're going to have to face us alone."

So I make a simple plan for the day: *Stay close to people you know.*

16
Man Troubles

Unfortunately, that's not so easy. First Hazel thought I was lying to her and brushed me off in Home Ec. Then, the minute I walk into Art class, strike number two is pretty clear: Stamp has turned on me as well.

How do I know? Well, it starts when the sub for Mrs. Witherspoon greets me with a hearty "Hello there. Mrs. Witherspoon's judging an art show in Tallahassee this weekend, so we'll be having a 'free day' in art this morning. Why don't you grab a seat and sit wherever you like? You can thank me later."

Then I see that Stamp's already gotten the message, given that he's surrounded himself with no less than five slobbering Art Chicks who are hanging on his every word. He's talking about last night's party (natch) when I sit down—alone—a few tables away.

" . . . then I told him, I'm not drinking out of that beer bong unless you fill it with *two* cans. None of this wussy one-beer crap for me."

And, oh, the girls do laugh—and laugh and laugh and laugh.

I sneer, open my pad, and begin sketching (for some odd reason) two beer cans sprung to life and attacking a certain tall, dark, and handsome football kicker.

"So who was there?" one of the Art Chicks asks, loudly enough for them to hear in the cafeteria (three schools away).

"Oh, everybody," he says as loudly. "Just . . . everybody." He looks my way, which I promptly ignore. "You know, I mean, everybody who's anybody."

And the Art Chicks sigh knowingly, even though none of them were there (probably) and could care less that he's doing this for show, only to make me jealous (I'm assuming-slash-hoping). And Stamp just talks, and they just laugh and laugh, and I sit and fume and fume, thinking how abruptly your fortunes can change when you're 17, lonely, and undead.

I mean, yesterday the world was my oyster. Best friend, hot guy asking me to parties, sneaking out of the window, Dad none the wiser, two blocks away from snogging with the new kicker for the football team, and then—*whack, zap, whammo*—game over. Do not kiss hot new guy, do not have understanding best friend, do not have heartbeat, go straight to Zombieville and stay there *permanently*.

And today? My best friend won't talk to me, Stamp obviously thinks I blew him off and won't give me the time of day so I can explain what *really* happened (well, a sanitized version of what really happened, anyway), clearly Bones and Dahlia want to add me to the long list of victims from Third Period Home Ec, and Ms. Haskins thinks I look grody enough to send home—four periods early.

As the laughter continues and Stamp brags about how cool the party was and how hot all the girls were and how rockin' the music was and how flowin' the beer was, I carefully fold my drawing into fourths, then eights, then sixteenths, then keep folding until I can't fold it anymore. And when I'm done folding it, I slip it in my pocket and sit there until the bell rings.

It seems to take forever, and in that time all

my hopes of getting with Stamp are dashed one phony, breathy Art Chick giggle at a time. Twenty-four short hours ago my future was bright, and it seemed a given Stamp would wrap that big white bicep around my shoulder and seal the deal. Today it's like I hardly know him.

He seemed so . . . sweet . . . yesterday, handing me my books after we ran into each other in the hall, molding his little clay figures at this very table, walking me back up the hill from the graveyard when I needed someone the most. And now?

He might as well be a stranger. I look at him out of the corner of my eye, telling his stories, drowning in his fans, and think about what could have been. As one of the Art Chicks carefully moves his little Superman curl aside and flirts ruthlessly, I blink away a few more nontears and stare at the clock, willing it to move forward one second, one tick, at a time.

Maybe it's for the best he turned out to be a jerk, after all. I mean, what kind of future did we have? Me, the Living Dead; and him, Drop-Dead Gorgeous? Did I think he was going to keep asking me to parties once he felt my cold skin, kissed my cold lips, felt my dead, nonbeating heart? Did I really think he was the kind of guy who was up for a little interzombie dating?

Finally the bell rings, but it doesn't bring the relief I'm looking for. Stamp is up and out in a heartbeat, never looking back, not even when his harem of Art Chicks scurry after him beckoning, "Stamp! Wait up, Stamp!"

I stand listlessly and walk past the sub, enduring the openmouthed stares and finger points of my fellow classmates as I wander through the halls, the loneliest zombie on the planet.

I've got my head down, and I'm not really looking where I'm going, or very much caring, when somebody bumps into me. I look up, but the person is already past, and even from behind I could swear it's Dane shuffling off down the hallway in his black hoodie and grody sneakers. Oh well, easy come, easy go; just another guy who can't be bothered to give me the time of day now that I literally look like death warmed over.

Believe it or not, the highlight of my day is emptying the shavings from Mr. Harvey's pencil sharpeners during sixth period. No, not because I'm addicted to the particular, peculiar, and quite powerful smell of pencil shavings (you know what

I'm talking about). It's because after being cooped up for six straight periods, I finally get some fresh air and freedom.

There's nothing else for me to do as library aide by this point in the day anyway; all the books have been reshelved by Mr. Harvey's previous five aides of the day, and Mr. Harvey is sequestered in the computer lab Googling himself. The only thing left to do is empty all 12 pencil sharpeners (one at the end of every other row of books), collect them in a plastic garbage bag, and spend the last 20 minutes of class out on a perfectly good, teacher-approved Library Aide Hall Pass.

"Write yourself a pass," he mouths behind the computer lab window.

I start to but can't find a pen on the reception desk. I'm digging through my pockets for one when I find a crumpled piece of paper that I know I didn't put there.

I open it up. It's a triangle of lined paper, roughly torn on two edges, like whoever did the tearing was angry, or in a hurry—or both.

ZOMBIES *Don't Cry*

Me shop class,
you Dumpster,
6th period.
Dane

So *that's* what the whole bumper cars imitation in front of Art Class was about? Shoving a piece of scrap paper down my pocket? I shake my head, throw away the note, and then empty out the pencil shavings in the same trash. I hold up the bag toward Mr. Harvey on my way out the library doors, but he's engrossed in some astronomy website, so I just walk out.

I'm tempted to throw the shavings out somewhere else, Dane's note be damned. I mean, who is he to demand exactly *where* I dump my pencil shavings during sixth period? By the same token, I'm vaguely curious as well. I mean, if Zombie Number 2 is going to all this trouble to pass me some stupid note, well, maybe it's worth checking out after all.

The Dumpster's behind D-wing, between the cafeteria and the hard Art classes, Remedial Auto Shop, Rocket Building 101, Power Soldering, ROTC—that kind of thing. I take the long way there, past the vending machines in B-wing, past the boys' locker room over by A-wing (you know, in case there's a sudden fire alarm and 30 wet, naked guys have to come rushing out the rusted double doors and suddenly feel the need to be rubbed down with pencil shavings), and out through C-wing to get a little fresh air.

Not that the air is always so fresh next to the Dumpster, but it beats sitting in the library listening to underclassmen giggle over the dirty parts in Judy Blume's *Forever* for 50 straight minutes.

By this time of day, most of the school is on autopilot. The jocks are saving up energy for after-school practice; the thugs have already been sent home, suspended, or expelled for the rest of the year; even the mean girls are cruising until their afternoon pedicures and spa treatments. So I walk in silence out the doors, round the corner toward the Dumpster, and find Dane Fields halfway through a sizzling Marlboro Light as he lingers a few feet outside the back door to Shop class.

The yard is full of scrap metal, rusty car doors, old oil drums, and dozens of other hiding places perfect for the sixth period smoker. And, with all that's going on in my life right now—no best friend; no boyfriend; and, oh yeah, I'm *dead*—this is my very first thought: *I didn't know Dane Fields smoked.* Interesting.

He's walking right up to me. "What took you so long?"

"Back off, Dane. You know how long it takes to empty out *all* the pencil sharpeners in the library?"

"You mean all twelve? Like three and a half minutes max."

I shake my head and dump the shavings in the Dumpster, practically one shaving at a time, just to make him wait another minute or two. I don't know why Dane is pissing me off so much today, but he . . . just . . . is.

I guess it's not Dane, per se, and it's not even Chloe so much. It's the way they've forced me into this unholy little family of theirs, hook, line, and zombie. I mean, of all the kids in this town who could be zombies, and I get stuck with . . . them?

He fumes. "Listen, Maddy, we have some serious shit to talk about, and you need to start taking me seriously."

"I get that, Dane. Really, I do." I look around for witnesses and, finding none, continue. "But *you* need to give *me* some time to get used to this, okay? I mean, I've been a . . . zombie . . . for, like, 48 hours, okay? Cut me some slack. I'm up all hours of the night, running around my room like it's a prison cell. I've got my dad eating brains by accident and thinking they're sushi. Now Hazel won't talk to me; she thinks I'm lying to her about something. Gee, what could *that* be? Every kid in this school is staring at me like I've got 'zombie' written on my forehead. I mean, I'm doing the best I can here, all right? Just . . . back . . . off."

He looks at me and says, more softly this time, "Okay, okay, I get that, Maddy. I do. I know it can't be easy for you right now, and trust me, I get that you'd rather hang out with your Normal friends like Hazel than Chloe and me, but you've got to start doing a better job of passing. This . . . look . . . you're sporting isn't cutting it."

I hang my head. Now even the *zombies* think I look like crap. I mean, talk about the pot calling the kettle dead. "I'm trying my best, Dane. I had Hazel give me a makeover before school, and she's practically a makeup expert."

Dane cracks a crooked smile. "Sure, with Normals, maybe, but helping a zombie pass takes a *very* particular skill set."

"Yeah." I chuckle. "Well, I guess I haven't acquired that one yet."

The bell rings, and we look at each other with

a kind of resigned frustration, like maybe I'm still a little peeved at him and he's still a little pissed at me but we're stuck with each other, so somehow we'll find a way around it.

Anyway, as we part, he says over his shoulder, "Don't worry, Maddy. I've made an appointment with someone who's an expert at passing. She'll be waiting for you after school."

"Yeah." I laugh on my way past the Dumpster. "If I make it that long."

17
Jock-Blocked

AND, AMAZINGLY, somehow I do. By the time the final bell of the school day rings, I've basically forgotten all about Dane and his unsolicited makeover advice. My mind is on about 1,001 other, more important things, like, you know, how I'm going to keep Dad out of my brains supply and keep Hazel in the dark about my zombie status when she is literally up in my business 24/7/365. So I'm halfway to the junior/senior parking lot, letting it all flood my brain, when I see Stamp waving me down.

I get a jolt as I see him standing there outside the boys' locker room, ready for Friday night's big game. He's in his football pants—short, tight little things that start just below his belly button and end right below his knees. But then he's also wearing this little half-shirt thing, I guess to go under his shoulder pads? So above his belly button he's got, like, two full feet of bare skin.

I'm staring at both of them when he says, uber-casually, "What's up?"

You know, like he didn't ditch me at some party the night before, like he didn't not come looking for me the next morning, like he didn't completely diss me in Art class. *What's up?* That's rich.

So, of course, I respond appropriately, really letting him have it. "Nothing. I just . . . I wanted to apologize for not making it to the party last night." (Okay, so I *didn't* let him have it, but you'd do the same damn thing if you were looking at the same two feet of naked man skin I'm drinking in.)

"Please." He snorts, waving it off. "I just figured you stood me up. You know, playing hard to get is all. No biggie."

"Really?" So *that's* why he didn't come looking for me the next morning. "I dunno, Stamp, I'd be pretty peeved if somebody did that to *me*."

He gives me that funny Stamp look. "Water under the bridge, Maddy, really. But listen, I've got a few more minutes until coach starts bitching about warming up for tonight's game. Hey, you coming, by the way? Anyway, I wanted to ask you something . . ."

In the back of my mind I'm thinking, *Fall Formal, Fall Formal,* but I don't want to jinx it, so I say, "Yeah, what?" as casually as possible. Which is pretty hard to do when you're already mentally making hair and nail appointments and predicting the color of his tux so you can match your eye shadow.

He blushes, looks away, spots something over my shoulder, and frowns.

I figure maybe it's the school PDA Police coming up from behind but turn to see Hazel slinking up instead.

Great. Where before there were merely half pants and six-pack abs and Stamp's stammering question, suddenly there's Hazel and her flowing red hair and her ample, man-magnet booty . . . and a dreadful, awkward silence.

After what seem like 10 full minutes, I look at her and ask, flat out, "What's up?" Girl talk, of course, for, *Back up off my man, biotch.*

"Oh, nothing. I just wanted to let you know Ms. Peppercorn asked me to be on the Decorating Committee for the Fall Formal. She wanted some male input, and since I don't trust any of the other guys in this school, I figured maybe I'd invite some new blood to participate."

"Me?" asks Stamp.

"Stamp?" asks me.

Hazel rolls her eyes. "Yeah." Then, she shoos me off. "This is a formal invitation, and I have to do it right, so . . . scram."

And, just like that, suddenly *I'm* the third wheel in my *own* conversation. I kind of stand there for a second, disbelieving, but Hazel is obviously serious, to the point of kind of turning her back halfway on me and forcing Stamp to look at her.

I say, "Okay, well, I'm going now. Bye!"

Stamp smiles helpfully, unsure whether to take any of this seriously, until Hazel snaps. "Focus, Stamp. Now, as I was saying . . ."

I stumble away, head down, taking little looks over my shoulders to see Stamp gazing forlornly after me and Hazel reeling him back in with a hand on his cheek. *Her* hand. On *his* cheek. Meanwhile, the question he's been meaning to ask hangs unanswered in the air.

I'm confused, hurt, hopeful, and embarrassed, all at the same time. I mean, what if he *wasn't* going to ask me to the Fall Formal after all? What if he was only asking, "Hey, what's up?"

I've never dated a jock before. What if that's just what jocks do? Hang their landing strips out to dry in front of the boys' locker room every day and see what sticks? What if it was all innocent and what I think happened didn't really happen?

But it did; I know it did. It doesn't take my superhuman zombie senses to figure out I was about to get asked to Fall Formal and Hazel just . . . just . . . *jock*-blocked me. I'm halfway through the parking lot, kicking every stone and blacktop pebble in my path, when I realize someone's leaning against my car.

Chloe Kildare.

"Get in," she says when I get close enough to the driver's side to hear her.

"Yeah," I say with my new zombie comeback cool, already pissed from Hazel's jock-block and in no mood for any other chicks I can't stand messing with the rest of my afternoon. "I plan on it. It's *my* car, remember?"

Ignoring her, I bend down, get in, and slam my door to avoid seeing her any further. Unfortunately, the electric keychain has unlocked all four doors, and before I can protest, Chloe is already riding shotgun.

I sigh. "Chloe, seriously, I don't have time for . . . this . . . today."

"Girl," she says without a trace of irony as she looks from my pale skin to the dark circles under my eyes, "you literally have all the time in the world."

"I may be immortal, but that doesn't mean my schedule's any lighter these days. My dad's been working all week and wants me to have dinner with him tonight, I've got a Sociology paper due next Thursday, and I *still* don't have a date to the Fall Formal, thanks to my best friend, so I have absolutely *less* than zero time for you to sit in my car and bully me around, and—"

"That's fine." She reaches for the door and pushes it open. From the seated position, she calls out to Stamp, now leaning against the wall outside the locker room as Hazel flanks him like a one-woman she-wolf pack licking her lips before dinner. "Hey, Stamp," Chloe cries out. From here, I can't tell if he can hear her or not. "I wanted to tell you a little secret about your girlfriend."

"Get in here," I shout, grabbing Chloe by the arm and yanking her halfway across the seat toward me.

As I fire up the Honda and peel out of the parking lot, she says, "God, you're so easy. Did you *really* think I was going to break about three dozen zombie laws and squeal your secret to Stamp? Right there, in broad daylight?"

"I dunno."

"Yeah, well, I wasn't."

I sigh, my head not exactly hurting, but my brain feeling like it's caught in a vise. "So, what is this, Chloe, some kind of zombie intervention or something? First Dane corners me in sixth period to tell me I'm not living up to my full zombie potential or whatever, and now you're staking out my car after school? What gives?"

"What gives," Chloe says as she looks me up and down in the unforgiving sunlight streaming through my windshield, "is that you look like 10 pounds of crap shoved in a 5-pound bag—and we can't have that. Dane and I have a rep to protect, you know, and now that you're one of us, well, we can't have you giving death a bad name."

I look at Chloe with her pancake makeup and pierced nose and cringe. "So *you're* the makeup expert Dane was talking about earlier?" I ask, unconvinced.

"What?" Chloe says. "You were expecting maybe Heidi Klum?"

I frown, but it's hard when I want to laugh. Who'da thunk it? Chloe Kildare? Cracking jokes? Giving me makeup advice? Riding shotgun like she owns the car, feet up on the dashboard and all? The world truly is upside down. Or, at least, *my* world is.

"I thought it would be easier, I guess," I say as we steer slowly through the long line of kids getting out of school on this beautiful fall Friday in sunny Barracuda Bay.

"Yeah, well, it *does* get easier, but not if you get outed by the whole school your first full day with the Z-disease. We've been watching you all day, Dane and I, checking to see how you'd do. I have to tell you, zombie to zombie, you failed. *Big*-time. I mean, kids who never look up from their textbooks were talking about you today. The whole school thinks you have malaria or something."

I brake for the next stop sign and peer into the rearview mirror. A stranger peers back—a dead, white, pale, broken stranger with no clue, no life, no future. "Is it *that* bad?" I ask for the dozenth time that day.

She doesn't answer the question. "Listen, you take me to the mall, and I'll make sure you pass and nobody finds us out. Deal?"

Instead of turning left toward home, I turn right and head toward the Barracuda Bay Galleria. "Do I have a choice?"

Chloe's dry chuckle is my answer.

18
Sentenced to Food Court

WE SIT IN THE food court, mostly deserted this time of day, two zombies slurping sodas like a couple of poodle-sweatered girls in a '50s diner. Aside from yesterday's grilled cheese sandwich, it's the first human food I've had since I died (do brains count?) but, more importantly, the first *non*diet soda I've had since I was maybe, what . . . eight years old?

A few tables away, a frazzled mother sits with her two young boys, yelling at one then another while trying to stuff a quick gyro into her stressed-out gullet. "Jeffrey, stop. Brian, don't *do* that. Jeffrey, *put* that down."

Chloe ignores them, staring out at the mostly empty stores beyond the food court perimeter.

"So remind me again why I'm not drinking diet." I take a tentative sip of the thick, syrupy soda. It's surprisingly good. So good I take two more long, big sips. The viselike tension from my head immediately lifts, as it always does when I've been too long without caffeine and drink my first snort of Red Bull—*wham*—32 grams of sugar straight to the cerebral cortex.

She shakes her head. "For starters, you'll never have to count another calorie again. Look at you; you're in the first stages of Assimilation. I bet you've lost at least 15 percent of your body fat already. Trust me, it doesn't take long. By the final stages, you'll be down to 4, maybe 3 percent body fat, tops, for the rest of your life.

"We're literally running on electricity now, Maddy, so your metabolism is crazy fast. So *this*"—she holds up her half-empty cup, as big as most popcorn buckets—"the liquid keeps your cells hydrated; the sugar gives your brain a boost. You don't *need* to drink it, not exactly; you *can* go without it; it just . . . helps you feel more . . . human."

Her voice has turned almost wistful, her eyes falling on the frenzied mother and looking downright sad. I give her the moment, although a thousand questions run through my brain. The biggest one being, *Why is Chloe suddenly being so nice to me?* The mother looks up, sees Chloe's stark white face, severe black makeup, scowling eyes, and T-shirt studded with safety pins, and gathers her boys to leave without cleaning up.

Chloe turns to me without comment.

"How long have you been, you know, like . . . this?" I ask.

"Thirty-seven years," she says nonchalantly, as if I've just asked her the weather.

"But . . . how?"

She turns to me, taking another deep, almost desperate slug of soda. She explains, too calmly, "I was holing up in an abandoned warehouse with my boyfriend. It wasn't only us; lots of kids did it back then. It was called 'squatting'; Google it sometime. Anyway, the cops got a tip, raided the place; everybody took off, even my boyfriend. I'd had a little too much to drink, maybe a few other things, so I couldn't move quite as fast as everybody else.

"Anyway, the cops tried to bust me, I resisted, they tased me; both of them at the same time, set Tasers to quadruple stun. I don't think they planned to; it just worked out that way. You have to remember, this was back when they first started using Tasers. They were pretty much brand-new, experimental, unproven—twice as big, plus twice as *strong*, as they are today.

"Anyway, I went through the Awakening; that's what they call it when you actually die and go into a kind of hibernation. But I wasn't totally gone; I could hear what they were saying, those cops. I mean, they thought I was dead; no pulse, no breathing, cold skin, the works. One said he had a family and kids and he wasn't 'going down for some punk skank.'

"I still remember that: 'punk skank.' Nice, huh? The other guy was young, only a kid himself. He said this could ruin his career. So they just left me there; didn't even throw a blanket over me or anything, like you would for a dog. When I came to a few days later, I stumbled off, figured things out, needed to get away from there as fast as I could. Didn't want the same cops catching me again, obviously. I went here, went there; soon enough I figured out what I was, learned what I had to the hard way and, well, here I am."

"How'd you find out about the whole eating-brains-within-48-hours deal?"

She shakes her head. "I didn't. I just . . . got

really, really hungry and . . . that was the only thing I had a craving for. I guess it's like when girls get pregnant; they know what they want. It got so bad after a day that I could literally smell the brains through the grocer's deli door. I waited and broke in that night and chowed down. It was . . . awesome."

The way she's describing it, I can almost taste the brains right about . . . Hold up, girl. Focus. Stopping myself from licking my lips at the thought of fresh brains, I ask, "And you never saw your boyfriend again?"

She sucks the last of her soda up and shoves the gargantuan paper cup away. "What, you mean that creep who left me to deal with the cops? No, Maddy, I didn't; didn't want to. Not like you and that football stud you were drooling over after school. What's his name? Stamp?"

I roll my eyes, sipping carefully at my soda. "Lot of good that's going to do me. You saw Hazel jock-block me."

Chloe smirks. "Thought you two were best friends."

"Me too."

Finally, Chloe points to her temple and says, "Lemme see it again."

"See what?" I ask, instinctively pushing my ridiculous beret tighter onto my head.

"The mark," she says, inching closer. "I saw you showing Dane in the trailer, but I want to get a better look. I've heard of zombies being reborn by lightning but never met one before. I just want to check it out."

When no one is looking, I snatch off the beret, bend toward the table, let her see, and then slip the hat right back on.

When I look at her, she's nodding admiringly. "Very nice. You know, hair grows for six weeks after you die, so by, say, Thanksgiving . . . that should be all covered up."

"Really?" I ask hopefully; here I'd thought I was stuck with it forever. (Oh, the things that pass for pleasant surprises when you're dead.)

"Really," she says, looking me up and down again. "But now enough with the show-and-tell. If you're going to pass, we need to do you up right."

Before I can protest, she stands and tosses her soda into the nearest trash can.

Helplessly, I follow.

A couple of hours and most of Dad's emergency stash later, Chloe and I are both weighed down with bulging bags from multiple stores. I'm used to shopping with Hazel, a fun, sunny person, in fun, sunny stores, for fun, sunny things. Shopping with Chloe is as dark and somber as the things she makes me pick out: black T-shirts, black slacks, black blouses, black jeans, black socks, black shoes—and that's *before* we get to the makeup counter.

"I can't wear that," I say as she makes me buy the thick, white face powder my grandmother used to wear to bed every night of her life. "It's not me."

"Look." She sighs, bullying the cashier into ringing it up anyway, along with the $30 of black makeup, lipstick, and nail polish she's piled onto the cosmetics counter. "Right now you're already a little—how shall I put this?—gray. And you're, what, not even two full days in? By Monday morning, trust me, you're going to need to either (a) wear enough blush to pass as a circus clown or (b) do what I do and go for the Goth look. Trust me, Maddy, this is more believable."

"Me?" I ask as we trudge out of the department store and head for the mall's main entrance. "Goth? *That's* going to be believable? I think most people who know me—granted, that's not a ton—but most people who know me would find it easier to believe I was an actual zombie before they'd believe I was a Goth."

She looks at my trademark khaki slacks, white

blouse, high collar, black flats, pomegranate scarf belt (and let's not forget "le beret") and frowns. "Okay, maybe not at first, but trust me, *every* teenager goes through some kind of phase: punk, Goth, rebellious, slutty, skank, whatever. Just pretend this is yours. This way your dad might question it, but at least he'll *understand* it—eventually. This way Hazel and your other brainiac buddies might cock an eyebrow, but if they're *real* friends, they'll get over it. It's the easiest way; trust me."

She pauses near the fill-your-own-bag-with-jelly-beans store to rearrange the bags in her hands and adjust her black bra strap and says, "Hey, at least Goth is still in. You should have seen me trying to pass this look off back in the '80s when everyone and their sister was still a preppy."

She gives me a quick glance up and down before adding grudgingly, "No offense."

19
Creature Features

I HEAR THE SHOWER running in Dad's room the next morning. Spotting his car keys on the foyer countertop, I breathe a sigh of relief. I hate it when he pulls these double, sometimes triple, shifts, given his line of employment. And especially now, given my new knowledge of the undead world. I mean, what's to stop the next cadaver in his next body bag from popping up and taking a bite out of his neck?

To make up for his long night, I start the coffee brewing, toast up some of his favorite whole grain Eggos, and put on water to boil for his other favorite: hardboiled eggs (one of the few things I can make for him without screwing up).

I step out the front doorway and grab a daisy

from his measly flower garden, find a little vase in one of the kitchen cupboards, fill it with water, pop the flower in, and set it between two place mats on the table in the breakfast nook.

By the time Dad's dressed for work and sniffing around the coffeepot, I've got three eggs on boil, his frozen waffles buttered and syruped exactly the way he likes them—heavy on the butter, light on the syrup—and hand him a fresh cup of coffee in his favorite oversized Christmas mug.

"To what do I owe the honor of my daughter fixing me breakfast-almost-in-bed?" he quips, sitting down at his place setting and admiring the fresh flower in his improvised bud vase. His voice is vibrant, but his eyes are tired, and I know these late nights are catching up with him. (Tell me about it!)

I lean against the kitchen counter next to the oven. "Nothing, Dad. I just . . . hate to see you working such late shifts at, well, you know . . ." I let my voice trail off, but Dad is too sharp to let my unspoken message go unnoticed.

"You mean 'to work such late hours at . . . my age'? Is that what you were going to say, dear?" He smiles even as he nails it. "I know you think your old man is ancient and decrepit, but you can stack six of those young whippersnappers they send my department fresh from the university every summer, and I'll outwork them, out-think them, and out-last them every time." His dander's all up and his coffee's half gone.

I top off his mug. "Whoa, pardner, I was just going to say I don't like you working such late shifts and such odd hours, period. No ageism was implied, honest."

He peers at me doubtfully, takes a sip of coffee, and looks at me again, more closely this time. "Tell me this." He sighs, turning toward me. "Did Hazel approve this new . . . look . . . of yours?"

And that's when I remember: today is Goth Ground Zero. I picture myself as I looked leaving my room only half an hour or so earlier: black duds from head to toe, two layers of white pancake make-up, plenty of mascara and eyeliner and, the pièce de résistance: maroon lipstick and black nail polish. Instant Goth.

"You're not digging the *Twilight* look, Dad?"

"Maddy, you're my daughter and I love you. And, let's face it, you'd look gorgeous wearing a hoop skirt and a raincoat. You're young; I figure I've had it pretty easy as far as fashion phases go. If this is as bad as it gets, well, color me happy."

189

And that's that: Dad in a nutshell. His daughter is a Goth; either I'll grow out of it or he'll get used to it. One way or the other, fighting about it isn't going to do either of us any good. No screaming, no yelling, no judging—just tells you like it is and that's that.

He yawns and gulps more coffee and slices off a square of perfectly toasted Eggo. After chewing it thoroughly and swallowing with pleasure, he says, "Aren't you joining your old man for breakfast today?"

I look at my empty place setting self-consciously. "I'm trying to lose weight, Dad, you know . . ."

He has that little twinkle in his eye. "Oh, I know, for the Fall Formal."

Not quite, Dad, but that's one less excuse I have to make this morning. One less lie I have to tell.

When I don't answer, he says, "Well, so, has your new guy asked you yet?"

I reach for a can of Mountain Dew from the fridge so it at least looks like I'm eating/drinking *something*. The fact that Dad doesn't have a hissy fit over me drinking one of his nondiet sodas or, for that matter, notice that I'm not drinking diet for, like, the first time ever, is a testament to his ongoing quest to find me a boyfriend.

"He's not 'my guy,' Dad and, for your information, no, he hasn't asked me to the Fall Formal . . . yet. I just, you know, I want to look good in case he does."

Around a mouthful of waffle, Dad says, "Well, he better not wait too long. Isn't it this coming Friday?"

I raise my can to my mouth just as he finishes asking so I don't have to answer. Then I notice him waiting, expectantly, with his fork in one hand and his knife in the other over his empty plate. I'm thinking about telling him to do his own damn dishes when suddenly I remember the pot of boiling water next to me and his three overly hardboiled eggs.

Without thinking, I put down my can, reach for his plate, and one by one snatch the eggs out of the boiling water.

With.

My.

Bare.

Hands.

I think nothing of it because my hands are so cold and the water is so warm (*hot, boiling,* whatever) and, according to page 68 of *The Guide*, zombies don't feel pain, so why not? I'm looking at Dad's plate, smiling and thinking, *Man, he's going to love those eggs,* and then my gaze travels up from his plate to his face and he. Is. Shocked.

Shocked, I tell you.

"Maddy," he shouts, leaping up from his chair to examine my hands with a practiced medical eye. "What were you *thinking*?"

"What?" I try to snatch my undamaged hands back, but his grip is too strong even for my extra-super zombie powers (at least, that is, according to page 32 of *The Guide*).

He's got my hands out in front of me, flipping them over and over, back and forth, up and down, studying them from every angle, and they look as pale as they did before I stuck them in boiling water to scoop out his eggs. Not a splotch, not a mark, not a blister, not a sore, not even a glossy pink sheen.

"Incredible," he says, as if he's got some new species of germ under his microscope back at the coroner's lab. "Not so much as a scratch."

Then he looks into my eyes and asks, more calmly now, "Maddy, I'm serious now, whatever *were* you thinking?"

I rack my brain for something sensible that a scientist like Dad would buy. "I don't know, really," I blurt. "We were reading in Science how, if you move fast enough, you can put your hand in freezing ice water or, in this case, boiling water, and not get a scratch. I guess I wanted to see if that was true."

He looks at me closely, like maybe he doesn't believe me. "You could have just asked me, Maddy, and I would've told you: it isn't true. By rights your hands should be severely burned right now, maybe second- even third-degree burns covering all the way up to your wrists. And yet you don't have a scratch on you."

"So the teacher's theory was right, then."

"No, in fact, far from it. It appears that my daughter is simply a freak of nature." He tries to pass it off as a joke, but he's clearly upset.

Inside I'm mentally kicking my brain cells. How could I be so stupid?

He sits down, stands up, sits back down, and then pushes away his plateful of uneaten eggs. "Well, Madison, it appears as if you've pulled off another impossible feat."

"What's that?" I hide my hands from view.

"You've made me lose my appetite for your spe-cialty: hardboiled eggs."

We make polite chitchat as he gets ready for work, me hiding my hands whenever possible, him scouring them for evidence of what he calls late-event trauma, which never quite develops. As he leaves, telling me how he's got to pull another all-nighter, he's still shaking his head—and I'm still feeling stupid.

But he's not the only member of this family with an inquisitive nature, and now that my official zombie diagnosis has finally been confirmed, I have a little research of my own to do. But not in any library.

Mega Movies opens at 10 a.m. on Saturdays; I get there at 9:58, sharp. In the two minutes I've got before opening time, I haul out my cell and text Hazel: *Up 4 a movie night l8r?* That takes less than a minute to type and send, and I know Hazel (a) is already up, (b) has her phone on, (c) usually texts me back in six seconds or less, and (d) is now trying to punish me with the silent cell treatment. I sigh, check the dashboard clock—which now reads 10:01—and get out of the car.

A chubby guy in Coke bottle glasses and a faded green Mega Movies golf shirt says, "Have a Mega Movie day," as I walk in and a little electronic bell chimes over the front door. Veiled in my hoodie and dark sunglasses, I smile and wave a pale, unboiled hand before rapidly shoving it into my front pocket. I head straight for the horror section while he tidies up and gets ready for another dull Saturday morning shift.

ZOMBIES *Don't Cry*

There are two full walls of horror: lots of sequels and prequels and dark, black covers with blood dripping red from titles like *Death Derby 6*, *Monster Camp 3*, and *Bloodsuckers 2*. Most are vampire movies; I skip those. (Frankly, I would have skipped those even *before* I became a zombie.) A few are about werewolves, ghosts, mummies, and the like; I skip those, too.

The stuff on zombies—what little there is— is mostly old, '70s and '80s stuff with hordes of brain-dead flesh eaters crowding the DVD covers and body parts lying around at their stiff, dead feet. I grab a few random titles that don't sound absolutely horrible—*Zombie Invasion 3*, *Night of the Teenage Brain Suckers*, *Zombie Family Vacation Getaway*— and ask the guy in the faded green shirt and thick glasses if he knows of any more that aren't out on the shelves.

"Zombies?" He scratches his head out of habit. Spotting my stack, he asks, skeptically, "What do you have already?" I show him my thin stash, and he pooh-poohs them all with a wave of his pudgy hand.

"Listen," he says, leaning in close even though I'm the only soul in the store. His breath smells of mint mouthwash but not quite *enough* mint mouthwash, if you know what I mean. "These are for amateurs. Keep them, if you want, but I hide the good stuff in the documentary section; you know, so they're always in. Nobody ever goes back there."

He leads me to a dark corner of the store, dusty and stocked with a big cardboard box full of rolled movie posters and a handwritten sign that says, *FREE! Take me home!* On one wall, scattered amidst lots of serious-looking nonfiction films—many in black-and-white, most with subtitles, all dusty—is the mother lode of all zombie movies: six by the time he gets through cherry-picking them off the walls for me.

"Now *these*," he says with obvious relish, "are what zombie movies are meant to be." He holds them close to his chest on the way back to the sales counter, as if a crowd of customers might storm the store at any moment and try to rent them away from me. Once we get to the register, he takes my other three, adds them to the pile, and studies me a little more closely.

I have to keep reminding myself that I'm dressed like a circus freak, as if my black fingernail polish isn't reminder enough when I hand my card over.

"Let me guess," he says, swiping my Mega Movies

membership card, "you and your Goth friends are having a zombie watching party. You know, getting a jump on Halloween?"

I shake my head. "Haven't you heard? Goths have no friends."

He smiles anyway, hitting on another bright idea. "I got it: the new boyfriend's a big zombie fan, and you're trying to play catch up so it looks like you share the same interests?"

Ha! I wish that (a) I had a boyfriend, (b) he liked zombie movies, and (c) he was down with dating one—indefinitely. I slowly shake my head. Not even close, pal.

He grows visibly worried. "We don't get many girls renting these," he says with a grin, scanning each zombie flick slowly as if he's suddenly having second thoughts about renting them to me in the first place.

"Well," I say matter-of-factly, "you do now."

"I mean, they're pretty gross," he says dramatically. "You sure you're okay with the walking dead?"

I am now. "Yup."

"Monsters chomping on raw brains?"

I actually have personal experience with that one. "Sure thing."

"I warn you"—he finally hands them over—"they'll keep you up at night."

"Not a problem," I say on my way out the door. "I'm kind of . . . an . . . *insomniac.*"

On the short drive home, I chuckle at the irony of it all: a real-life zombie renting zombie movies. Slipping through the front door and locking it behind me, as if one of the neighbors might see my towering stack of gore and suddenly put two and two together, I promptly load the top movie on the stack into the high-tech DVD player on Dad's beloved big-screen TV and settle onto the couch with . . . no movie snacks.

I realize it's the first time I've ever left Mega Movies without an armful of Twizzlers, microwave popcorn, Raisinets, and Goobers in addition to my pile of movies. It's weird. Not only am I not hungry at all (best diet *ever*); I just . . . don't crave those things anymore, at all. I wonder, will watching movies be the same without movie snacks? Only one way to find out, I guess. I push play on . . . what is it again?

Oh yeah, get this: *Zombie Homecoming.* Catchy, huh?

As the opening credits roll over a black-and-white screen that looks, cleverly enough, like a formal homecoming invitation on a silver platter, I check out the box it came in. The zombie on the cover is a mostly skeletal girl in a tattered red homecoming dress, a crooked tiara resting on her flat green forehead (so . . . what, I'm going to turn green now? *That's my future?*), and a black sash hiding a thick gash in her throat, where you can almost, just barely, see the exposed vocal cords. (Nice. You stay classy, *Zombie Homecoming* filmmakers.) She looks all kinds of dead, not very attractive—or fun, for that matter—and about as lifelike as a dollar store Halloween mask on a half-price mannequin.

I sigh, watch the opening scene where the homecoming queen somehow takes a detour past the high school gym (why?), where it's clearly homecoming (I can tell by the big *Homecoming* banner over the double gym doors), and straight to the nuclear plant, presumably to make out with her boyfriend, who, uhhm . . . works there?

Late at night?

Even though he's still in high school?

And it's . . . homecoming?

What, he couldn't get the night off?

It goes downhill from there. (But then, what did I expect?) In the first 10 minutes of the movie, our plucky heroine (a) parks her car next to a stack of rusty yellow canisters with a red toxic waste symbol plastered all over them, even though two inches away there's clearly an empty parking lot full of much better spaces, (b) trips, twice, for no apparent reason, (c) finds her boyfriend in the Porta-John (???), (c) makes out with him (in the Porta-John, no less—grossness), (d) follows him back to her car, where (e) he leaves her without saying good-bye (rude), and (f) the toxic canisters magically open up and drown her in her car with a toxic green goop (that looks suspiciously like gallons of neon mint jelly). By minute 11, she's become a great green ogre, her toes falling off as her clueless date slips on her size-10 dress shoes on the way into the homecoming dance; hilarity ensues.

I turn it off shortly after that and stick in *Zombie Groom* next. Wow. Just, wow. At least *Zombie Homecoming* had a *little* charm; *Zombie Groom* is just gross. And not only gross but single-minded, charmless, *and* gross.

One minute the lead character is this semihandsome groom (look, we're not talking A-list stars here) who steps outside his wedding reception for a quick smoke; the next minute, some random zombie walks—sorry, stumbles—over, bites him on the neck, and suddenly he's . . . drumroll, please . . . Zombie Groom.

Zombie Groom is a lot hungrier than Zombie Homecoming Queen, who took at least five minutes to chomp her first victim after catching the Z-disease; Zombie Groom goes in for the kill almost immediately, biting his best man on the arm—right before he tears it off and gnaws on the elbow bone (elbone?) like it's a giant chicken leg. Then his best man, with only one arm, bites the caterer in the neck, blood gushes all over the pigs-in-a-blanket and, once again, hilarity ensues.

I watch for a few minutes more as the zombies get grayer and grayer, hungrier and hungrier, and less . . . human . . . by the minute. Half an hour into each of the first two flicks (or about as long as I can stand each one) the zombies have dragging arms, missing teeth, shrunken eyes, hanging jaws, blood-soaked chins, and they're eating small intestines for appetizers and human thighs for dessert.

I suffer through a few more—*Zombie Picnic, Zombie Cheerleader 4, Zombie Biker Gang 2*—until I've had about all the standard zombie dialogue I can take: "Brains, eat! Eat brains!" Then I slide the last disc out, put it back in its box, and spread the cases out, side by side, on the coffee table.

You know, kind of like a zombie lineup.

I stare at my future—rotting skin, sunken eye-holes, bad skin (gray or green seem to be the prevailing choices), holes in my clothes, bad prom dresses, torn sashes, grave dust in my hair, intestines like sausages hanging out of my mouth—and wonder, *Is this what I have to look forward to?*

I mean, when did the world decide vampires were the sexy undead? In the movies they could fly, flirt, seduce, sparkle, transform, kick butt, *and* look good doing it. Even werewolves got to look human 29 days a month, right? Could go out in the sun, enjoy a fresh burger, play Frisbee with their buds with no one the wiser?

But zombies? I haven't seen one zombie, anywhere, ever, that looks even remotely . . . human. They are dismal, dead, dying, and gray (or green, whatevs); dead eyes, dead mouths, dead brains, dead souls.

They don't say anything (except "Brains!" or, occasionally, "Eat brains!" or, once in awhile, "Brains, eat!"), don't do anything, don't . . . *feel* . . . anything.

So how come I can feel *everything*?

And just how long will it last?

20
Batter Up!

HAZEL SHOWS UP later that night as I'm watching the last of the zombie movies. (I can't help it; if I rent nine movies, I've got to watch all nine—even if they *are* degrading to zombies, in general and me, in particular)

She doesn't knock on the door, doesn't rap on the glass by the door, just uses her key and walks right in. "Break and enter much?" I say from the den, mostly so she'll know where I am. (As if the screaming victims running from the dead-eyed zombies wouldn't clue her in.)

"Bitch much?"

I snort out some of the Mountain Dew I've been sipping.

She flops down on the couch and grabs the cup from me and takes a sip. "Eewwww, where's the diet?" she asks, a wrinkle in her nose and a gag in her voice.

"I'm not buying diet anymore." I'm little-white-lying easily now that I've done it so often. "All that fake sugar is bad for you. My dad read a study where—"

"Really?" She interrupts, putting the cup down like it contains radioactive waste. "Well, tell him to read the study where high school girls who quit drinking diet soda get fat, lonely, and unpopular. I think he'll find it highly interesting. Maybe he'll even share it with you."

"Hmm." I sigh, glad to have Hazel back, on my couch, in my life, riding my ass. "And what respected scientific journal would that be in? *Liar, Liar, Pants on Fire*? Or maybe it's in volume 8 of *I Don't Know Jack; I'm Just Making All This Up*?"

"Uh, yeah, you'll actually find it in *Common Sense for Loser Girls*, volume 1."

"Touché." I giggle and, at last, she joins me.

We sit comfortably for a minute.

She leans back and turns her head my way. "I'm sorry, Maddy."

I look back, still smiling. "Sorry for what, Hazel? The part about accusing me of lying to you?" And even as I say the words, I kind of feel guilty for giving her grief when, actually, I totally *am* lying to her.

"Yes." She groans.

"Or the part about you stiffing me in Home Ec?"

"Yes." She groans again.

"Well, wait, I wasn't finished yet. Or the part about you not texting me for the last 24 hours?"

"Yes, yes, and whatever *else* you've got stored up for me, yes, I'm sorry for that, too. Maddy, I'm sorry; it's just—"

"Whoops, just one more. Or the part about you interrupting Stamp when I think, *think*, he was going to ask me to the Fall Formal?"

"*What*? You didn't tell me that. Why didn't you say something?"

"Uhhm, I did say something—with my eyes. I believe it was, 'If you don't get the hell out of here, I will poison your dog, if you ever get one,' or something along those lines."

Hazel is rocking back and forth, laughing, "God, I'm so stupid. I really thought I was doing you a favor."

"What? How? By getting Stamp to *not* ask me to the Fall Formal?"

"By getting Stamp involved *in* the Fall Formal.

I figured, you know, that way I'd have his ear more than his stupid football friends and, you know, could talk you up."

"Hmm." I sigh, shaking my head at Hazel's circular logic. "So let me get this straight: rather than letting a half-naked hottie ask me to the Fall Formal on the spot, you figured you'd interrupt me, blow me off, send me away, and lure him onto the Fall Formal Decorating Committee so you could convince him to do sometime next week what he was already willing to do yesterday? That is really awesome, Haze; thank you *so* much."

She's giggling so hard she almost—*almost*—forgets to notice my new Goth style. But she wouldn't be Hazel without quietly—and then not so quietly—judging me, so eventually she notices and gives me the proper best friend once-over.

Making sure I notice every eye roll, tongue click, and sigh of desperation over her best friend's fashion faux pas, she gradually works her way up from my black sneakers past my black sweats to my black hoodie and beyond to my pale face and dark eyeliner and maroon lipstick.

"Hmmm." She finally sighs, staring me in the eye. "Seriously? We're seriously doing this Goth thing? In public and everything?"

I wince. "Well, not permanently, Hazel. I mean, only until I figure out what this . . . sickness . . . I've come down with is and get back to normal. Once I'm feeling like myself, when total strangers aren't stopping me in the halls and asking me how long I have to live, yeah, I'll go back to khakis and white linen, but for now . . . like it or lump it."

She rolls her eyes and notices my hands on the back of the couch. "The black nail polish is a classy touch. Very eighth grade; so retro."

"Thank you." I laugh.

Just like that, Hazel is back: bigger, stronger, happier, sadder, funnier, and more judgmental than ever.

After a few more minutes of busting my balls over the new Goth look, she looks away from me and toward the TV screen. Before I can react and hit the pause button, she sits up, eyes wide. "*What* are you watching?"

I was so happy to see Hazel, I forgot all about the TV. I look at the screen to see the star of *Zombie Gardener 3* using his trimming shears to slice off the toes of his latest victim. At that precise moment, his mouth opens, and black, oozing goo pours out all over the floor of his nursery.

"N-n-nothing, just . . . some old movie that was

on. Saturday night, you know. What's really on?"

But Hazel is smart and sees the stack of zombie movies towering on the coffee table right next to the clicker. "This isn't on TV right now, Maddy; you actually *rented* this crap. Like, actually left the house to go and pick these titles out, specifically."

She reaches over and sees the zombie titles. "*Zombie Gardener 3*? Who knew there was a *Zombie Gardner 1* and *2*? *Zombie Biker Babes on Spring Break*? Maddy, what's gotten *into* you? I ditch you for one measly day and you resort to this—"

A knock on the door interrupts her tirade. What's left of my decaying heart flickers, but she smiles to beat the band and says, "Oh, *yes*. Please tell me I got here before Stamp was supposed to come over and take you out on a date. Please let that be my reward for saying 'I'm sorry' first this time."

I get up and go to the door to prove her wrong, dead wrong, but naturally she's there before me by a half second (damn her warm and fleshy human muscles) and whips open the door. The doorstep is empty; no one is there—but, no, that's not quite right, either.

I'm getting ready to shut the door when Hazel stops me and points to the middle of the deserted street, where two figures stand under a streetlamp. One is petite, dressed fashionably; the other is tall, dressed ridiculously—Dahlia and Bones.

"What the—?" Hazel stands stock-still, her hand still on the doorknob. "Aren't those the creeps from Home Ec? What are they doing prank knocking you on a Saturday night?"

I feel her pain. It's not exactly that I'm surprised to see them that's giving me the willies. I mean, after all, they *did* promise to get me alone and I suppose, in a way, I've been waiting for this moment ever since they bushwhacked me, Dane, and Chloe on the way back from our little late-night visit to the Council of Elders. It's the way they're standing there just so, stock-still, in the middle of the street, under that streetlight.

Creepy?

Creepy doesn't even begin to describe it.

I leave Hazel in the doorway for two seconds and reach into the hallway closet, where Dad keeps his weekend softball uniform. Resting underneath it is an aluminum bat. I grab it and walk past Hazel straight out to the driveway. She goes to follow me, and I say, "Hazel, lock the door and call the cops."

She does neither, following me out to the street instead.

"My, my," says Bones, not moving, not smiling, his lips barely fluttering as he watches Hazel's red pigtails bounce behind her. "Looks like we hit the jackpot tonight, Dahlia. We came here looking for Victim Number 4 and found Victim Number 5, too."

"What are they *talking* about, Maddy?" Hazel asks, her always minty breath stale and hot on my shoulder as she crowds next to me for safety.

"Nothing," I shout, as if her ear isn't two inches from my lips. "These fools are just talking nonsense, as usual."

"That's right, Hazel," says Dahlia, dressed in sleek, formfitting black from head to toe. She's done up her eyes and nails to match. "We're just fools, talking nonsense. Nothing to worry about here."

"N-n-no, no," Hazel stammers, sounding for the first time in, I think, her whole life somewhat less than confident. "You said something about victims. What were you talking about?"

Bones smiles. "Do we have to spell it out for you, Hazel? After all, *you're* the one who insists our Home Ec class is . . . cursed."

And I see the look in Hazel's eyes, and I see her

putting things together, and I think of the cold, hard Sentinels in their blue jumpsuits and what they'd do to me—to Hazel—if they found out I let a civilian know about the Zerkers, the Truce, and zombies in general. (Or me, in particular.)

So even though I don't want to, even though it is, in fact, the last thing in the world I'd like to do, I pick up the bat and start moving forward.

Bones is laughing as I walk, stiff but strong, out to meet him in the middle of the street.

Dahlia isn't. She moves swiftly to my side, and while Hazel screams for me to stop, they're suddenly on me, around me, and things move very, very slowly after that.

The bat is powerful in my hand and sounds blissful as I bring it down on Dahlia's shoulder blade with a thwacking, shuddering *crunch*.

She goes down immediately but not for long, and in the meantime Bones reaches for the bat with a long, spectral hand. I thwack it away with the bat, the hollow aluminum cracking along his bare knuckles once, then twice. He laughs, but I see him snatch his hand away and know that if I haven't exactly hurt him, I've at least surprised him.

Meanwhile Dahlia launches into me with a

lurching tackle, sending me sprawling onto the pavement, but I have a vise grip on the bat and pound it into her shins as she wrestles me back onto the ground. She shrieks and backs away, hobbling in her big black boots.

Then suddenly Bones is hovering over me, smiling before he kicks me halfway across the blacktop and practically into the tires of my car.

Hazel screams again, kneels to help me.

I murmur, "Hazel, get lost."

But she doesn't. She sits there, stupidly, as I stand and try to protect her as best I can.

It's freeing, not feeling the pain, but with Hazel right there I know that could all change at any minute.

So I rush to meet them back in the street, but they're slippery and know I've found my strength. I drag the bat along the street, liking the harsh, bare aluminum sound it makes on the even harsher blacktop, liking the vaguely startled look in the Zerkers' eyes even better.

Bones winces ever so slightly as Dahlia tries to blitz past me, but I catch her just under the chin when she thinks I'm not looking, and down she goes, pale and momentarily dazed.

But Bones is right there behind me, grabbing me

up in his arms until the bat is useless, and he's squeezing me tightly to punish me for laying a finger—make that a *bat*—on his precious, broken Dahlia.

I hear things cracking, things inside me—things I'm pretty sure I'll need later on—and know I'm not strong enough to fight Bones yet. Not like this; not all alone, Zerker-to-zombie. I struggle and squeal, wriggling and kicking and biting and clawing, until, like a gardener who's stumbled on a wasp's nest, Bones finally flings me down, hard, onto the pavement, just to get rid of me before he'd squash me like a bug.

I lie there dazed for a second, thinking of Hazel, and scramble up to protect her. But I'm already too late. At least, too late to save her by myself.

Miraculously, Bones lies on the ground, his neck under Dane's knee as Chloe holds Dahlia high overhead, threatening to crack her like a walnut over her thick, rather unladylike knee.

"Sorry, Maddy," Dane says, trying his best to keep Bones under control. "We came as fast as we heard."

"Heard what?" I say, walking up to meet them, grateful and proud that I'm only limping slightly.

"Heard *you*"—Chloe nods toward the bottom of our hill—"from the graveyard." Then she looks at Hazel, cowering by the hood of my car in her pink outfit and glitter nail polish and bright red pigtails and frosty crème lipstick and ruby red Converse high tops, and adds, "Or rather, heard Hazel screaming."

Bones grunts and knocks Dane off him.

Dane recovers speedily and I'm at his side, retrieving my bat from the ground and giving it that extra-noisy pavement slide. Dane gives me an approving, if somewhat startled, glance.

As Bones inches forward, Chloe clears her throat, inching Dahlia a fraction higher as if to say, *Move another inch, and Dahlia won't survive the night.*

Bones grunts. "Fine, fine, put her down, and I'll behave. For now . . ."

Chloe does, and Dahlia scampers to join Bones. Together they inch back into the spotlight as Chloe, Dane, and I follow closely on their heels.

"Did you think we'd leave her unprotected?" Dane asks with a smile.

"Ah, but you did," Bones says while Dahlia smirks beside him.

I smirk, too, noticing Dahlia's favoring one of her legs.

"Better yet"—Dahlia leans on Bones for support— "you will again."

And with that they're gone, out of the spotlight

and into the bushes beyond our street. I start to follow, to prove them wrong, to let them know I'm ready to finish this right now, but then I feel Dane's hand on my shoulder.

"Later, Maddy. For now we have to figure out what to do with your friend here."

"Hazel?" I turn to find her squatting, cross-legged on the ground, crying, and I run to her.

"What's happening?" she asks, fear in her voice. "Who are these people, and why are you holding that bat, and what happened to our weekly movie night?"

"W-w-what do I tell her?" I ask Dane as he stands over us both.

"Tell her the truth," he says.

"What's that?" I ask.

Chloe has joined us, her expression blank. "The truth? Simple: that you're a zombie, that Dane and I are zombies, that Bones and Dahlia are, well . . . bad . . . zombies, that they've already sucked the brains out of three of your classmates and, if we hadn't shown up, would've sucked out your brains, too."

21
The Z Files

"B-B-BUT THAT'S IMPOSSIBLE," Hazel insists a few minutes later, once she's safe in our cozy breakfast nook and I've placed a Christmas mug full of hot cocoa in her trembling hands. "I've read all of the articles about those girls from our Home Ec class, and none of them ever mentioned the word *brain*, to say nothing of *zombies*."

"Well, now, they wouldn't, would they?" Dane says as I pour him and Chloe a glass of Mountain Dew.

"Well, not unless she was reading *Fangoria*, they wouldn't." Chloe laughs, and when Dane joins her, I cut them a hard glance.

Hazel shivers in her chair, outnumbered by zombies—one of which used to be her best (human) friend.

217

Chloe snorts indignantly, but Dane sees what's happening and says, "Come on, Chloe, let's let Hazel . . . absorb . . . all this."

At the sound of her name, Hazel looks up. Her eyes are distant, as if she's seeing Dane but not seeing him.

Chloe drags him out of my kitchen and toward the front door, and I follow. "We'll be in the cemetery if you need us," she says ominously.

Dane looks at me with an apologetic little half smile. "Seriously, though, Maddy," he says as I linger in the doorway, "you need to make her understand how . . . sensitive . . . a situation this is."

While Chloe pounds stiffly down the sidewalk, Dane and I glance at Hazel, who's peering into her Christmas mug. "If she's strong enough to keep a secret, Maddy, I'll trust you to tell us so. But if she's going to cause trouble, then I have to know that, too. I mean, you've seen the Elders; you've seen the Sentinels. You know what's at stake here."

I stand back, vaguely insulted at the implications. "She's my best friend, Dane. I trust her completely."

"She's a Normal, Maddy. You keep forgetting; you're not *like* her anymore."

I nod but don't feel the need to make more promises.

"Fine, Maddy, whatever," Dane says. "If you

trust her, that's good enough for me. But don't forget, it's not safe for either of you with Bones and Dahlia pissed off now. We've got to stick together from here on in."

His words stay with me long after he's gone, long after Hazel's untouched cocoa has passed the lukewarm stage and gone straight to cold. Something has changed tonight, something fundamental. *Who* has to stick together from here on in? Hazel and I: BFFs? Or Dane, Chloe, and I: ZFFs?

As a best friend forever, my loyalty is with Hazel. If she knows, I have to trust her to keep my secret.

As a zombie friend forever, my loyalty is with Dane and Chloe. Long after Hazel and Dad and everyone I know on this planet are gone, they will still be there, watching my back.

We've got to stick together. Who's the "we" in that sentence?

I don't have to look far for the answer. "Hazel," I say, shocking her gaze out of the depths of her cold chocolate. "I'm sorry I didn't say anything before. The zombies, the Elders, they . . . wouldn't let me."

She merely shakes her head. "I knew something was up." Her tone is filled with failure, with sadness, with disappointment. "I knew something was wrong. I knew you'd . . . lied . . . to me."

I give her the moment; she's absolutely right.

Then she looks up and says, "Prove it, Maddy."

"Prove what?" I ask, but already I know the answer.

"Prove what you said; what *he* said, that creep in the hoodie. Prove you're a . . . a . . . zombie."

I was afraid of this. I stand up and walk to her and place her hand on my chest, where it stays while I count, "One one thousand, two one thousand, three one thousand . . ."

By the time I get to "forty-two one thousand," she's finally had enough and pulls her hand abruptly away. "Okay, so you're a zombie; that doesn't mean that Bones guy and Dahlia sucked the brains out of Amy and Sally and Missy. That stuff doesn't happen in real life."

"Oh, but your best friend turning into a zombie *does*?"

She opens her mouth to answer, to dispute, to one-up me, but can't.

I feel bad for Hazel. I had time to deal with my Assimilation. Well, not much, but still; more than she's getting.

"What if I can prove to you that those girls didn't show up in the morgue with their brains intact, Hazel? Will you believe me then?"

She looks up and simply nods.

I don't even have to sneak into Dad's office to peep his files. Well, not his work office, anyway, which is fortunate because the county morgue is set up in the sheriff's office, where there's someone manning the front desk 24/7/365.

But Dad does have a home office and his computer is linked to the Cobia County Coroner's Network. I log on to the county website, click on "Current Deceased Files" and, when asked for an account number and password before logging in, simply look under Dad's keyboard, where I find, on a faded sticky note, *account number and password*, and all the info I need.

I key both in and, just like that, Dad's autopsy files for the last six months are at my fingertips. I go to *search by name* and fill in all three girls' names, separating them with semicolons. "Amy Jaspers; Sally Kellogg; Missy Cunningham."

Like magic, the PDF files of their autopsies appear on the screen. Hazel, who's been standing over me, breathing onto the top of my head, suddenly looks away when Amy's autopsy photos pop up. I close that link and search instead for Dad's official findings, which I know from experience have the names of each internal organ and a blank next to each one to record its weight.

I find Amy's, then Sally's, then Missy's and print them out, one by one, before logging out of Dad's account and clearing his history bar so he won't see what I've been doing while he's been working another double shift.

From the printer, I grab the three sheets of paper. From the pencil holder, I grab a yellow highlighter. I look around, but Hazel has disappeared and, by the time I've highlighted the empty line next to where the weight of each girl's brain *should* have been recorded (but wasn't), I find Hazel sitting in the breakfast nook, her house keys on the table, her big pink purse in her lap.

"Well?"

I lay the sheets out for her, one next to the other, next to the other.

She looks at them skeptically until I point out the highlighted boxes. "So? This could mean anything. The lab misplaced it, the cops couldn't find it, any number of things could have—"

"That's why I highlighted Dad's notes at the bottom, Hazel."

She glances briefly at the big highlighted box at

the bottom of each form before shoving the print-outs away.

"Okay," I say, snatching each one up and reading them in order. "Amy Jaspers, cause of death termed accident. Only anomaly a deep gash in back of skull and her brain ripped out at the stem. Sally Kellogg, cause of death is termed by this coroner to be accidental. Only anomaly a deep gash in back of skull and her brain ripped out at the—Hazel, where are you going?"

"Fine." She walks toward the door while rubbing away tears from her eyes. "You've proved your point, okay? I'm suitably freaked out, all right? So, not only do zombies exist, but my best friend is one. Awesome. And she's not alone. There are four others in town. Yippee. And two of them are going around eating the brains of our entire Home Ec class, one by one. But thank goodness, the other two are hanging out in the cemetery watching over us, making sure we're not next. Happy now, Maddy?"

"Me? What'd I do wrong? You think I asked to be a zombie, Hazel? You think I *wanted* all this?"

She stops at the door, her mascara running, her

upper lip shiny with wasted tears. "I dunno, Maddy. I don't know anything anymore. I know you weren't very happy when you were alive, so I just hope you're happier as . . . as . . . a zombie."

22
Formerly Yours

MY FIRST WEEK as Barracuda Bay High School's newest Goth doesn't exactly go very well in just about every department. Lots of stares, lots of finger pointing, daily lectures from Ms. Haskins, from Hazel, and, well, let's just say it goes downhill after that.

By A-lunch on Wednesday I'm so ticked off—with everybody, everywhere, in every class, during every period—that the thought of suffering through another of Hazel's insufferable lectures about the difference between glam and Goth literally has my stomach turning.

So I avoid the cafeteria altogether and head out past the quad to the track and field, where B-lunch is still sweltering through a mild October noontime as their PE class winds down. Hey, as far as lunchtimes go, it's not a bad way to spend half an hour.

There are lots of strapping young guys in tight gym shorts and tighter tank tops, but I don't really even notice them as I climb into the bleachers and fume in my new Goth wear. I'll give you this much, though: the sun feels good on my face. I blink and put my sunglasses on top of my head, Princess Grace style, and stare off into the nothingness behind my thick gray eyelids.

"Maddy?"

Seriously? Now?

His legs look funny in shorts. Don't get me wrong; they're still hot. It's just . . . funny to see them so bare and so . . . close. "Stamp?"

"I've been looking all over for you," he says sincerely, sitting down backward on the bleacher bench in front of me. "Your car was already gone when I came by this morning, you haven't been to your locker in forever, you keep ditching Art class; it's like . . . like you're avoiding me or something."

Bingo! But not for the reason he thinks. "Stamp, I'm *not* avoiding you, really. I just—"

"Is that black lipstick?" He reaches to touch it.

ZOMBIES *Don't Cry*

I don't want him flinching from the cold of my skin, so I instinctively shrink back.

He doesn't seem hurt, just . . . more curious. "And, why are you, I mean, when did you go . . . Goth?"

"What? You don't like it? Well, you don't *have* to like it, Stamp. What, just 'cause you ask me out to a party—*once*—you think you can tell me how to dress? What to wear? Who to hang out with?"

He smiles, then laughs. "No, no, not at all. It's just, one day you look like little miss bookworm with the beret and the scarf and the stack of homework, and now, all of a sudden, you look like . . . like . . . a vampire chick. Actually, it's kind of . . . *hot.*"

I tilt my head. With the sun blazing right behind him, it kind of looks like he's wearing a halo. "Really?" I ask hopefully. I mean, if a guy like Stamp can go for the Goth look, maybe there's hope for me passing among the Normals yet.

"Yeah," he says, inching forward. "I mean, I always thought Goth chicks were kind of sexy."

"Yeah? Really? You're not just saying that?"

"All the girls in Wisconsin were so . . . blonde," he says. "And, I mean, they all looked the same. I dunno, I just, I'm digging the new look."

Oh boy; this is going to be harder than I thought.

227

"Listen, Stamp, about the other day—"

"Tell me this," he says, idly fingering the laces of my new black boots. "Are you going to wear this when we go to the Fall Formal on Friday?"

My stomach falls, and my mouth drops, and my eyes close, and I think, *Great. Your first official week as a fully Council-of-Elders-approved zombie, and you're about to break the Number 1 Rule of All Zombie Law Ever: "thou shalt not date Normals"?*

"I can't," I say, inching back like maybe I just saw a bug scamper across his thigh.

He blinks—twice—but never stops smiling. "Sure you can, Maddy; just say 'yes' and we're good to go. I mean, it's just a dance."

"No, I mean, I *can't* go, Stamp."

"Look, if your dad's not cool with it, I can talk to him and make him see . . ." He keeps blathering, the little black curl dangling over his forehead moving with each smarmy come-on.

No matter how attractive he's making it sound (and look), I have to shut him down completely, no questions asked. It's not even a Zombie Law thing so much as a common courtesy thing.

Even if it wasn't against the Law to date Normals, why would I? Why would I take a kid like Stamp and lead him on when it can't go anywhere? I mean, what am I going to do when it's time to go to second base? (Or is it third? I always get them mixed up.) Make sure it happens not merely near a sauna but *in* a sauna?

And what about after *that*? What if it's really the real thing and he wants to get married? Have kids someday? Can zombies even have kids? I'm doubting it since they have no heartbeat—and don't nutrients move through the blood?

And no, just . . . no. This has to stop. *Now.*

Whatever Stamp is saying, I shut him down in the worst way possible. "I don't mean I can't go to the dance, Stamp. I mean I can't go to the dance with . . . *you.*"

Ouch. And now his eyes go soft, not tearful soft, just . . . hurt soft. Great. So now I'm the creep at the end of *White Fang*? Tossing sticks at the wolf to get him to go away because I know he has to go live in the wild but *he* doesn't know that?

"I don't understand. I mean, I thought we had . . . something?"

"We do, Stamp; I mean, we did. But I'm not who you think I am. I'm not *what* you think I am. A good girl, I mean. I'm not, really, a good girl."

He shakes his head. "There's someone else?" he says, almost like he can't believe it.

And suddenly—right then and there—he gives me the out, the really mean, nasty out I've been struggling to find since he walked up the bleachers. "Yes, I mean, I didn't want to tell you but—"

"Who?" he asks. "Who is it?"

"You wouldn't know him."

"I don't care, Maddy. I want to know who it is."

Now his face is ruddy, and I'm mad that I have to do that to him, and mad that he's pushing it so hard, but most of all I'm mad that he can get red in the face when I never, ever will again.

"Fine, Stamp," I shout, standing in the bleachers, making a scene now. "You want to know why I can't go to the stupid dance with you, Stamp? I can't go to the Fall Formal with you, Stamp, because I'm already going with . . . with . . . Dane Fields."

Wow, *that* comes out of nowhere. He looks momentarily confused; then the clouds clear and the light shines and he smiles, thin and mean, and says, "What, that creep who's always hanging out with that Goth Amazon chick? The one who never takes down his hoodie, even in class? The one who smokes out by Shop class every day? *That's* the loser you chose over me?"

I want to say Dane's not a loser, that *I'm* the loser, but this is for the best. I keep telling myself this is for the best. So I let it go, I let him rant, and with every word, with every fleck of spittle that flies from those beautiful, full lips, I thank him, thank him for doing what needed to be done when I was too weak to do it myself. Because whatever he thinks of me, whatever lies I've had to tell, whatever happens next, at least he'll never know the truth.

Not the *real* truth.

"Fine, Maddy," he says, standing now, towering over me, his curl wagging left and right like that hanging ball in a grandfather clock. "Whatever. Take your little punk loser to the dance. I don't need you, Maddy. I can ask two dozen, three dozen chicks right now to go with me."

"Well then," I shout over my shoulder as I stomp down the bleacher steps, "I guess you better start stocking up on corsages."

23
Any Grave Will Do

LATER THAT DAY, sketch pad in hand, satchel over my shoulder, feeling desperately in need of a little grave rubbing therapy, I come across Scurvy toiling earnestly at the cemetery gates. He's pruning some bushes, looking ruddy with his sleeves rolled up and his gardening gloves on.

Blinking against the late afternoon sun, he asks, "What's got you smiling?"

I shake my head, taking in the strong scent of his clean sweat, his health, his . . . normality. "I shouldn't be smiling about anything with the day I've had, but sometimes you just gotta laugh to keep from crying, right?"

"Ain't that the truth?" He says it earnestly, like

maybe a guy named Scurvy would know all about it.

I stand there beside him and dig around in my satchel until I find the little freezer Baggie full of oatmeal cookies I made after school and hand them over.

"Ah." He slips off a glove and digs into them straightaway. "If only I wasn't married and 11 years older than you and you weren't the coroner's daughter," he says jokingly.

I wave him off over my shoulder and scuttle deeper into the graveyard, leaving behind the sound of Scurvy's headstone teeth chewing on warm cookies.

I've gotten here early because I don't want to be caught in the cemetery after dark. Not anymore, not with Bones and Dahlia on my case and this whole zombie and Zerker Truce thing resting in the balance. And it makes me feel better to think Scurvy will still be here even after I'm done with my latest grave rubbing. Okay, okay, so maybe I *should* have told Dane and Chloe about it; maybe I should have let them know where I was going to be, but you know what? I'm already dead. What's the worst that could happen? I'll die again?

I try to put the zombies, and especially the Zerkers, out of my mind for a minute. I attempt to forget how much Hazel and Ms. Haskins and pretty much everybody else at school hate my new "life-style choice." Instead, looking for exactly the right grave to rub to forget all my troubles, I think of Stamp. The way his face looked when I told him no, the way it practically fell, like all the life had gone out of him. I've never had anyone look at me that way before; chances are I never will again.

I think so hard I find myself in front of a not particularly cool headstone, with no real flourishes or distinguishing characteristics, but I'm so eager to start the process, so anxious to lay down my satchel and fondle my tools, so quick to be calm, that I don't really care.

I'm too sad to visit any of the girls from our Home Ec class; sadder still now that I know the real reason behind the Curse and how close I came to becoming Victim Number 4. I mean, Dane said the Zerkers liked to stalk their prey, to toy with it awhile and make sure the victim's brain was in fear over-drive before chowing down.

Is that what they were doing the last few days, tripping me in Home Ec? Following me to the grave-yard? Stalking me, putting my brain in a frenzy?

I think of Amy and Sally and Missy and what might have been happening to them in the days before they died. Was Bones shadowing them all around town? Was Dahlia giving them the evil eye up until the day they died? I shiver at the thought and try to blink their happy, sad, smiling, or crying faces away, glad I chose to stay far from their graves today.

So I sit at the generic grave. I empty my satchel and take out the brush, and the brushing feels good; so good I clean that headstone like it's probably never been cleaned before. (No offense to Scurvy, of course.)

Then I rip out a sheet of onionskin, tape it up tight, grab a perfectly new charcoal pencil, and start rubbing, just . . . rubbing, the sound of black charcoal dust on white paper, the scratch of the onionskin against the stone, the rushing, rushing back and forth and soon I'm in my place; the special place rubbings take me, where no one or nothing can get me—not even in a cemetery.

Scurvy stumbles over when I'm halfway through my rubbing, his shovel dragging business end down in the dirt, stray twigs, and grass. I look at my watch and realize I've already been at it for over an hour by now. One blissful hour with no Stamp, no Elders, no Dane or Chloe or Hazel or Goth or preppy or Bones.

"What's up, Scurv?" I say, happy to see him. Happy, at this point, to see *anyone* with a pulse.

He shakes his head. "I dunno, Maddy. I don't feel so hot."

He's standing over my gravestone now, looking red in the face but white in the throat, like a candy cane mixture of freezing and hot skin. He drops the shovel and wipes his brow. Some sweat drops on my rubbing, ruining it completely.

"Eewwww, Scurvy. Are you okay? You don't look so good."

"Look who's talking," he snaps, eyes yellow and angry.

"What?" I say, blinking the sight away.

"What?" he says, almost whispering now, his eyes suddenly back to being kind—and white. "What did I say? Why are you looking at me like that?"

"Scurvy, this isn't good. You're insulting me for no good reason. You're sweating all over my rubbing. You're standing way too close to me. Seriously, back. Off! You look like you're having a heart attack or something."

Scurvy's eyes go round and wide and all kinds of yellow, his throat and chest doing that crazy candy cane thing again. "Yeah, well *you* look like that lady on *The Addams Family*."

"Scurvy, that's *enough* now. Why are you *talking* to me like that?"

"I don't know." He practically whimpers. He looks at me, eyes white again, almost crying now, and whispers, once more, "I just . . . don't . . . *know.*"

Then he stumbles again, ripping my onionskin etching in half with his big, dirty, size-12 work boot. The tape holds the onionskin together at the top and sides, but still. Then I see the gash in Scurvy's neck, right below the collar, bright red and full of pus, bulging, almost throbbing like a cocoon getting ready to spurt out some strange new life form. When he straightens himself, the collar moves again and I see more clearly now; I see it's a bite mark, and I know. I know that Bones, or Dahlia, or maybe even Bones *and* Dahlia got to him.

And here I am, alone in the graveyard. No Dane or Chloe to save me this time. How could I have been so stupid? I back away toward his shovel, making sure it's close enough—just in case. Scurvy looks at me funny, like maybe he's seeing me for the first time, and now his skin is no longer red, or sweaty or, for that matter, Scurvy's.

Scurvy is gone; now something hard and gray and leathery and mean is standing there in his place. Yellow eyes burn above licking lips and he looks at me like I'm dinner. Or maybe dessert.

"What are you doing in my graveyard?" His voice is gravelly and strange and no longer Scurvy's. He is big and muscular anyway, and now he knows no sense of personal space. He keeps inching forward, leaning in, and then stumbling back, so that with every woozy, boozy movement he creeps closer.

And the closer he gets, the more I can see the emptiness that is Scurvy. The folksy 28-year-old I've been bribing with apples and oatmeal and peanut butter cookies for the last 3 years is now a brain-thirsty zombie; a Zerker, wanting one thing and one thing only: yes, the dreaded brains. But not just any brains; *my* brains. By now his arms are already knotty and tense, jerky and slow. His face is pale, dried out, no longer alert; no longer smiling.

Suddenly, those yellow eyes light up and he looks at my head like it's a pinata. "Brains," my friend the gravedigger says. Friend . . . human . . . no more. "Me . . . eat . . . Maddy's . . . brains."

I lean down, grab the shovel, and he lunges at me, barely missing my flesh with his teeth but clawing at my arm just the same with his rock-hard fingernails. I hear the tearing of my new black hoodie and feel his nails break my skin; they're like claws.

One of his fingers, maybe a thumb, gets stuck

in my hoodie, and down we go. He is like two tons of bricks in a pair of jeans, and I hear a *whoosh* seep out of my mouth. His arms are flailing, his yellow, gnarly, bent teeth chomping against each other—*clack, clackety, clack*—as he tries to find purchase in my skin.

The shovel went somewhere; as I slam one fist into his head and both knees into his crotch, I use the other hand to root around in the grass. I finally grab hold of the wooden end and yank it around for all it's worth.

I lash out with the shovel, hearing a thick *clank* against his knee as he goes down—again. And still he's coming, scrambling to follow me as I jump up. Bum knee or not, he's like a runaway train, so I *clank* the shovel into his shoulder, watching blood spurt out of a fresh wound, but still he comes.

It's like he's not even feeling it.

He's on all fours now, broken, bent, and still I whap him with the shovel, and still he murmurs, groans, shouts, screams, "Eat brains! Brains, eat!"

"Scurvy," I'm shouting. "Scurvy, stop!"

"Brains!"

I scream and close my eyes and slice the shovel into the wind, and I don't hear him coming anymore, don't hear him moving or shouting or anything much at all until . . . something . . . rolls against my feet. Then I look and see Scurvy's head lying there, between my bloody new army boots, and then I hear it all right: the screams—the screams.

My screams.

Part 3
The Afterlife

24
And So It Begins

LATER, AT DANE and Chloe's trailer, they're cleaning my wounds and bandaging them and wrapping them tight. It's not that they hurt, exactly (zombies don't feel pain, remember); it's just kind of hard to explain gaping wounds to your teachers and friends the next day in school, you know? "Oh, that? That's . . . nothing. I was just shaving my . . . ears, see . . . and the razor blade slipped and cut out a big chunk of my throat. What? You're saying that never happens to you?"

"They got to him, Maddy," Chloe says. "They bit him, maybe an hour before you got there; that's about all it takes to turn them."

I can't believe it. I can't believe I can be giving a

guy I've known for years—*years*—oatmeal cookies and a smile one minute and the next he's ready to rip off my head and snack on my brains.

"But then, why was he so nice to me when I first got there? We had a conversation, for Pete's sake. He even ate some of the cookies I gave him, made a joke—flirted! I mean, one minute he's Scurvy; the next he's a . . . a . . . Zerker."

"It's called the whiteout phase," Dane explains. "A kind of no-man's land between being a Normal and skipping being a zombie and then becoming a Zerker. They've been bitten, sure, but sometimes they don't feel it; sometimes they don't even remember it. So they go on thinking they're Normal because, well, why *wouldn't* they? Meanwhile, inside their body, their heart is slowly shutting down, their lungs are giving out, and the circuits are all switching over to electricity only. It takes about 30, 45 minutes to take effect. Then another 10 or 15 minutes or so to switch into full Zerker mode."

Chloe adds, "They must have been following you, Maddy. They know you dig the rubbings; that's where they found you the first time they threatened you, back when this all started and you were merely some Normal they wanted to suck the brains out of. So when they saw the satchel and the pad this afternoon, they knew where you were going. They headed down to the cemetery, bit Scurvy first thing. They knew how long it took you to do the rubbings. They knew Scurvy would turn long before you finished. And, let's face it, they were right."

I'm leaning against a counter in their tiny kitchen, my hands trembling, blood on my hands, when Dane says, "You should probably wash up."

I look down at myself and see why. Gheez, and I drove this way? With blood splatters on my clothes and gore on my hands? What if I'd been stopped by a cop? As the water runs over my hands, turning red to pink and washing the last of Scurvy down the drain, Dane sidles up behind me and says, quietly, almost apologetically, "You did the right thing, you know."

"I thought only Zerkers killed humans," I say, looking out the tiny window above the sink into the tiny patch of lawn they call their backyard.

He turns me around forcefully, yet gently. "You were defending yourself, Maddy. And remember, it was Zerkers who turned your friend."

My hands are dripping onto his shoes. He grabs a nearby dishtowel and gently, very gently, dries them off for me.

"That's just it," I say, snatching the rag from his hand and finishing the job myself. "He *was* my friend. He looked out for me, and you and I both know the only reason they bit him in the first place was *because* of me. So how do you live with that?"

Dane nods. Then opens his mouth to say something, probably some Dad-like platitude that I'm ready to bust him for the minute it comes out of his mouth, but I guess he thinks twice about it; I'll give him that much.

I hear a wooden chair scrape against clean linoleum, and Chloe joins us at the sink. This many people, in this tiny kitchen, it's like wedging three freshmen in a locker.

"If it helps any, Maddy," Chloe says, "he wasn't your friend anymore. The minute they bit him, he stopped being Scurvy."

I nod, glad for once that I can't cry because it's not very ladylike blubbering in a tiny kitchen in a green double-wide trailer.

Then she clears her throat and looks at Dane. "We should probably go see about the . . . body."

25
Home Ick

MY CAR IS idling in Hazel's driveway early the next morning. She's been so busy with decorating for the Fall Formal since Wednesday that she's ditched me the last few afternoons and caught rides with Tracy Byrd (aka Cheer Club captain, junior class president, leggy Southern blonde, and all-around Stepford Teen). But if there's one thing I need right now it's a friend who knows my secret—even a passive-aggressive one who vaguely resents me for being undead—so I stalk Hazel and force her to ride with me to school.

"But Tracy will wonder where I've gone," she says, biting her lip and leaning in my driver's side window. Her red hair is still wet, and she has two Styrofoam cups of coffee, one in each hand, which makes it even more difficult than usual for the *so*-not-a-morning-person Hazel to finagle her way into my car. When I look vaguely unsympathetic, she says, "She's the head of the Decorating Committee this year, you know."

"Is that for Tracy?" I ask as I guilt her into the passenger seat. When she doesn't answer, I say, "I've been driving you to school for a year and a half and you never once brought *me* coffee before school."

Somehow she wedges the steaming cups in my undersized cup holders. "You don't drink coffee, remember?"

I think of how long it's been since I've had human food. "How does your precious Tracy Byrd take her coffee? Sugar? Cream?"

"Two sugars. No cream. Gheez, carb much?"

"Perfect." I grab the second cup, whip off the lid, and take two big chugs.

"Careful! It's still hot." Then she remembers my secret, remembers what I am, and sits back.

I don't flinch but keep drinking until I feel semihuman.

Halfway to school, she says, a little vaguely, kind of standoffish, like, *oh, ho hum,* "I hear Stamp finally asked you to the Fall Formal."

"Yes, he did," I say, knuckles white on the

steering wheel. I wonder how she heard, seeing as I haven't talked to her since then. Stamp? Or one of the clowns in his PE class who no doubt heard my little temper tantrum on the bleachers the other day? Who knows? Maybe she has ESP.

"I hear you turned him down," she says.

See what I mean?

"Yes, I did."

"Hmmm." She sighs judgmentally over her steaming coffee. "Any particular reason? Or are you just bound and determined to sabotage what's left of your junior year?"

I pull up to a stop sign a few blocks from school and shoot her a sideways glance. Rather than whipping off her lid and tossing it in the backseat, like moi, Hazel has actually used that little bend-it-back-and-stick-it-in-place feature and is sipping through the little open triangle. I shake my head. Dead or alive, can't I do *anything* right?

"Hazel, let's quit pretending like this is any old school year, okay? Let's quit pretending like what happened Saturday night never happened, like you don't know I'm the Living Dead. Now, given that I have a few bigger things on my mind than the Fall Formal right now, do you really think I give one *shit* about the rest of my junior flippin' year?"

She doesn't answer. At least, not until we're finally angling for a spot in the student parking lot. Then she says, quietly, calmly, like she's been giving it a lot of thought, "So what am I supposed to do, Maddy? Sabotage *my* junior year, too? Just because you're dead, just because *you* don't care about school anymore? It still matters *a lot* to me. A *whole* lot, and I can't . . . afford . . . to waste a whole year following you around while you finish learning what it means to be a zombie. I mean, I still have to get into college, find a man, you know . . . things most human *beings* care about. So you're not entirely alone in this, okay? When your best friend turns into a zombie, well, there's . . . there's . . . collateral damage."

I turn to touch her arm, but she's already clattering the seat belt out of its clasp and grabbing her purse and bolting from the car.

"I'm sorry, Hazel," I say, not caring that she's turned it all around—again—and made it about her; not caring that it hurt me more than she'll ever know to dump Stamp like that. Just wanting, just needing, my best friend back.

She pauses before slamming the door, then

slams it anyway.

She takes a step away, pauses, turns back, and leans in. For a second there, I think she's going to apologize. I mean, I actually believe she's going to realize becoming a zombie trumps being unpopular.

But instead she says, "I know you didn't choose this, Maddy, but for once I wish you could think about how *your* actions affect *me* for a change."

And instead of blasting her, instead of slamming her, instead of pointing out that all I've ever done was think of her—even in the Afterlife—I cave, I whimper, I practically beg. Before she can walk away I ask, hopefully, desperately, "See you in Home Ec?" (Desperate much?)

She looks at me like I've just spoken Farsi or something. "Are you crazy, Maddy? The Fall Formal is *tonight*, remember? But then, why would you? You only turned down the hottest guy in school. Anyway, the Decorating Committee is in lockdown mode for the next 12 hours. I won't be in any of my classes today. Sorry." (Not that she sounds it.)

She's clattering away now, waving at some of her stupid new Decorating Committee friends, when I shout, a tad desperately, "So, when *will* I see you?"

But she doesn't answer; doesn't even turn around.

Nice, Maddy. First Stamp, now Hazel. "You're running out of people to hurt," I murmur to my Goth reflection in the rearview mirror. Then I fix my black lipstick, shut off my car, down the rest of stupid Tracy Byrd's stupid coffee, and head into school.

Homeroom is intolerable. Over the intercom it's nothing but *Fall Formal* this, *Fall Formal* that, *Night of a Thousand Stars* here, *don't forget to personalize your corsage* there. Even after the announcements are over, the whole class is abuzz with talk of tuxedo rentals and dress sizes and hair appointments and the going rate for pedicures down at the Clip 'N' Curl.

I picture Stamp in his tux, looking just about ravishing with hair slicked back, a shy, eager-to-please smile, and a corsage for me. I wonder who he'll take in my stead—which one of those "dozens" of girls he's asked since our little tiff—and I'm glad, actually, that I won't be there to see the two of them walk arm-in-arm.

Homeroom finally ends, but Civics class is no better. Most of the class must be on the Decorating Committee because they're nowhere to be found. With so few people, the teacher lets us text whoever we want for 50 full minutes. With no one on my friends list who's actually still my friend, it's a long, *long* 50 minutes.

Finally, I scuttle through the halls to the Home

Ec room, where, surprise, surprise, Bones and Dahlia are leaning against the wall outside. Seeing them standing there, so smugly, I suddenly remember the shovel in my hand, Scurvy's head at my feet, and I would love nothing better than to shove both of these Zerkers through the wall.

Instead I shuffle right up to them. "Sorry I missed you guys last night," I say, the span of the last few days making me angry, coarse, and fearless.

Dahlia makes big O eyes and says, "Who . . . *us*?"

"Where?" asks Bones.

"You guys know *where*, you guys know *who*, and you guys know *why*. But it doesn't matter. I'll never be a Zerker; *never*."

They chortle, and before I barge into class, Bones whispers, "Maybe we don't need you after all, Maddy."

"Yeah," Dahlia says. "Your friends are so . . . *delicious*. Much better-tasting than these pathetic Home Ec losers—"

I've never hit a girl before, or a boy, for that matter, but I have to confess it feels absolutely divine. No, wait; that's not quite right. What's the word Dahlia used right before I punched her square in the nose? *Delicious*. That's it—delicious!

"You *bitch*," she screams, both hands covering her nose as she squats down to the ground.

Bones turns to her and gently peels her hands away. Underneath them, her nose looks crooked, like a boxer's. (Ha! Like a 72-year-old boxer's.) There's no blood, of course, but I can tell just by looking I scored a direct hit.

I glance down at my knuckles, which appear slightly pink but none the worse for wear. I smile, Dahlia whimpers, but Bones stands up to his full six feet four inches and looks down at me with his evil, yellow eyes.

"Come on," he says to Dahlia, "I'll get you to the school nurse. I think Ms. Haskins has Home Ec covered today."

The way he says it, so delighted, so thrilled about Home Ec, I can't imagine what he means. That is, until I walk into class and see Ms. Haskins for myself.

The class seems oblivious that their teacher is the Living Dead. They murmur amongst themselves, idly cracking eggs and sifting flour as Muffin Month continues. (Today's flavor? Cranberry raisin.)

Ms. Haskins, so normally put together, so freshly fashionable, so sexily sophisticated, now looks tired, beat, and thoroughly worn. She's still dressed to the nines, still presentable (obviously Bones and Dahlia have given her the broad strokes about passing among the Normals), but something has clearly changed. Now I know what Bones meant about my "friends" being so tasty.

Apparently, Scurvy wasn't enough; they've gotten to Ms. Haskins, too.

But this is no wild-eyed Scurvy; this is no frenzied Zerker. Whatever they made her, they made her like . . . them. Her black hair, once so raven-like and enviable, is now a dusty shade of gray. Her eyes are yellow and dazed, like maybe she's waiting to wake up from a bad dream. Her clothes are still snug and sexy, just somewhat . . . off; the hem of her slutty red skirt is crooked, and it looks like she missed a button in her too-tight, too-white blouse. (Hmm, guess now that she's dead herself, she's no longer in mourning for her three former students.)

As the class clusters and mixes, banters and bakes, Ms. Haskins kind of . . . hovers . . . around her back desk area, silently pacing from one end of the room to the other like a gear in a groove. I hold my purse close, ignore the other kids, and walk slowly back to where she's pacing.

"Ms. Haskins?" I say, tentatively, the marks

from Scurvy's stealth attack still fresh on my mind and, literally, torn into my skin.

She looks up, eyes and teeth yellow, smile grim between two thin, razor-tight lips. "Yes . . . Maddy?" She says it like maybe she's not sure it's me or, for that matter, who I am or why she should care.

I clear my throat. "I just was wondering, I mean . . . are you . . . okay?"

She cocks her head, just so, and where her high white blouse collar formerly hid the bite marks, now I see them plain as day. They're not fresh and bubbling, like Scurvy's were, but scarred over and pale, like maybe they turned her first—and she's had all night, or even longer, to calm down, smooth out, and come to what's left of her senses.

"I'm fine." Her voice croaks, like maybe overnight she smoked 42 packs of cigarettes nonstop while downing a dozen pints of 100-proof whiskey. She looks somewhere over my shoulder as her eyes refuse to focus. "Why do you ask?"

"Oh, nothing. It's just . . . forget it. Listen, I'm not feeling so hot myself. Do you think I could have a hall pass to—"

Before I can even finish coming up with an excuse, she reaches down to her desk and tosses me the whole pad of her personalized "From the Kitchen of Ms. Haskins" hall passes. I shake my head, take them all, and slip out of class.

Boncs and Dahlia are gone by now, but I'm pretty sure they didn't go anywhere near the nurse's station. I imagine them roaming the halls, chomping on anyone I've ever known or loved or cared about or borrowed a No. 2 pencil from. I cower in the C-wing girls' room for as long as I dare, leaning against the busted hand dryer under the window and frantically texting Chloe and Dane: *Wher R u guyz?!?!?!*

Neither one answers right away, and I'm scared of getting trapped in some small space alone, so I wander over to the biggest place I know: the gym. I've never been honored enough to be asked to decorate for the Fall Formal (let alone attend), so it's quite something to see the auditorium in frantic, festive behind-the-scenes mode.

The posters around school have been touting the "Night of a Thousand Stars" theme (real original, guys) for weeks now, and when I walk into the gym and see the preparations for myself, it's like they're taking the theme literally. Okay, so maybe there aren't technically a thousand, but there *are* hundreds and hundreds of cardboard stars slathered with glitter spread out across the entire gym floor.

Rows of Decorating Committee members loop fishing string through the holes in the tops of stars for hanging later; they look like they're picking strawberries or something, bent over and focused, moving shoulder-to-shoulder, step by step, row by row.

I hear Hazel's voice before I see her. She's laughing, naturally; with a boy, double naturally. Only, it's not just any boy. In the middle of the gym, surrounded by shiny cardboard stars at my frozen feet, I watch as Stamp makes Hazel giggle, as Hazel reaches up to toy with his Superman curl, as Stamp reaches back to move a wisp of red hair from her face, as he leans in with googly eyes, puckers up, ready to plant one on Hazel's—

"Hey," someone shouts. "Look where you're *going*."

But I can't look where I'm going. I can't even see what I'm doing as I'm backing out of the gym, crunching stars beneath my feet left and right, glue and glitter stuck to the soles of my new army boots, desperate to leave the auditorium and never, ever look back.

26
Eternally Yours

GRADUALLY, THROUGHOUT THE rest of that endless day, order breaks down at Barracuda Bay High School. Whether it's the four or five people missing from each class to paint and glitter and hang stars in the gym, or the two or three more who simply skipped school to alter their dresses or get their hair done, or the lazy teachers handing out word searches and crossword puzzles to the kids unpopular or lame enough to actually come to class, the whole school has that lazy, do-nothing, care-about-nothing, day-before-summer feel.

Anticipation fills the halls, kids are abuzz, and even the teachers—at least, the ones the Zerkers haven't turned into zombies, that is—are in a festive mood. I make it a habit as I enter each class to address each teacher. If their clothes are all buttoned properly, their eyes aren't yellow, and they respond promptly with my name, I smile and say, "Oh, never mind."

So far, so good.

All except for Ms. Haskins, that is.

I walk into Art class prepared for the worst, but Mrs. Witherspoon is bright-eyed and the class is nearly deserted. The Art Chicks who actually bothered to show up for class are hanging out together at one of the long, black drawing tables in the back, flipping through a new copy of *Elle* and ignoring me with their droll expressions and knowing eyes and whispering mouths.

Stamp is there, fuming in the back, arms crossed, lips tight—not zombie tight, just . . . pissed tight— waiting for me. With so many empty seats available, I skip the one beside him and sit in front of him instead.

"Real mature," he says. I hear his chair scooting and then, just like that, he's right next to me.

"Back off," I say, forgetting my new zombie strength and shoving him away. His chair scoots literally to the next table over.

Mrs. Witherspoon cocks an eyebrow above her big goofy glasses. The Art Chicks giggle and one says, "Lover's spat," in a singsong voice, but Stamp just picks up his chair, walks back across the room, and sets it down even closer to me.

"Bench-press much?" he asks, face red from being flung across the room by, of all things, a girl.

"A little," I lie. *The Guide* said I'd get stronger over time, but this? First I'm beheading gravediggers with a single swing; next I'm breaking Zerker nose from the standing position; then I'm tossing 200-pound jock hunks halfway across the room? A girl could really get used to this.

"So . . . you know about me and . . . Hazel?"

"Whatever do you mean?" I say, playing it innocent.

Stamp frowns. "We saw you in the gym, Maddy. *Everyone* saw you in the gym."

When I don't answer, he adds, "I didn't want you to . . . find out . . . that way."

I groan and roll my eyes. "How *did* you want me to find out, Stamp? Were you and Hazel going to rent out one of those sign planes and announce it to all of Barracuda Bay at once so my humiliation could be complete?"

"Hey, *you're* the one who turned me down, remember?"

"Okay, fine, but then you have to turn right

around and run and ask Hazel? Hazel? Really? My *best* friend? What happened to those three dozen *other* chicks you were going to ask first?"

He's quiet, looking down at his shoes, not defending himself, and suddenly I get it. Hazel and her moody ways lately, Hazel jock-blocking me the day Chloe took me shopping, Hazel ditching our before- and after-school rides all week, the frustrated look on her face this morning as she was getting out of my car, as if she wanted to say something but then, at the very last minute, thought better of it.

"You didn't ask her, did you, Stamp? *She* asked *you.*"

He doesn't shake his head, doesn't nod, but I know.

Suddenly a thought occurs to me. "Just tell me this, Stamp. Did she ask you *before* you asked me . . . or after?"

Stamp blushes, opens his mouth to answer, then stops himself. "I . . . I can't answer that, Maddy."

"You just did."

Then the door bursts open and suddenly Hazel storms in.

"Hazel," we shout, halfway out of our seats by the time she starts marching down the aisles.

She looks . . . bad. My stomach drops. Even from

across the room, I can see the fresh bite marks on her shoulder where her rapid pace makes her roomy peasant blouse bunch and gather, then unbunch and ungather.

Oh God; oh God, no. Not Hazel; not *my* Hazel.

"Get away from him, Maddy," she shouts, spittle flying, eyes wide, cold and—yellow. Flashlight-in-the-dark yellow. Black-cat's-eye yellow. Zerker yellow.

Oh God, not her, too.

In a flash, everything is gone. All of it. Everything we've built together—wasted, utterly and truly abandoned. I picture Hazel as I first met her: pigtails then, pigtails now; a little frilly pink dress as we drew on the sidewalk with pink and blue chalk. (Guess which color she chose?)

I think of all the firsts we've shared since then: first day of junior high, first locker combinations, first periods (and not the kind you go to when the bell rings, either), first kisses, first crushes, first sips of beer at Rob Blonsky's pool party, first driver's license exams, first—everything.

I can't imagine a time when Hazel and I *weren't* sharing firsts together; I've known her for most of the years I've been alive—and now neither of us is alive. And even now, suddenly, I can't stand the sight of her.

Knowing what she is, knowing what Bones and Dahlia have done to her, what they've made her, how—ugly—they've made her, the sight of her clenching white jaws and glowing yellow eyes makes me want to look away, to deny her, to deny all those firsts.

But I can't. Even now, she's still my best friend.

Stamp stands up, his chair flying back into the table behind us with a clattering explosion of plastic and metal. As Mrs. Witherspoon and the Art Chicks watch on in amazement, Hazel launches herself across the table at me. (I mean, this is some serious soap opera shit right here.)

Stamp is fast but not fast enough. I am, though. With my new strength, I grab her wrists with one hand and the back of her neck with the other, slamming her—hard—into the table. With her face hanging down off the table, I lean in and whisper into her ear, "I know what you've done; I know what they did to you. Back off, Hazel; you're not up to this."

She hisses, spits, and I stand up, inch away so she's out of range before releasing her. Then I shove Stamp out of the way as she bolts upright and wheels around. It feels wrong, unnatural, taking sides with Stamp against my best friend, but I've already seen what the Zerker strain did to Scurvy. If it's going to do that to Hazel, she's already gone. But then a strange thing happens. Suddenly a little of the old Hazel is back—the popular one, the one who takes extracurricular activities to round out her college applications, the people pleaser, the teacher pleaser.

With Stamp safe behind me and the Art Chicks clustered in the other corner of the room protected by a quivering Mrs. Witherspoon, Hazel stands up, straightens her frilly dress, tucks a strand of red hair behind her pink ear, and says, "I'm sorry about that little . . . display . . . Mrs. Witherspoon. I don't know what got into me. Stamp, if you'll be so kind, the Decorating Committee needs your . . . help."

Without asking for permission, Hazel yanks Stamp from the class. He goes willingly, not looking back. In their wake, I'm left to clean up the pieces, and now I'm no longer the Maddy Mrs. Witherspoon, or even the Art Chicks, knew. Busted, I slip from class, ignoring Mrs. Witherspoon's protests and waving Ms. Haskins' pad full of free hall passes in her face on my way out the door.

I chase after Hazel, catching her as she rounds the C-wing corner headed for the commons. "Hazel!"

She turns, whispers something to Stamp, and shoves him in the general direction of the student parking lot.

"Stamp?" I whimper, but he only pauses, giving me those "it's not my fault" eyes before turning and scampering away.

Hazel turns and takes a battle stance, as if I might follow him and she has the right to stop me. I stop, take one step back. "Whoa," I say soothingly, still a few yards from her. "Hazel, I just . . . I want to talk to you. This is . . . this is crazy."

She stands her ground, doesn't move a muscle, and already I can see the gray pallor has her, the dark shadows seeming to deepen under her eyes even as she speaks. "What's so crazy, Maddy?"

But even as she waits for the answer, I know nothing I say is going to change what she's become, what we've become.

"This, Hazel. Can't you see? *This* is crazy. You storming in here, dragging Stamp away like some cavewoman. This isn't like you."

"That's because I'm the new me, Maddy, and there's nothing you can do about it."

Even as I'm mourning the death of our friendship, she seems almost . . . happy . . . about it. She's smiling, and I know it's not to look brave; her smile goes deep down to the heart of her, as if she's glad we don't have to be friends anymore.

"Sure there is, Hazel. I'm still me, dead or alive. I'm still me. I *can* help you; Dane and Chloe can help you, the Elders, the Sentinels . . . somebody . . . can help you. You have to fight it, Hazel; fight it for a little while longer so we can get you some help."

"Fight what, Maddy? Why would I fight feeling this . . . good? For once in my life, I can be exactly who I want to be and nobody can stop me. Not even *you*."

At this, of all things, I laugh. Out loud. "When in the *hell* have you ever not done exactly what you wanted to, Hazel? I mean, you didn't have to become a Zerker to get your own damn way. You've been getting your way since we met."

Now she takes a step forward, but not to fight; at least, not with her fists anyway. But then again, Hazel was always a warrior with words. "That's what you think I've been doing all this time, Maddy? Getting *my* way? You think I've been doing this all for *me*? You think being friends with *you* has helped *me*? Bitch, please. You've been holding me back since day one. Why couldn't we have moved onto a street with popular bitches? With cool chicks? You think I enjoy movie night with you every Saturday? You think I enjoy passing up invitations from prettier, more popular girls—and guys—to babysit your sorry ass every weekend? I've been doing *you* a favor, Maddy; but no more. Now it's my time."

My lips quiver but, of course, no tears come. I take a step forward and she flinches, but I keep coming until we're face-to-face, and I slap her with the open part of my hand. Hard; hard enough to where, if she were still alive, her jaw might crack. Instead, she flinches, and it's my marble hand against her marble skin.

"You take that *back*, Hazel. You take it *all* back, right now. I know you didn't mean it; I know you've been a true friend. You couldn't have been faking it all these years. Know how I know? 'Cause you're not that good an actress. This is just, just . . . some . . . disease making you say all this."

She doesn't fight back, doesn't rush me and tear my blouse or yank my hair or try to shove me in a freshman locker. She just rubs the place where I slapped her and says, "Bones was right; I really can't feel anything."

It's like her eyes are empty; like she's already gone. Like nothing we've ever done together, talked about, laughed or cried about is still up there behind those empty yellow eyes. Like it's all been erased for good. "I don't understand how you can be this . . . brutal." I whimper, hating myself for saying it, powerless to *not* say it.

Hazel actually laughs; the sound is cruel to start with, but even crueler as it bounces off the floor and wall tiles until I'm in a pure vortex of hateful Hazel laughter. "Bones was right about you, too, Maddy. He said you were weak, and I thought he was wrong. But he was right; you *are* weak. And you had your shot at being a zombie first; now let me show you how it's really done."

"That's what you think this is, Hazel? A big competition? This is life and death, Hazel; this is forever. You don't go through a Zerker phase and tap out when you're done; you're in it for life. And if you think I'm happy about being the first to die, Jesus, kid, you've got a *lot* to learn."

"Me?" she says, inching forward before backing away. "We'll see who's teaching who when it's all said and done, Maddy."

And with that, she's off, turning on her heels and scrambling away in jerky movements. Though I know she can no longer hear me, I shout, "Whom! It's 'We'll see who's teaching whom.' You never were good in English. I've been carrying *you* for years."

In her wake, the halls—and my life—are empty.

It's like my own personal Armageddon or something.

I head straight for my locker on hollow legs, planning on grabbing a few books for the weekend and . . . heading home, hiding out, and trying to forget the last two weeks ever happened. (Damn, has it only been two frickin' weeks?)

I key in my combination, open my locker, and out falls a shiny silver envelope. On the front is my name, my full name: *Madison Emily Swift.* It's written in loopy, feminine script.

For one split second my dead, nonbeating heart thrums to life. I think it's from Hazel—a sorry note or some other heartfelt missive—but then I reason, *How could she apologize in advance for something she just did?*

I open it and find these words:

Dear Maddy,

You are cordially invited to tonight's Fall Formal. Please bring your two new friends, Dane and Chloe. We promise you _won't_ be disappointed. In fact, it could be a night to _die_ for.

Eternally yours,
Bones and Dahlia

A boot squeak on the hall floor startles me, and when I turn from my open locker, I see Dane and Chloe waiting for me, shiny invitations in their hands, already open and read.

"I guess the Truce is over," I say.

Dane looks like he just ate a pound of bad brains, then another, just to make sure. "You have no idea."

27
Breaking & Tasering

"**D**O I REALLY have to *do* this?" I ask half an hour later, pulling up in front of the Barracuda Bay Sheriff's Office.

"It's the only way, Maddy," says Dane, who's riding shotgun in my tiny green Honda Civic.

"But it's my dad. What if somebody finds out they're missing? He could lose his job."

"No one's going to find out, Maddy," Chloe says from the backseat. "They're just Tasers; three stupid Tasers. It's not like you're breaking into the Pentagon and stealing government secrets or anything."

"I just don't want my dad to get hurt. I'm done for. That's fine; I get that. But he's still alive. He still needs to eat and make a living and have a roof over his head."

"For now," Chloe says.

I whip around. "What does *that* mean?"

Dane touches my shoulder and waits until I turn to face him. "Maddy, if we don't do this, your dad's going to get hurt in a way that can't be reversed. Like Ms. Haskins; like . . . Hazel. If we don't stop the Zerkers tonight, and stop them dead, this whole town could be infested by morning."

"Fine," I say, getting out of the car and slamming the door for good measure.

Inside the sheriff's office, I smile demurely at a few of the folks I know from backyard barbecues or softball games or the annual Cobia County Employee Christmas Party, which Dad drags me to every year.

I get a few odd looks before I remember none of these people have seen Goth Maddy yet. (Oh, the grief Dad will be getting in the break room after this little visit.) My backpack is snug on my arm, emptied of books and papers and folders to make room for the three police-issue Tasers Dane and Chloe want me to steal from the ammunition room.

Dad's office is across from it, but then again Dad's office is also across from just about *everything* in the tiny building: the coffeemaker, the vending machine, the ladies' room, the broom closet—you get the picture.

Dad is surprised to see me but not too surprised. It's a small town, and the police station isn't too far away from school. I've been known to drop by once or twice a week with a to-go dinner when I know he's working late or a box of donuts and thermos of coffee if he's working early.

"Maddy!" His eyes light up as he stands up from his desk chair. "What a nice surprise."

"Hey, Dad." I try to keep the sad sound of betrayal out of my voice. "What's up?"

"What's up with *me*?" he says, sliding his bifocals down to the tip of his nose so he can see me better. "What's up with you? Isn't tonight the night of that big dance you've been looking forward to?"

I slump down in a squeaky gray chair across from his desk and make a big show of being all tired-like. "Yup," I say, between fake yawns. "That's why I came to see you. I knew you wouldn't have time to come home and snap pictures of me and my . . . date . . . so I thought I'd give you a sneak preview."

Dad looks toward the doorway. "You brought your date?" he asks hopefully.

"No," I say, looking pointedly at the display skeleton hanging in one corner of the room. "You think I want my date to think of corpses all night?"

He laughs and then looks at me more closely. "Well, you're not wearing *that*, are you?"

I snort, looking down at the full-on Goth gear I chose for school this morning. So far, Dad's been pretty understanding of the whole Goth phase. Not overly enthusiastic, mind you, but more understanding than, say, Hazel. (Of course, now I know why.) I fiddle with the short hem of my black pleather skirt and say, "Naw, I've still got to go home and change. That's why I wanted to swing by here first; in case I missed you." More fake yawns.

He looks at me funny. "Well, you need to perk up, Maddy. You've got a long night ahead of you, and you want to enjoy it. Hey, can I get you a cup of coffee? I've got a few minutes before my next autopsy; you can tell me about your dress."

Bingo!

"I thought you'd never ask," I say (and at least *that's* no lie).

When he disappears across the hall to get me the coffee I've been angling for ever since I walked in, I reach over his desk, open the top drawer, and snag his key ring. Yes, I feel bad doing it; yes, I know I'm a rotten zombie, but I *am* a zombie and, after all, it's for his own good.

It's like Dane said: steal the keys now and feel like a jerk for a few minutes; don't steal them, don't stop the Zerkers, let the town be infested, and feel even worse when your dad becomes one of the Living Dead and tries to eat your brains after work one night.

The keys are safe in my pocket by the time Dad comes back with two steaming cups of coffee. I look into mine, and he's put cream in there. I stop myself from making a face and take a sip to make him happy. We make small talk, and he says, "So, is this that new guy you were telling me about? The one who plays football? The one who looks like Superman?"

I nod, hoping that by not actually saying the word "yes" the lie is only half as bad. (You know, as compared to, say, stealing your dad's keychain and a couple of Tasers from the ammunition room.)

"Oh, good," Dad says. "He sounds like a nice boy."

I nod noncommittally, picturing Hazel dragging Stamp from Art class and his helpless look as she ordered him away in the commons. Then I think of Hazel—poor, undead Hazel.

Dad kind of senses something's amiss and says, actually says, "And Hazel? Do you approve of *her* date?"

I almost spit out the coffee I'm pretending to enjoy. But what might have been a slapstick moment

24 hours ago finds me in a kind of sad, heartbroken limbo.

When I don't answer, when I can't answer (no more lies!), Dad stifles his hopeful grin and says, "Maddy, you look like you've seen a ghost. What's wrong? Goodness, dear; you've been waiting for this dance for the last two years. I thought you'd be happier than this."

And God, how I want to spill it all. To confess about stealing the Tasers, to explain what for, but most of all to tell him Hazel—his sweet caretaker Hazel—is gone and not coming back. And still I can't talk, and still his concern grows more apparent by the second, but I can't help it. I'm powerless to fake it anymore, to pretend my entire world isn't collapsing around my head, that my best friend isn't merely dead but worse than dead—a Zerker who in a few hours is going to try to kill me with her bare hands if she gets the chance.

A buzzer sounds somewhere, and soon enough I see a vibrating beeper shake itself across Dad's desk like a Mexican jumping bean.

"Oh booger," he says absently, pushing his glasses higher on his nose. "I thought we'd have more time. Listen, I'm really happy for you, dear.

Maybe tomorrow morning you can tell me all about it?"

Sure, I think. *If any of us are still alive, that is.* Out loud I say, "Sure, Dad. I'll make you breakfast and fill you in on all the gory details."

"Splendid." He hugs me on the way out. We stand in the hallway together, and he says, "Shall I walk you out?"

I wave the thought away and point to the ladies' room. "I'm going to powder my nose, and then I'll see you back home . . . whenever."

"Whenever. Right." He smiles mischievously. "Do you need a curfew, or can I trust you?"

I pause and blink twice. Dad? Asking *me* if I need a curfew? Has he forgotten his own house rules? He seems to read my mind and shrugs. "Hey, I've already broken one rule by letting you go to the dance with a guy I've never met; I might as well let you choose your own curfew, right?"

"Seriously? No curfew?" It's not like I was going to obey it in the first place, not after what Dane and Chloe have planned for the evening, but the fact that he's offering means a lot.

He doesn't answer. His beeper buzzes again, and he presses it to shut off the annoying sound, then ambles away down the hall, turning back to wink at me before entering the autopsy wing.

I sigh, look around, find the right key, and let myself into the ammunition room. It's not much bigger than a broom closet, just much better armed. The real guns, of course, are locked up tight. Dozens of rifles line one wall, locked safely behind a mesh wire gate. Ditto for the ammunition clips and pistols.

But the bulletproof vests are fair game, as are the walkie-talkies and Tasers. The Tasers are in plain view, stacked next to each other in their identical wall chargers. Time is ticking away. I don't know how long I've been inside, but it feels like an eternity and every footstep outside seems to be headed right for the ammunition room door.

Finally I commit, I dunno, a misdemeanor— or is it a felony?—by yanking three supercharged Tasers from their solid black outlets. I shove them in my backpack, zip it up tight, and listen at the door before I can tell the coast is clear.

The Tasers are bulkier than I thought, and heavier, too, as I lean over Dad's desk and return his keys. I stand by his desk for a minute, steadying my nerves for the final phase of Operation Dick Your Dad over to Keep the Whole Town from Being Infested.

On the way out of the sheriff's office, I keep

waiting for one of Dad's colleagues to stop me, frisk me, lock me up, and throw away the key, but they just smile at Dad's leggy 17-year-old Goth daughter, shaking their heads at the idleness of youth and eyeing my short black skirt on the way out the door, ignoring the three clearly Taser-shaped bulges in the backpack jostling directly above my dead derriere.

I stow the backpack with the Tasers in the trunk and barely stop myself from peeling out of the sheriff's office and making a scene. "Where to next?" I ask cheerfully, almost casually, as if I do this type of stuff every day.

"You got them?" Chloe asks doubtfully.

I nod curtly and head downtown, our zombie shopping spree now in full swing.

First stop, the fireworks store. While Dane pops inside with a twenty dollar bill, I turn to Chloe to ask, "Are we going to scare them with firecrackers or something?"

She snorts but doesn't look up from inspecting her chipped black nails. "Cherry bombs, actually. Zerkers hate them. Something about the sulfur reminds them of their graves, I guess; whatever the reason, they *really* freak out."

"Does it kill them?"

She finally looks up and frowns apologetically. "I wish. No, it only makes them weak and panicked for a few minutes. Kind of like garlic to a vampire. You know, if they actually existed or anything. The goal is, freak them out with cherry bombs and tase them before they know what's happening."

I note her dour expression. "You don't sound too confident of that working out."

She shrugs. "You know why we call them Zerkers, Maddy?" When I shake my head, she explains, "It's short for 'Berserkers.' So, the thing is, you can plan on this and hope for that; you can go by the rules of what's *supposed* to happen, but at the end of the day, you have to remember that these are just plain crazy, strong, mad, angry, mean, vicious zombies who occasionally go berserk."

I frown, staring over her head and expecting Dane to stride out of the fireworks store any second. When he doesn't, Chloe explains, "It's the Fall Formal. Kids like to stock up on fireworks and set them off on the beach afterward. You know, kind of like a tradition. It's probably a madhouse in there right now."

"Is that what you and Dane like to do?" I ask, girlfriend to girlfriend.

She thinks for a second, smiles. "What, you

think Dane and I are . . . an . . . *item*?"

"Hmmm." I sigh, chin still on the back of my seat as I stay on the lookout for Dane and his cherry bomb stash. "Let's see, you've been inseparable since you showed up at Barracuda Bay High at the beginning of this year. You drive to school together, eat together, *live* together. What *should* I think?"

She looks nonplussed, like maybe she doesn't care *what* I think. "We're just trailer mates, Maddy. I've already told you my sad story; his is not quite as bad."

I start to ask, but she barely pauses before plunging ahead and granting my secret wish to know what turned Dane the boy into Dane the . . . zombie.

"When his car went off the road and slammed into that power plant, well, the body they pulled out of the wreckage was dead. When he woke up in the morgue, late at night, Dane just . . . walked away.

"No one ever reported the body missing. His parents already figured he was dead; no reason to muddy the waters, right? He wandered from town to town for a few weeks, walking at night, lying low during the day. I was the first zombie he met, so I became his chaperone; that's all. Kind of like we did for you. That's it, Maddy, really."

"Yeah, but you guys live together; I mean, surely

you must be tempted every now and again."

She snorts and smiles. "Tempted? By Dane? Maddy, he's still a zombie baby compared to me. He's still a little . . . young for my taste."

"Hmm, zombies have a taste?"

"Not every . . . impulse . . . dies, you know. Electricity goes everywhere. Yeah, I have a taste—"

Suddenly the passenger door opens, cutting her off midsentence.

"Taste for what?" Dane says, clutching his bag of cherry bombs triumphantly as he clambers into the shotgun seat.

"Nothing," I say, turning forward in my seat and backing out of the parking lot. "Just . . . girl talk." Looking in the rearview mirror, I wink at Chloe; she winks, too—a first!

It's slim pickings at the formalwear shop at the mall, where the best dresses were snatched up weeks ago. I find a sleek little emerald number, just formal and sexy enough, but a size too big.

"I can alter it," Chloe says confidently.

"You sure?"

She smiles. "I'm going to have to alter anything we wear anyway, so . . . sure. I think you'll look good in that."

ZOMBIES *Don't Cry*

She finds something in burgundy, which looks a little too . . . ruffly . . . for my taste. But hey, at this stage of the game, beggars can't be choosers, right?

We find Dane in the men's department picking out a smooth powder blue tux—the only color left in his size. He looks embarrassed, but as Chloe settles up the bill (who knew zombies had credit cards?) I lean in and whisper, "I think you'll look good in something other than . . . black . . . for a change."

He bites his lower lip doubtfully.

Our last stop is the cemetery. "Seriously?" I ask as we pile out of the car.

"I'm sorry, Maddy," Dane says. "We need some fresh grave dirt; it's like Kryptonite for the Zerkers. Plus, I think, well, I think you'll feel better if you see where Scurvy was laid to rest."

They lead me to a grave in the older part of the cemetery that looks like all the rest. Well, at least until you take a closer look; then it's easy to see where the earth has been disturbed.

"After you told us what happened," Chloe says, filling her backpack with cemetery dirt, "Dane and I came here and found Scurvy. It would have attracted too much attention to leave him like that, so we found an old grave we knew nobody would be visiting anytime soon, dug it up and, well, buried him above the old casket."

"You did him a favor," Dane says as Chloe fills her bag to the brim and zips it up.

"What, by beheading him?" I ask, shuffling my feet.

"Better to rest in peace here," Dane says, "than to wind up a Zerker for eternity."

He squeezes my shoulder gently, lets his hand linger there, and then follows Chloe away from the grave. They linger for a minute, then start walking away.

"Maddy?" Chloe asks over her shoulder.

"Five seconds," I say, holding up a hand for emphasis. "I want to . . . pay my last respects."

When they're out of earshot and heading for the open cemetery gates, I say, quietly, reverently, "Scurvy, you were always nice to me, and you were the only person on the planet who liked my oatmeal and peanut butter cookies, and I'm sorry I got you into this. I know it wasn't your fault, and you won't understand, but tonight, with a little help from my new friends, I'm going to make it up to you. I promise."

28
The Business End

BACK AT THE trailer, we get straight to it.

Chloe and Dane have moved the living room furniture into their (separate) bedrooms, so all that remains of the main living area is just carpet and bare walls. On top of the kitchen counter are three stakes, each about as long as your standard slasher movie butcher knife.

Chloe has changed into black gym shorts and a tight gray T-shirt that says, *Demons Do It Longer.* (Gross.) Dane is in sweats and a tank top, his skin fat-free and hairless, his muscles pronounced. He is sitting Indian style on the living room floor, working out the kinks in the Tasers.

Chloe picks up one of the stakes and says, "It's

nearly impossible to cut a Zerker, Maddy. Their hides are tough."

"Like leather?" I ask, eyeing the three identical stakes.

"Like stone," she says. "Tougher than our skin; harder."

I remember Dahlia's bent nose under my knuckles and agree. "So what are these for?" I ask. Before she can stop me, I grab one of the stakes by the copper end.

When I come to, I'm lying on the kitchen floor, Dane and Chloe standing above me, shaking their heads, parent-style.

"Wow!" I say, the electric current still sizzling through my body like the best three-candy-bar sugar high imaginable. "What just happened?"

As they help me up, Dane says, "You grabbed the business end first, Maddy."

"But aren't they stakes?" I say, kind of enjoying the whooshing of current still flooding through my body.

"Well, technically I guess you could consider them stakes, only . . . in reverse. The wooden part is the handle," says Chloe, a slightly bemused expression on her face. "You hold it like this." The wooden part's in her hand and the flat, circular, copper end—kind of like a notary stamp—faces out.

"Well, that's not very dangerous-looking."

She smirks. "Maybe it doesn't *look* dangerous, but it knocked you out cold for 20 or 30 seconds. That's enough time to do some serious damage if you get the chance. And if you can get it past the skin and shove it in far enough, for long enough, well—it *will* kill them."

I look confused, reaching for the stake and—as they gasp and reach to stop me—picking it up by the wooden end at the last minute.

Dane explains, "Copper conducts electricity. To Normals, it's no big deal. But to Zerkers, it creates havoc on the system. You stick them with one of these and, *boom*, out go the lights."

"Or, at least, in theory anyway."

I'm twirling the stake like a baton, careful to avoid the copper end, when I say, "Wait. Hold up. 'In theory'? What does *that* mean?" When they don't answer me right away, looking at each other sheepishly, I shout, "Don't you guys *know* already?"

They stand awkwardly, side by side, looking down at their feet. "I mean, you *have* done this before, right? Right?"

"Well, technically." Chloe hems. "I mean, we've

already taken Zerker Slaughter 101—"

"And we've read the chapter on Zerker massacres in *The Guide*." Dane haws. "But—"

"But *what*, you guys? You come off like you're some big, famous, lethal Zerker hunters. Now I find out you've never actually *killed* any before?"

Nothing. More floor staring and feet shuffling.

"Chloe?" I ask, taking the direct approach. "How many Zerkers have you killed before?"

"None, okay?"

"Dane?"

"Well, I buried one once."

"Hmmm." I sigh. "Would that have been . . . yesterday?"

He nods, still avoiding my eyes.

"So, basically, I've been a zombie for, what, less than two weeks and I've already killed more Zerkers than you two? Unbelievable, just . . . unbelievable."

29
Three's Company

"Ruffles?" I ask skeptically as Chloe picks at my hemline and slowly sews it into place a few hours later. "Really? Ruffles? I'm not trying to sound indelicate here, Chloe, but you *were* a pubescent zombie way back in the '80s. You *do* know fashion has moved on since then, right? That 'Like a Virgin' is no longer at the top of the charts?"

Dane smiles from the living room doorway, handsome and sleek—if a little stiff—in his powder blue tux. Rather than highlighting his pale skin and dark eyes, the tux complements them; he looks kind of like a zombie 007, and I smile shyly.

Chloe notices and yanks on my ruffles to get my attention.

"The ruffles contain the dirt from the grave-yard," Dane says, patting his shoulders. "That's why they feel a little . . . heavy."

"Yeah, well *you* don't have to wear ruffles." I pout as Chloe ties a knot on the underside of my hem and bites the thread off. "Where are you hiding your graveyard dirt, huh, Mr. Aloof and Mysterious?"

He smiles and flips up the collar of his tux. Underneath are hastily sewn blue pouches bulging with grave dirt. "Right here," he says. "Neat, huh?"

Actually, it is; even from five paces, you can't really see the bulges when he puts the collar back in place. "And look here," he adds, digging into his hip pockets and pulling out handfuls of more grave dirt. "In a pinch, I can even blind them with this."

"And Chloe?" I ask. "She's got no ruffles."

"No," says Chloe, standing from the floor and pointing to her hips, "but I've got these." She points to the frills at her narrow waist, graveyard soil buried in a round, tubelike belt hidden beneath a row of white roses in the pattern winding around her like a garden vine.

"Still, you guys look downright fashionable compared to me."

"Maddy," Chloe says, handing me a copper-tipped

stake for my purse. "Get your head in the game, will you? We're not actually going to the dance to see and be seen, remember? We're going to kill us some Zerkers, right?"

I make a "ghee whiz" face, and Dane laughs.

"Look," Chloe says, beckoning Dane to the full-length mirror she's hauled into the living room to help with the alterations. She pulls me close so that the three of us are standing in front of it together.

Dane looks dashing and robust in his tux. Even Chloe looks (almost) ladylike and demure in her slimming, satiny gown. And my emerald ruffle nightmare doesn't look *that* bad when combined with the pancake makeup, thick plum lipstick, deep dark eye shadow, and frills of rich, black hair cascading from the do Chloe gave me right before I slipped into my dress

The trailer is quiet as we grab our mini stakes and slide them into our formalwear. Chloe and I weave them into the folds at the front of our dresses, making sure to keep the deadly copper from touching our skin, while Dane slides his into his tux pocket. These are easy to hide, but the bulky Tasers provide more of a challenge. They're shaped like cell phones but twice as big—and solid, fatter, and heavy; really heavy.

Dane can fit one in his pocket without looking too ridiculous, but he wants us each to have one in case we get separated in the gym. Mine fits in my purse without looking too obvious, but Chloe's clutch purse is smaller and clam-shaped.

"Chloe," Dane snaps, "that purse won't work; get another one."

She looks at me conspiratorially and I frown; that purse really *does* match her dress (something a clod like Dane would never understand). Still, a massacre is a massacre, so she dutifully replaces the purse with something big enough to fit a Taser in. (Unfortunately, it's a rather clunky black affair with a rhinestone skull for a clasp.)

By now, the crisp fall afternoon has turned to dusk, the dusk to twilight. Orange shadows bathe us on the way back to school. As we slowly inch forward in the growing line of traffic waiting to park, I have to admit that, despite the circumstances, I get caught up in all the high school excitement that is the Fall Formal. Most of the cars in line are limousines, where alternating douche bags in white tuxes stick heads through the sun roof and hoot at the girls in convertibles in front or behind.

Chloe and Dane look disgusted, but whether it's

because I haven't been a zombie as long or because I'm just a romantic at (nonbeating) heart, part of me wishes I could turn back time and say "yes" when Stamp asked me to the dance.

Yes, it would've been breaking all kinds of zombie laws and, no, it wouldn't have stopped Bones and Dahlia from turning Scurvy and Ms. Haskins . . . and Hazel . . . into zombies, but at least I would've been able to go to the Fall Formal without grave dirt in my ruffles, a stake hiding just below my cleavage, and a Taser in my purse.

As we finally pull into the jam-packed school parking lot, I notice the assistant principal and the dean dressed in three-piece suits (no tuxes for them) checking girls' bags on the way in.

"Uh, guys," I say, pointing to the unanticipated checkpoint.

In the rearview mirror, Dane flashes me a yellowing smile. "Don't worry, Diva; I've got it covered."

As Dane fiddles with something in his lap, Chloe nudges me in the arm and mouths, "Diva?"

I shrug and muscle my way into one of the last remaining spots in the lot. As I park, I have to wonder, *Has Dane Fields just used a term of endearment?*

As we walk toward the school, Chloe and I adjust

our purses full of Tasers and sulfur-spewing cherry bombs. Our heels are low (all the better to fight Zerkers with, my dear), but after a week of clomping around in polished black army boots, the sound of them scraping on the asphalt sounds funny.

A line has formed at the purse-frisking station, and I shift nervously from one foot to the other, craning my neck for any wandering hordes of Zerkers in sparkly black dresses and shiny white track suit tuxes. Instead, all I hear is Dane chattering with the two thugs behind us, identically decked out in satiny tan retro tuxes and matching gobs of spiky hair goo.

"You two guys together?" Dane asks when we're only a few couples away from the check-in point.

"Dane," I whisper, elbowing him as the two thugs bow up. "We don't have time for this now."

"Let him be," Chloe whispers as she jabs an elbow in my ribs. "He knows what he's doing."

"No," one of the thugs says.

"Why?" asks the other, preening. "You interested, pretty boy?"

Clearly these two hunks of meat aren't smart enough to be offended.

"No," Dane says sarcastically. "But your boyfriend sure is. He's been checking me out all—"

Finally, I hear one of the thug's fists break on Dane's forehead as he hurls the first punch, followed by what I think is girls screaming but what is, in fact, the thug squealing in pain.

"Inside, ladies," the assistant principal shouts to us poor, defenseless girls, instantly abandoning the checkpoint to rush to the thug's aid.

While the dean and assistant VP are trying to get the story out of the bumbling boobs in tan, Chloe grabs one of Dane's arms and I grab another as we hustle him inside before the rest can be sorted out.

We keep going, plunging deep past the punch bowl and frosted grapes at the snack table and right onto the dance floor. If you ever get the chance to see a zombie dance, avoid it. We are pretty bad, but fortunately it's a medium tempo song and nothing that will twist our subtly moving hips out of joint. When the song is done we figure the coast is finally clear, so we amble off the dance floor and find solace at a blue, curtain-draped high-top table toward the back of the room.

"That was close," I say because, hey, I've always wanted to.

Chloe and Dane are scanning the crowd, looking for the Zerkers. It isn't easy, even with zombie vision. The dance floor and its periphery are dotted with swirling teenagers, all in some form of evening wear.

The lights are rotating, swirling, first thousands of white pinpoints cascading across the floor, then flashing strobe lights, then multicolor spotlights randomly roaming the dance floor until they fix on some random couple who's then expected to show off, at least until the spotlights move on to humiliate someone else.

Thinking I see a flash of ugly yellow Zerker eye on the perimeter, I step away from the table only to be promptly yanked back by Chloe. "Stay together," she whispers. "That's what they want: to pull us apart, get us alone. If we're going to survive, if we're going to win, we *have* to stick together."

"Okay, okay, sorry," I say, wrenching my arm away from her cold, titanium grip. "But I thought I saw—"

"Dahlia!" Dane points with a half-empty plastic punch glass to the dead, yellow eyes and zombie stiffness I saw moments ago. I make a face at Chloe as we slowly stalk the Zerker through the crowd.

She's standing alone at a tall table, like the one we just vacated. We stop a few tables short, elbow our way to an empty table, and watch carefully. She seems to be alone; no glass in front of her, only a clutch purse like mine, and her expression is serene.

After five minutes, no one has come to join her. Not Bones, not Ms. Haskins, not Hazel—not anyone else they may have infected since they dropped those shiny gray invitations in our lockers earlier this morning.

"How are we supposed to do this?" I say over the thumping bass of another fast song. "There are so many people."

Chloe nods. "We've got to wait until the crowd thins; get each one alone." She pulls her cell from her clutch purse and says to Dane, "Text me when she goes to use the bathroom." To me she adds, "You follow her in; we'll try to ambush her."

Dane shakes his head. "I don't like it." He cranes his neck to look for a sign—any sign—of Bones or Hazel. "It just feels too . . . easy."

"It is what it is," Chloe says before departing. Even though she passes within inches of Dahlia, the Zerker never even looks her way.

"Hey," Dane calls after her. "You forgot your purse!" To me he says, "She always does that."

"Where do you think they are?" I ask Dane, inching closer to him so I won't have to shout over the spastic DJ (or so I tell myself).

He shrugs, his shoulders big and broad in his flattering tuxedo. "Maybe they're waiting till the crowd thins, too."

I'm looking at him under the twinkling stars, the strobe lights, the alternating spots. In school, he never changes his ever present hoodie, never wears anything but jeans and scuffed shoes. I've always pictured him as slight and frail, at least skinny and tall, but all the while he's been hiding a fairly hot zombie bod under all those protective layers.

He catches me looking, waves a large, pale, dismissive hand, and says, as if zombies are mind readers, too, "Relax. It's just the muscles; they harden over time, the fat melts away, the muscle takes its place, they get bigger is all. It has nothing to do with me. I mean, it's not like I work out or anything."

I smile. "Will that happen to me?"

He looks into my eyes and says, "You don't need any help to look beautiful."

Then he abruptly looks away, as if something has caught his eye.

It has. Dahlia is gone.

We leave the table as a pair, him grabbing my hand to tug me through the still healthy crowd. Finally, we get within eight paces of Dahlia and see her heading straight for the ladies' room.

"Go," Dane says as I hurry to follow. He clicks on his phone and says, "She's coming. Chloe? Can you hear me? Chloe?"

He calls after me, but the music is too loud for me to respond and, anyway, I'm totally focused on Dahlia and couldn't—wouldn't—pull back even if I wanted to. Instead, I follow her straight into the bathroom.

And, of course, straight into the trap.

30
Zombies in the Girls' Room

BY THE TIME I get there, Chloe is already hog-tied with jump ropes; they must have brought them in their purses. She is facedown on the bathroom floor, her chin up defiantly, her mouth moving violently behind a gym sock gag.

Meanwhile, all the sinks are overflowing, gushing over their sides and into a veritable lake on the girls' room floor. I'm already three feet in, with water halfway up my shoes, when I notice Dahlia at my back. She shoves me forward so hard, so fast, I almost fall face-first in the running water. (These stupid heels don't help matters any.)

Then I see her.

In the same slinky evening gown I helped her

pick out weeks ago, Hazel stands triumphantly over Chloe, who writhes and struggles against the tight, polyester ropes.

"Don't even try it," Hazel says to me, holding a portable radio high above Chloe's head.

At first I laugh. Were these Zerkers *that* stupid that they didn't even know electricity brought zombies *back* to life—not put them out of their misery?

Then Chloe wriggles free from her gag. "Get out of here, Maddy. One shock to bring us back to life, remember? And one shock to kill us. If you get zapped twice, that's that."

Just as quickly, my amusement turns to fear—not for me so much; I never expected to make it through this night in the first place, not really—but for Chloe, who's only in trouble *because* of me.

If I'd never bumped into Stamp that day, if he'd never invited me to that stupid party, if I'd never snuck out that night, none of this would be happening right now. Chloe would be Chloe and Dane would be Dane and Hazel would be Hazel and I'd just be the girl in the background, watching it all from the very last row.

Dahlia has the door, so there's no way out (even if I were chicken enough to leave Chloe lying there alone).

ZOMBIES *Don't Cry*

Hazel has the radio, and at any second she could put us all out of our misery. She leaves it teetering carelessly on the hand dryer as the sinks continue overflowing, cascading sheets of water onto the already deluged floor.

Hazel walks over to me, a sneer on her pale, dead face, not even trying to hide the puncture marks above the spaghetti strap of her little black formal dress. "I thought all zombies knew that."

"What would you know, Hazel?" I ask, my voice a shade deeper since the last time we talked, a shade tougher as well. "You're not a *real* zombie anyway. You're a watered-down version of these half zombies you call friends."

"Maybe so," says Hazel, her triumphant smile slightly dinged, "but I'm not the one with my friend lying hog-tied on the floor, now, am I?"

"Why are you doing this, Hazel?" I ask, stalling for time, inching forward, tougher than her, a zombie longer than her, my muscles and legs and bones and will stronger than hers could ever be. "You were my friend. You were my *best* friend. We've known each other for 11 years, Hazel. And you turn on me that fast? Like . . . like you're a stranger; like you've *always* been a stranger."

Hazel barely flinches, impatient for my little trip down memory lane to come to a swift and certain end. "And the first day I met you I told you not to lie to me, Maddy. And what did you do?"

"When, Hazel? *When* did I lie?"

"When you didn't tell me you got struck by lightning, Maddy. When you didn't tell me you were a zombie. When you let me believe you were just sick, when all the time you were . . . dead."

"But I *did* tell you, Hazel. I mean, eventually I came clean."

"Only when you couldn't hide it from me any longer. Only when I saw it with my very own eyes."

"Okay, so maybe I omitted a few pertinent facts, Hazel, but I *never* lied."

Hazel shakes her head. "It's the same thing, Maddy. And besides, whatever we had, whatever we *thought* we had, it's nothing compared to what Dahlia and Bones have given me."

I turn to Dahlia, who says triumphantly, "I told you we'd get you all alone, Maddy. All I needed was your friend here to make it happen."

"They're using you, Hazel," I shout, turning back to my former best friend. "Using *you* to get to *me*. Can't you see that? It's all a big game for them, turning people, making them Zerkers, then leaving them to die. Or killing them themselves. They don't care about you. They turned Scurvy, too, Hazel. I had to kill him, put him down."

I pause and shoot a look straight into her evil yellow eyes. "Don't think I won't do it to you, too."

By now she's inched back to the hand dryer, picked up the radio, and holds it over her head. Her fierce red hair is in an updo, no longer quite so fierce but certainly stylish.

I look down at Chloe, her eyes closed against the coming shock.

Hazel says, "Not if I do it to you first." With that, she drops the radio.

"Don't forget, you're a zombie, too," I shout before leaping up on the nearest toilet seat.

The floor ignites in a snaking ripple of pure, blue current. It's like a thin, blue flame branching out over the black-and-white tile floor. From the stall next to me, Dahlia laughs as Chloe goes limp and Hazel crashes to the floor next to her, wilted and lifeless like a giant rag doll; a well-dressed rag doll, but a rag doll just the same. I scramble to crawl up the bathroom stall, up out of Dahlia's reach, as the electricity boils my friends—old and new.

The bright bathroom lights flicker, then go out altogether. In the darkness I see the Zerker crouching in my way as I race across the tops of the stalls for the bathroom door. The ceiling is right above my head and low so I have to crouch and scuttle, almost like a crab. I stop, barely out of reach.

An emergency light over the sink mirrors flickers on as the generators kick in, casting a hazy red glow over the waterlogged bathroom. (All the better to see you with, my dear.) From beyond the doors, I can already hear screams. The screams of Normals. The power must have shorted everything, everywhere, plunging the dance floor and the rest of the gym into darkness.

There is a knocking at the door, somebody big and strong, and just when I think Dane has come to save us, an adult voice bellows, "Anybody in there? The main power's been cut and there's not enough juice in the generator to run your precious disco ball; the dance is over. Report outside immediately for a head count. Everybody's going home . . ."

In the glowing red light, Dahlia jumps from the top of the stall, catching the railing above with gymnastlike reflexes. As if lowered by a tether, she slides almost effortlessly to the ground, her muscles

obviously much more accustomed to the zombie life-
style—and the effects of gravity on deadweight—
than mine will ever be.

"All according to plan," she says, stepping on
Chloe's lifeless body to avoid the electric blue current
still sizzling along the black-and-white floor.

I crouch on top of the nearest stall.

Dahlia looks up. "Don't stay too long, dear;
you'll miss all the fun."

I wait until her back is turned and she's heading
for the bathroom door to make my move. I leap down,
down, my heavy zombie body landing with a *thud* on
poor Chloe's back. I hear a *crack* but ignore it.

Dahlia turns at the sound, her hand scrambling
for the door handle, but I leapfrog from Chloe's
body to Hazel's and slam the retreating Zerker
hard against the bathroom door. Her nose cracks,
again and again. I yank her head around and lift her
up and over me, tossing her over my shoulder and
through the air.

She lands on a sink; a slippery, flowing sink.
Her hands scramble for purchase, her thickly veined
muscles holding her aloft as long as possible while her
legs scamper and scurry to avoid touching the floor.
Her heels fall off, her black stockings drenched, her

eyes panicked as finally, at last, her hands slip off the cool, wet porcelain and down she goes.

There is a faint crackle, then a whiff, of electricity before she goes out completely. I groan, the tension inside flowing out through my vocal cords and into the dead red air of the sizzling bathroom.

Like a frog leaping from lily pad to lily pad, I step from body to body until I hear the crunch of Dahlia's ribs beneath my new heels. Next to her is the radio plug, still live thanks to the school's stupid generator; I yank it out of the wall right before sliding off of Dahlia's slick, dead body and onto the flooded floor.

Now the water is just water; now the bathroom is just a bathroom. I stare at the cluster of bodies jumbled on the bathroom floor, Dahlia lying halfway across Hazel, Hazel jammed up gracelessly against Chloe, like a zombie traffic jam.

I check Chloe first, turning her over onto her back and snapping her jump rope bonds with two stiff fingers as her legs intertwine with Hazel's. Her arms fall limp to the floor, making a sad splashing noise in the three inches of water struggling to bleed through the overworked drain in the middle of the floor.

"Chloe," I say, but she is already gone.

ZOMBIES *Don't Cry*

I feel a stirring beside me and look to see Hazel sitting up and rubbing her head. Only then do I really consider where she's fallen after she dropped the boom box and electrified the entire room: half on the floor, half on Chloe's lifeless body. She must have avoided the full shock of the current by being just far enough off of the watery floor.

With my purse drenched and ruined and across the floor, much too far away to get to in time, with Chloe's purse resting uselessly on some random table out in the gym, I reach slowly for the stake in my dress, carefully avoiding the business end this time.

"Hazel!" I shout as she struggles to her feet, her eyes live and electric yellow, her hair wet and matted, her skin pale as the white floor tiles. "It's me, remember?"

She cocks her head, smiles. "Who's the zombie *now*, Maddy?" She lunges for me, zombie strong and Zerker angry; she moves so swiftly, so stealthily, the stake gets knocked out of my hand and slides into a lonely, wet corner of the bathroom floor. With equal parts regret and anger, I watch it clatter across the tiles, tumbling end over end. I curse, loudly, and fling her off, hearing something snap as her back hits the metal corner of the nearest stall.

She lands with a yelp, sliding down to the still

wet floor, but recovers on wobbly knees; one has a hole over it where her stocking's been torn. Her dress is also ripped and tattered. Her shoulders are crooked and off-kilter as she stands, like maybe I *did* break something important after all, but her smile remains intact.

She looks hungry, ready for anything—and eager to get it over with.

She circles me, kicking off her high heels for better traction on the slippery bathroom floor. One hits me in the leg and she cackles ruthlessly; the other lands harmlessly a couple of feet away. I stand my ground, watching her waiting, sad and grim and three kinds of pissed off.

"Look!" I say as she circles, endlessly circles. "Look at what you've done. I hope you're happy with yourself."

"Not yet," she says, lunging again.

This time I'm ready for her. As she ducks slightly to pick up momentum, I move to one side—kind of like a bullfighter—and elbow her in the back of the neck even as I grab hold of the back of her dress and use it like a luggage handle to propel her, headfirst, into the nearest wall.

While she sits, legs splayed out, rubbing her

head, smiling against the wall, I tumble to reach for my stake. She catches me across the floor with a stiff foot to the chin, which knocks me back, back, back. I would stop if the floor were dry, but now it's like a Slip-N-Slide in this grim, death-filled bathroom. As I slide and glide, my attempts to stop myself with wet hands on wet tile only propel me farther back.

Hazel, always smart, always quick, now spies the stake I've been trying to get to and inches toward it, one bruised hand at a time. She is stiff and pale, hard and crooked and wild-eyed, but inching forward with every ounce of Zerker energy in her dead body. Her dress is ragged, the back of her red hair dotted with plaster from the wall, her stockings worn to shreds, her feet bare.

"You don't want to do that, Hazel," I say as I crawl slowly back to her on the slippery tiles. Still too far away to do any good, I try to reason with my old friend.

"Reverse psychology." She scoffs. "You were reaching for it, so it must be some kind of weapon."

"Not the kind you want, Hazel."

She is almost there, smiling gleefully now, so eager to find something to hurt me with, to stab me with, to kill me with, that she can't hear the reason, the fear, the concern in my voice. With real relish, with eyes wide open, with something like a victory smile already playing at the corners of her lips, she reaches for the stake.

"Hazel!" I shout, but it's already too late. Maybe it's always been too late.

She grabs the business end first, assuming wrongly that the sharp wooden end is designed to kill me. (And how wickedly eager she is to kill me.) I thought she'd go down, out for the count and lie there like I did when I grabbed the copper end in Dane's trailer earlier.

Then I remember: she's a Zerker, not a zombie.

Instead she springs to life, sizzling like a frankfurter on the end of a stick as it roasts over a summertime campfire. Now that she's headed that way anyway, I race to help her cross back to the other side. I slip once on the wet tiles but use the bottom of the nearest stall to propel myself forward, jamming her bare chest against my stake as her back meets the bathroom wall.

It goes halfway in, and she screams, whimpering, "But I'm your friend, Maddy! I'm your friend."

"*She* was my friend," I say, jerking my head toward a fallen Chloe before I shove the stake the rest of the way in, copper end first. "*You* were just my . . . neighbor."

Suddenly, as if they've been waiting for our little dance of death to be over, someone is pounding frantically on the bathroom door. I rush to open it and see that Dahlia locked it from the inside. I turn the lock and throw it open, and Dane is there, still pounding thin air as the door opens.

When he sees me, he grabs me, clings to me, squeezes me tight. Then he pulls away and asks, immediately, "Chloe?"

I try to shove him out of the doorway before he can see her lifeless body on the bathroom floor, but he is far too strong. He brushes past me and kneels next to Chloe, his lips moving silently, like mine next to Scurvy's grave earlier that afternoon.

He stands and says grimly, "I should have known they'd be expecting us. I should have planned this more carefully."

He looks around, spots Hazel's body still buzzing with the copper stick wedged in her chest, and says, "Hazel?"

"I had to do it." I sigh.

"So the copper works then, huh?"

I nod, my lips curling into a sad, scary smile. Then I see Chloe's still army boots and frown all over again.

"What happened?" I ask, turning to the dance floor. Last time I saw it, the place was hopping with kids, swirling lights, blaring music, life, and laughter. Now it's deserted, emergency lights illuminating an empty dance floor, plastic punch cups turned over and lying on the floor, streamers and glittery stars hanging haphazardly over rows and rows of empty tables. Without the music blasting, it's like watching TV with the sound off.

"When the power cut out," Dane explains, "everybody scrammed."

I gently guide him away from the bathroom toward the dance floor and ask, "What now?"

Just then the back doors of the gym open and three figures plow through; two willingly, one being dragged along reluctantly like a man doomed to the gallows.

"Now," says Dane, turning to meet them with clenched fists, "we find out how this story ends."

31
A Pimp Called Death

BONES HAS TURNED his track suit into a tuxedo. How, I have no idea, but there it is just the same: shiny and white, with a crisp white fedora on top of his skeletal head instead of his trademark skullcap. The topper? A cheesy red carnation sticking out of his shiny white lapel.

He looks like a pimp called Death, and if things weren't currently going to hell in a handbasket, I would laugh out loud in his face. Preferably while shoving said face into a big, fat mirror so he could see how ridiculous he looks. (Not that he would. I mean, you leave the house in a track suit tuxedo thinking it's stylish and you've obviously got a fashion blind spot; am I right?)

In contrast, Ms. Haskins is wearing a sleek black number, not so shiny, much more sophisticated, stunningly at odds with her pale white skin, harsh red lipstick, and cold, dead eyes. Beneath her black fishnet stockings, her legs are marble white and it makes me wonder how long it took her from being confused in Home Ec to warming up to the idea of spending the Afterlife hot for teacher.

Between them, Stamp trembles in a simple black tux, cheap and ill-fitting, like maybe they grabbed the last one in the store and shoved him, kicking and screaming, inside of it. His lips are pressed tightly together, silent and grim, but the look in his eyes squeals, *Help me!*

He doesn't look too bad, for now, but the Zerkers' unspoken message is clear: *try anything, and Stamp gets it.*

Dane steps in front of me, protectively, but I shove him aside until we stand shoulder-to-shoulder. (Hey, I've earned it!)

Bones is smiling, so happy and self-satisfied is he with his well-orchestrated plan. He looks over our heads to the darkened bathroom door. "Am I to understand Chloe and Dahlia won't be joining us this evening?"

Ms. Haskins follows his glance and, with a

sultry pout, asks, "And what about Hazel, Maddy?"

I shake my head. "What do you care, Ms. Haskins?"

"I don't, actually." She sighs, checking her nails as she raises her hand in front of her face. "This may come as a surprise to you, Maddy, but I never liked Hazel all that much. I know it sounds horrible for a teacher to confess something like that, but, well, the cat's out of the bag."

"I don't think they'll fire you for it. I mean, becoming a Zerker, dating one of your students, crashing the Fall Formal with your new boy toy here, any of those might be a firing offense, but when we get through with you, losing your job will be the least of your worries."

She stares daggers. "Such big talk from such a *little* girl. And I'd always had such high hopes for you, Maddy. Oh well."

Bones laughs. "You've got it all wrong anyway, Maddy. We don't want to kill you; we just want to . . . *turn* . . . you. Now that Dahlia and Hazel are gone, well, we've got a few openings on Team Zerker."

"Never gonna happen," Dane says decisively.

"Don't be so sure, hero," Bones says. "After tonight, you won't be around to protect your little girlfriend here anymore."

I go to defend myself, but Dane beats me to it, saying, "Who says she needs protection? From the looks of it, she's racking up a higher body count than you are."

"For now." He looks bored. "Now, onto business. The way I see it, you have two choices: join us right now . . . or die where you're standing."

"Before you decide," Ms. Haskins says, "just think about the future. You stick with us and, by the end of the night, we'll *own* this school. A teacher and a couple of her former students? This place will be crawling with Zerkers by morning. No more passing among the Normals, no more playing with your little Goth makeup. With a school full of Zerkers, there will *be* no Normals; we'll all look alike."

Dane whistles. "That's some plan. I can't wait to hear what the Elders have to say about it."

"You act like you're *already* an Elder, Dane." Bones scoffs. "The Afterlife is for the Afterliving, my friend. If you can't enjoy it now, quit taking up space and getting in the way so the rest of us can have our fun."

"That's just it, Bones," I say, walking slowly forward. Dane matches me, step for step. "Even the Afterlife is about more than just having fun. Otherwise, it's just . . . anarchy."

Bones leers at Ms. Haskins. "Who says there's anything wrong with that?"

"What are you going to do a week from now, Bones," I say, "when the whole school is full of Zerkers—every jock, every skank, every brain, every nerd—and they're all as strong as you, all as smart as you? You've been top dog for some time now, Bones. You really want to fight to stay on top of the hill every week, every day, every minute?"

Bones doesn't like that. He inches forward and snarls. "I think you overestimate the qualities of the student body here at Barracuda Bay High, Maddy."

"Let's just do this, all right?" Dane says between clenched teeth. "Enough of the playful banter; enough of the one-upmanship. Let's end this thing."

"Oh, we'll end it all right." Bones laughs before turning to Ms. Haskins. "Dear, why don't you invite our friends in to join the . . . party?"

"Gladly." She eyes me wickedly, destroying whatever image I've ever had of her as a teacher, as a mentor, as an adult, as a . . . friend. She opens the double doors they've just walked through, moonlight flooding in on a wave of pitch darkness. The motion is so dramatic, the setting so serene, the actress playing her part with such flair, I half expect a waft of B-movie fog to roll in across the floor and tickle our feet while she's waiting.

Then she whistles with two fingers between her lips (sex-ay) and, beyond the doors, the singularly recognizable noise of mass . . . *shuffling* . . . begins. It's a most unsettling sound—it's not only shoes against the parking lot gravel or clothes against dead skin, but the growling, the mewling, and shouting of Zerkers gone wild. I have no idea what to expect and, unlike zombies or the older Zerkers, these new ones are frickin' slow.

Step by step, they begin inching into view, but the emergency lights and Bones' white fedora and the crisp moonlight and the late-night dark all camouflage most of what I'm seeing until it's far, far too late.

Dane looks at me with the closest I've ever seen to fear in his eyes and says, "Whatever happens, Maddy, just . . . stay close."

As the shuffling continues, I steal a glance at Stamp. He must know what's coming through those doors because he's violently yanking his arm away from Bones, trying to get free at any cost. Bones yanks him back, roughly, whispers something in his ear, and Stamp gently calms down.

While I'm wondering what Bones just said, both boys look at me: Stamp with an apologetic smile, Bones with menacing glee.

I close my eyes for a second and try to swallow. When I open them again, the doorway is filled with . . . teachers. *Our* teachers. (Or, what's left of them anyway.) Seven or eight of them, pale as the moon-light above, dead as the fall leaves under their feet, slow as molasses but strong as oxen.

Their eyes are wide and vacant, their mouths moving, some making sounds, some merely clattering jaws, shadowy eyes buried in dark circles hidden in doughy white faces, licking their lips. Our teachers are Zerkers. So Bones and Ms. Haskins were right about one thing: after tonight, there really is no going back.

"Say hello to the new and improved staff of Barracuda Bay High School," Ms. Haskins says grandly, as one by one the Gym teacher, the high school counselor, the assistant principal, and finally even Mrs. Witherspoon herself shuffle in, Zerker style.

God, will this ever end?

I think of Scurvy's head at my feet, of Hazel's jolting body at the end of my stake, and now of all these teachers and what will become of them. How is one supposed to dezombiefy her Gym teacher?

Her assistant principal?

Her favorite Art teacher?

"And thanks to Stamp here," says Bones, finally shoving the poor kid forward and onto the ground, Stamp's bare hands making awkward squeaking sounds on the harsh gym floor as he slides forward on all fours, "we were able to invite the football team as well."

From behind the teachers a swarm of thick-necked, muscle-bound Zerker jocks stumble in. Even as they shuffle toward us in their huge, shiny dress shoes and size XXXL tuxedoes, I ignore them.

"Stamp," I shout, and he wastes no time scrambling toward me, looking puny and helpless as he crawls on all fours.

"I'm sorry," he says.

Dane shoves him behind us protectively, making the motion look easy as we inch closer together to form a kind of zombie seal in front of what might be the last human in the room.

Stamp looks remorseful. "They made me do it, Maddy. I had no choice."

"Did he bite you?" Dane asks impatiently as the crowd around the gym doors swells to one or two dozen angry, hungry, thick-necked Zerkers. He checks under Stamps' collar, turning his face toward him roughly to inspect for teeth marks on his ruddy neck. "Did *any* of them bite you?"

Stamp shakes his head, looking at me innocently. With all that's gone on, after Scurvy and Hazel and now Ms. Haskins turning, I don't trust him. God forgive me, but I don't trust anybody.

Anybody, that is, but Dane.

"Did Hazel bite you, Stamp?" I ask bluntly, pushing up his sleeves, yanking up his pants cuffs, inspecting every inch of his body (okay, not *every* inch) for any signs of Zerker bite marks. My hands are rough, and his skin is soft. It doesn't seem like he's turning, but what the hell do I know? It didn't seem like Scurvy was turning either, at least not until his teeth were two inches from my skull.

"Honest, Maddy," he says, his voice pleading and frantic, "she didn't bite me, I swear. They said they were just using me—as bait. Hazel tricked me into coming with her on a double date with Bones and Dahlia. I was mad at you for dissing me at the party. I was . . . confused. I figured, 'What the hell? I'll make her jealous.' The minute they picked me up, they had me call all the football players and made them meet me in the locker room. They told me if I didn't, they'd . . . hurt . . . you."

I take his hand, and it's trembling. I touch his cheek, and it's wet with tears. I tell him, "It's not your fault, Stamp."

"Maybe not," Dane says, turning his attention to the grumbling linebackers, the eager running backs, the brain-hungry wide receivers, "but thanks to your boyfriend here we're knee-deep in 300-pound jocks. As if Bones and Ms. Haskins and 10 of her favorite teachers weren't enough."

"Didn't you hear?" Stamp snaps back. "We're not an item anymore."

"Seriously, you two," I say. "We've got bigger fish to fry right now than my dating status."

They both give me, then each other, dirty looks; then back to me again for another trip to the dirty looks buffet. Meanwhile the horde is approaching across the gym floor, the space between us and certain death (again) dwindling.

Spotting the threat, preparing for it, Dane hands Stamp a Taser. "Listen, let's split up. Stamp, you take the jocks. Jab them in the neck with that, and they should go down hard and stay down. Maddy, you take the teachers. Use my copper stake." He hands it to me. "They're still so new they shouldn't put up much of a fight. Me, I'll grab Bones—"

Before he can finish with his best laid plans, Bones barks some kind of a command and the Zerkers begin to advance in earnest. I inch to the left, toward the buffet table and the long line of slender, high tables that I imagine might be some good obstacles against the approaching teacher onslaught.

Ms. Haskins follows, leading the teachers after me, her skirt slit high and her blouse buttoned low; Lolita of the Living Dead.

"Nice look," I say, jabbing Dane's copper stake in her direction.

"Nice try," she says, avoiding it as the copper tip plunges into Coach Potter's stomach. He sizzles, jolts, and goes down for the count. His body lies in a heap. She uses the opportunity to slap me across the face. "I never *did* like teacher's pets."

I slap her back, hard, with every word: "Yes"—*slap*—"you"—*slap*—"did!"—*slap!*

She is older, but I have been dead longer. She is bigger, but I am stronger, my muscles and bones stiffer, harder, more marblelike and, thus, heavier. It's like my hand is no longer my hand, more like it's some rubber glove filled with fast-drying cement. With every slap, I hear a little bone break, a chunk of cheek, an ear bone, maybe her jaw crumble beneath her smooth alabaster skin.

She falls to the floor with a frustrated yelp, and I reach again with the copper stake but, out of nowhere, Mrs. Witherspoon knocks it away, taking off her big red glasses and holding them in her hands like a weapon. She jabs at me with the eye frames, her hands still plump and fleshy.

I avoid them easily and roll away on the floor, grabbing the stake just in time as my zombie teachers gather around my flailing body like Boy Scouts at a campfire. I kick at each of their shins, and they're still new enough to react to the pain.

They grab at their legs, mouths forming black, round Os of discomfort. They howl as they tumble to the ground and, one by one, I short-circuit the Afterlife out of them with the copper tip of my handheld stake. It's like Whac-A-Mole, only with human beings. (Whac-A-Teacher? Whac-A-Zerker?) One by one by one they fall, overlapping each other on the floor in their writhing, foaming electric agony.

They pile up like lumber and as their life forces drain away, I have to keep reminding myself they're only Zerkers now and that the teachers I knew, and loved, and sometimes hated, and occasionally even feared, were dead and gone the minute Ms. Haskins bit the Afterlife right into them—and the Normal life right out.

Finally only Ms. Haskins remains, but while her comrades have fallen, she hasn't rushed to their aid. Instead she's inched away from me, far away, until she has her back to Bones and he has his back to her while he faces off with Dane.

It wasn't going well when it was one on one; it's definitely not going well now that it's *two* on one. Dane looks battered, scared, and I rush to help.

Out of the corner of his eye, he sees me coming and shouts, "*Stamp*, Maddy! Go help Stamp!"

I stop, torn between the two. Though battered, Dane *is* a zombie, has been a zombie, and can hold his own—even against an angry monster like Bones. But poor Stamp is a Normal—flesh and bones and blood and soft tissue—and currently surrounded by the entire Barracuda Bay defensive line and dying the death of a thousand hard jabs from his former teammates.

A few of the big, bulky players are down on the ground, limp and lifeless, but the rest—about a dozen of them left now—are slowly picking Stamp apart. His tuxedo is in tatters, one shoulder ripped through to the stiff white, bloodstained shirt beneath it.

I shiver, flinch. I keep forgetting he's not a

zombie, not immune to pain. That his heart still pumps blood, that his body can be hurt, torn, can spill blood; that he can . . . die. I leap on the two nearest linemen, stabbing them each in the back of the neck with the copper tip of my stake. One goes down right away, and I think this is going to be as easy as silencing the teachers was, but the other goes down with a fight, tossing my stake across the gym even as he falls, sizzling and dead, to the ground.

Great, no spike, and my Taser is lying, useless and wet, back in the ladies' room. While a few of the linemen pummel Stamp, I struggle to my feet, dazed but not hurt from the fall to the floor with the 300-pound lineman on top of me. Meanwhile, two more gigantic Zerker jocks corner me against one of the tall Fall Formal tables.

One is thin and I snap his arm with a swift roundhouse kick to the shoulder. He flinches but keeps coming, so I repeat the process and break his other arm. Now he's like a cat with no claws, a marionette with no puppet master. While I push the thin one over easily, the other jock moves in behind me, and before I can lash out, he scoops me up in his arms for the mother of all bear hugs.

I squirm and stretch my arms out, his muscles

tightly coiled. He is strong, physically stronger than me, but still he's only flesh and blood, while I am now granite and wiry muscle and dead, solid bone. I bite at his flesh, spit it out, kick at his knees, all while his grip grows stronger. I struggle in vain, until I remember the ruffles full of grave dirt.

I growl, kick, turn, squirm until I'm finally facing the gigantic beast. He looks surprised as I head butt his face, but even his broken nose doesn't stop him from trying to grind my spine to dust in his huge, python arms. The cemetery dirt does, though. I inch closer, not squirming anymore but embracing him, reaching around his back and clasping my hands together in a kind of finger lock to pull him closer to me, scrambling up his chest to his face until his nose is buried deep in the ruffles, into the dirt-filled ruffles Chloe sewed into my dress and we both laughed about once upon a time.

His scream fills the auditorium; the howling nearly shatters my eardrums. He tries to drop me, but I'm fused to him now, following him like a second skin wherever he turns, wherever he falls, wherever he runs, my granite fingers piercing his thick hide and sticking to him like a rodeo rider to his bucking bronco.

The footballer leaps away, falls to the ground, rolls, and still I cling to him, his nose sizzling, his face seared black and crusty by the effects of grave dirt shoved straight under his broken nose. I stick close until I know he's gone, and out, and down for the count, his face still smoking, his eyes open and coated with a thin, gray film.

Shoving him away, I look for a weapon of some sort and spot Chloe's clutch purse lying on top of a nearby table; I'd know it anywhere—it's the only purse in the room with a rhinestone skull clasp. Reaching inside, I grab the lighter and a handful of cherry bombs.

They feel pebbly and rough, and I've never been a big fan of the Fourth of July—or boys' room pranks, for that matter—so I don't exactly know what to expect from the little suckers. But I trust Dane, and he said they work (although he only read about them in *The Guide*), and it's too late to stop believing him now.

Standing slightly back, listening to Stamp's screams, desperate to help, frightened that I will suck at this, I light the first cherry bomb and toss it into the crowd of growling, chewing, snarling Zerker jocks. The sulfur spews like a great green gas,

following the first bomb as it circles end over sparkling end, the fizzing and sulfur spewing from my
hand to the crowd.

One by one I light, *sizzle*, toss, and throw; light,
sizzle, toss, and throw.

They land, spew, spout, *sizzle-crack-boom-BOOM!*

Suddenly it's a sulfur explosion, sparks spitting
where one left off, explosions shattering the floor,
the tables, the very air I don't breathe anymore.
Immediately, the Zerkers freak out, fighting each
other, pounding fists to faces, kicking bent knees
with shiny shoes, and punching bloody knuckles in
order to get away from the thick sulfur smell filling our corner of the gym. Seeing his opportunity,
Stamp scrambles away, favoring one awkwardly bent
leg, his left arm limp and twisted, his face scratched,
scarred, bruised, and bloody.

He reaches me in a heap of trembles and tears,
his boyhood back, his manhood gone, obviously
grateful and embarrassed and hating me and loving
me all at the same time.

And here is Stamp, at my side, and there is
Dane, screaming in frustration, trapped between
two Zerkers, and I have only the slightest, barest,
craziest notion of what might possibly come next.

I ignore Stamp's thanks, drown out his pleas, and reach for his Taser, yank it from his bloody, trembling hands, apologize profusely with my eyes, and zap every one of his former teammates until the spasms stop and they crumble to the floor, heads hitting the polished hardwood with thickening, crunching finality.

They lay in a twisted, beefy pile, more like a heap, slashed tuxedos, bleeding eyes, skin seared from the sulfur, necks fried from the Tasers, Zerkers no more, their skin pale and already yellowing, their eyes black and dead, and even *that* is sad to me; more pawns in Bones' crazy, twisted game of Zerkers versus zombies.

In their short, violent Afterlives, the jocks have managed to succeed at one thing. By Tasering them all, I have wasted precious time, and steps, putting me farther away from Stamp, separating me from Dane. Now we are at three points of a distant and dangerous triangle: Dane battling Bones, Stamp in grave peril as Ms. Haskins gets him in her sights, and me standing awkward and triumphant above a pile of twisted corpses still sizzling and cold: Queen of Jock Mountain.

Behind me, Stamp is whimpering, his ankle

twisted, his arm sprained, his face bruised and flushed with pain and fear and shame.

Across the room, Ms. Haskins is advancing on him. Her eyes are full of Zerker hate, her circuits fried by Bones' bite, her only goal to serve him, to ruin us, to separate Stamp from his brains and me from the only guy at Barracuda Bay High who ever looked at me twice.

I watch helplessly, too far away to reach them with my stiff limbs and with only one cherry bomb left, sitting squat in the middle of my trembling hand.

Behind me, Bones is lifting Dane high, his strong, granite arms rising. They are both in tatters, their formalwear ripped to shreds, their skin exposed, their mouths open and angry.

"What now, Maddy?" Bones cackles casually, as if lifting Dane above his head is no more trouble than flicking a fly across the dinner table. "Who do you save? Stamp from Ms. Haskins? Or Dane from me? Who do you let die? Which boy is worth risking your Afterlife for?"

He is only too right. I watch helplessly while Bones brings Dane down onto his knee like some WWE wrestler even as Ms. Haskins yanks Stamp up by his collar and gnaws on his neck like a fat kid with an all-day sucker.

I scream, Bones laughs, Stamp squirms, and as I stare at the ceiling, praying for help from above, I suddenly see a tangle of pipes and nozzles. Bones lifts Dane up again, cackling even louder this time, and I light my last cherry bomb behind my back, scramble to the top of the nearest tall table, and throw it as high as I can. It ignites on the way up, the scent acrid and coppery, already spewing thick black fumes as it spins and spins, one sparkling end over the other.

Bones smells it first, his head snapping to one side to watch the cherry bomb ignite and climb, climb, climb into those pipes and nozzles. Meanwhile he holds Dane high over his head like some kind of zombie umbrella. Ms. Haskins ignores it, her head buried too deep in Stamp's life force to bother with anything as paltry as the end of her own.

And Stamp? Stamp is too far gone to know what's happening when the sprinklers spring to life, showering the entire gymnasium floor with hundreds of gallons of water in a huge, gushing tidal wave.

And me?

I pray and curse and lean down from my table, ignite Stamp's Taser with a crackling sizzle of bright blue voltage between its two metal vampire fangs, and plunge it so far into the gymnasium floor I can see the crack in the varnish even through the searing wave of pure electricity flowing out like a bright blue mushroom cloud across the rippling, sizzling waterfall.

32
Maddy's Choice

TIME DOESN'T STOP, exactly; it just slows wwwaaaayyyyyyyyy doooowwwnnnnnn. In my head I know the events are whipping by at lightning speed, but my eyes reveal them one at a time, almost in slow motion. The scene plays out not in real time but frame-by-frame-by-frame; death by slideshow.

Frame 1: Bones screams.

Frame 2: Bones looks up at Dane.

Frame 3: Bones looks down at the floor.

Frame 4: Bones drops Dane.

Frame 5: Dane does one slow roll through the air.

Frame 6: Then two.

Frame 7: Ms. Haskins stops biting Stamp.

Frame 8: Ms. Haskins screams.

Frame 9: Stamp groans.

Frame 10: Ms. Haskins drops Stamp.

Frame 11: Stamp falls to his knees.

Frame 12: Then his hands.

Frame 13: Stamp slumps over.

Frame 14: Ms. Haskins pivots.

Meanwhile, in a million simultaneous frames all at once, the floor flickers to life as electricity sears across the football-field-sized varnished floor. It spreads like an oil fire, with a faint crack and swift sizzle. There is not an ounce of rubber in sight, only gallons and gallons of gushing, rushing water.

As the electricity races, the frames speed up now, from slo-mo to fast-forward. Dane topples silently to the floor, his eyes wide as gravity sucks him down to earth. Nothing in his zombie powers is strong enough to stop the downward pull.

I hold my breath and at the last minute, just as Dane passes Bones' head on the way down to the floor, he reaches out and grabs the Zerker in a choke-hold. His arm in its torn tuxedo sleeve looks like a thin log against Bones' white throat. From across the room, I hear the powerful Zerker's Adam's apple crunch and watch his face erupt into a map of surprise and rage—mostly rage.

It's too late. Buck as he might, struggle as he must, time is finally against Bones this time, and the slow-motion replay mode continues speeding up until it's almost back to normal. Down they go, water sloshing, Dane toppling, death in the balance, his arm still clipped tight to the Zerker's throat.

I close my eyes, can't stand the suspense, open them again, and suddenly Bones is on the floor, jerking like a fish on the deck to buck Dane off of him and reverse their positions. Dane is on top of him now, wiggling frantically to stay there like a vacationer on a life raft coursing through the gnarliest part of the raging rapids.

I drop the Taser into the water; let it go completely. It fries, sizzles, and sends out one last blunt wave of flickering blue electricity before shorting out altogether.

Dane rolls off of Bones roughly, splashing to his feet awkwardly and racing across the room as puddles turn into steam around his ankles with every stiff, jerky step. He tries to stop in time but can't, the untested bottoms of his slick new tuxedo shoes sliding even when his legs stop moving as he topples into the table, into me, and spills both of us on the floor.

"Maddy! You're all right. Maddy!" I've never in my life seen anyone so happy just to see me; to see me alive. To touch me, to hold me in his arms as if the future really *does* depend on it. His eyes, usually so dark and brooding, are now electric and full of life. His smile lights up his pale white face, his mouth wide and inviting.

And I'm so safe in his arms, so far and removed from the teachers and the footballers and Bones, and when he kisses me, gently, so gently, I laugh and smile and cry without tears and kiss him back (not quite so gently), and he's laughing and saying, "I guess this makes you Zombie Number 1 from now on, huh?"

And still I'm kissing him and laughing and crying without tears. He helps me up from the cold, wet, dead floor, holds my hand as we walk toward Ms. Haskins' once sexy, now lifeless body. Her eyes are open and, instead of closing them, I tear a cloth off of the nearest table like the world's worst magician and, as punch glasses and paper plates and centerpieces topple to the floor, I toss it gracelessly on top of her.

I know it wasn't really *her* doing all that evil stuff moments ago, but sometimes evil is enough to wipe away our fondest memories. Gone are the warm, fuzzy images of her in Home Ec, offering to write me a letter of recommendation and nurturing me toward the art world. Now all I see is a dead Zerker, her mouth drenched in Stamp's blood, her cold white feet sticking out from the other end of the blanket; one shoe on, the other off.

Gone now, lost forever. Like the rest of them, like *all* of them. Everyone in this room, all the bodies scattered on the floor, teachers I loved, feared, laughed with, laughed *at*, respected, ignored—all gone, all dead, silenced forever.

The athletes, so promising, so young—all gone, all quiet, all corpses destined to join Scurvy in the graveyard—may they all rest in peace. And Dad, my dad: he will touch every one of them in the morgue, with care and tenderness, weeping, probably, to see life snuffed out so young, so violently, so unnecessarily.

If only he knew it was his own daughter who had snuffed most of them out for good.

Next to Ms. Haskins, Stamp lies dead and cold, his eyes closed, his expression peaceful, his poor battered face (that face!) a picture of pain and grief. He is like a giant rag doll, arms and legs akimbo, face slack and empty, a lifeless bag of bones and guts. Already his skin is pale and waxy, the gash in his throat where Ms. Haskins bit him bright red and garish in contrast.

My poor Stamp, gone and cold.

I kneel next to him, crying dryly, throat raw from too many sobs and no tears.

Dane's hand is on my shoulder, his breath cold in my ear as he says, "You have to bite him, Maddy. You have to . . . *turn* . . . him. Before it's too late."

"W-w-why?" I stammer. "He's gone; let him be. Why can't we just leave him in peace?"

"He's *not* in peace, Maddy," Dane says. "Not really. Think about it: Ms. Haskins bit him right before you electrocuted her. Before you fried them all. He hadn't *technically* turned yet. Right now, electricity or not, he's theoretically in the Awakening stage. It's like, how do I explain it? It's like he's in death's cocoon, wrapped up deep and tight, where nothing—and no one—can reach him. Not even 10,000 volts; not even a million volts. You know how you get a surge protector to keep your computer from frying when the power goes out? The computer doesn't take the jolt; the surge protector does. Right now Stamp's body is like a giant surge protector."

"What's it protecting?" I choke out the words.

"His brain. I could tase him for 10 minutes

straight and nothing would happen; nothing would change. He'll still wake up a Zerker, Maddy. That's his fate. Unless . . ."

"Unless"—I finish for him—"unless I . . . *bite* . . . him."

Dane's face is cautious and kind. He is leaning against me, his tuxedo still wet, his skin so dreadfully cold, his face so pale, his eyes so dark and . . . kind? He is definitely not who I thought he was. Then again, I'm not who he thought I was.

Together . . . what could we be?

If we were to leave here, to turn right now, to ignore the bodies, the corpses, the friends, and the BFFs we left behind? At the moment, it's so tempting to just hold him, to close my eyes, to hide from it all, to bury my head against his cold, lifeless chest and let him whisk me away to where there is no warmth, no family, no familiar faces or places—only a blank slate and our eternal future.

A future together.

On the floor, Stamp lies lifeless because of me. Bones turned Hazel because of me; Hazel seduced Stamp because of me. Because Bones wanted to use them both, because he knew if he did I would weaken, crumble, falter, and fail. He didn't care about the threads that wound out from his plot, touching our lives and ruining them completely.

Dane clears his throat. I look from Stamp to Dane, and he blinks, his lashes long and tender—I never noticed before. Then he explains, almost reverently, "One way or another, Maddy, he's being reanimated as we speak. Deep inside, the Zerker rage is coiling through his body, rewiring his circuits, frying the guy you knew. The guy you . . . loved. Still love, might love, whatever."

He stops, touches my chin, drops his hand, continues, "You can either turn him to our side and make sure he's safe or let him wake up a Zerker in his grave, angry and mean and hungry—and alone. Do you want Stamp to wake up alone? With no memory of you or Hazel or me or Bones or any of . . . *this*? Someday, we might even have to do to Stamp what you did to Bones and Ms. Haskins."

I think of Dane's kiss, so gentle yet hard; his hands, cold like mine. I think of eternity with him, his deep black eyes, his dark ways, his strong presence. I look at him, now, and can see he's thinking of it, too.

And yet, he's making it so Stamp and I can be together at last.

Together forever.

Why?

He could have let me leave Stamp lying here. Knowing he'd wake up a Zerker, knowing he wouldn't be the Stamp I knew or loved or cared about or wanted. And, worst of all, knowing that I wouldn't know any of this. He could have kept his mouth shut, kissed me, whisked me away, and I would have never known. And yet now he's giving me a choice, even if it means bringing my first crush back to life.

I tremble. "Dane . . ."

He picks up my copper stake and hands it to me. "Of course, there's another option."

I take the stake. "What?"

"If you stake him now, while he's out, if you plunge this into his body and leave it there, stuck inside, when he finally reanimates, it *will* kill him."

"But I thought you said . . ."

"You can't *shock* him to death, Maddy; not with a Taser or a dozen Tasers or a thousand Tasers, but according to *The Guide*, the copper will scramble his system, rewire his life force. It'll be like a circuit breaker he won't be able to turn on, won't even be able to reach. He'll just . . . never wake up."

"Wow, Dane," I say, oozing sarcasm in place of tears, "that is just great! Oh, joy. What fun. Why didn't you tell me earlier? So, I can either turn Stamp into a zombie and watch him rot for the next thousand years or kill him now. Is *that* what you're saying?"

"I didn't say it would be an *easy* choice, Maddy." His voice is quiet, eyes deep and dark and sad and tender. "I just said you *had* a choice."

He gives me a long look and says, "I'm going to check on Bones, Maddy. We've all seen those movies where you turn your back on the dead guy and then turn around and he's not there anymore. I don't want him coming back in the sequel, you know what I mean? I just want to make sure he's out for good; that's all. Whatever decision you make with Stamp, just know that . . . know that I care for you. That I'll always care for you, whether *we're* a couple . . . or you and Stamp are."

He turns without saying another word. I go to speak his name, but that's not enough. I stand and follow and grab him, turn him around and kiss his cheek, his eyes, his nose, finally his lips. It's like I'm starving and can't get enough Dane, like I'll never kiss again. He accepts it passively, neither giving nor receiving, and when I've had my fill, I hold his face in my hands, look into his deep, dead eyes, and whisper, "Thank you."

Then I watch him go, his shoes squeaky on the damp gym floor, his legs stiff from the effort, from the cruelty, from the exhaustion. His shoulders are broad but slumped; it's like he's aged a century overnight. I watch him until he kneels gingerly next to Bones, until I hear something breaking and then tearing and see parts of Bones—pieces, really—start to pile up next to what's left of the Zerker's bent, broken body. I shudder, tired of the violence and the fear, of hearing it and seeing it up front and center, and turn to Stamp.

He looks pale already, long and lean as he lies stretched out on the floor, deadweight from head to toe. I try to picture him as one of . . . us. He has the hair for it; I'll give him that much. Dark and thick and strong at the roots and, hell, I sure wouldn't mind staring at that Superman curl for the rest of eternity.

But is that what I *really* want for him?

Is that what I really want . . . for *me*?

I listen to the breaking, to the tearing, as Dane turns Bones into, well . . . bones, once and for all. And I look at Stamp, and think of his family, and how they'll miss him, how they'll miss him either way. And how, selfishly, *I'll* miss him.

With the stake in my hand, Stamp's hand in the other, I choke back the last of the night's tearless tears and kneel to finish what I started.

Epilogue
Maddy in the Middle

DANE IS WAITING in the truck after Stamp and I finish our zombie picnic. As we stumble out of the cemetery together, Stamp kind of leans in and asks, like maybe he knows he should know but still doesn't know, "Who *is* that?"

And I want to tell him, "That's the guy I thought I'd be with forever," but I don't (for obvious reasons). Instead I kind of whisper, because we're getting close to the truck now and Dane's feelings are going to be hurt enough, "That's Dane, Stamp; he saved our Afterlives."

And he nods, like a little kid who doesn't want to admit he had to ask. "Oh yeah, I knew that."

And the smile on my lips fades. I thought I

would be so happy reuniting with Stamp; and I am, sure. Of course. He's alive, he's still sweet, he's here and safe, and, yes, dammit, I know I made the right choice. But seeing Dane there in the driver's seat, his pale fingers tight on the wheel, after waiting patiently for me to go dig up my boyfriend and drag him away with us, makes me feel guilty for all kinds of things.

"Hi, Dane," Stamp says, winking in my direction as I slide in next to Dane and then gently haul Stamp up next to me. (Can you say, *awkward sandwich*?)

Dane smiles sadly and says, "Hey, buddy," gently, like you would if you were picking up someone from the hospital or the nursing home. And his voice is so bleak.

I mean, I know he's trying to be brave, but it's like every word hurts, and I can see in his eyes that all he wants to do is dump us both out, hit the gas, and speed away. And I wouldn't blame him one bit. I'd chase his ass down wherever he went, sure enough, but I wouldn't blame him one bit for trying to ditch me and Stamp.

As I slide over, Dane leans in and whispers to me, "I wonder how long it will be before he remembers he hates my guts."

ZOMBIES *Don't Cry*

I want to say, "He doesn't hate your guts yet, Dane. But he would if he knew we kissed."

Instead, I snort and grab the morning paper from the dashboard, trying to act all casual-like as I read the banner headline to myself: *Tragic Accident at Fall Formal Claims 31 Lives: Students and faculty mourn their own as Barracuda Bay High School struggles to pick up the pieces . . .*

Up the hill past the cemetery, Dane drives slowly by Hazel's house. Inside, every light is burning and a somber black wreath marks her parents' door. There are windows in nearly every room facing the street, but her parents aren't in any of them. I imagine them in their bed, still dressed up, sobbing quietly into each other's arms. Or maybe just their pillows.

And I imagine they'll be the kind of parents who will keep Hazel's all-pink room as an all-pink shrine, until one day they're forced to sell the house and leave her memories far, far behind, and even then they'll cart her stuff away and put it up in her next house, exactly as it was in this house: Hazel the Museum Exhibit. (Just the way she would have wanted it.)

Gradually I tense, knowing my house is only a few numbers away. Dane seems to sense it, too, and rests his shoulder on mine. For once, the ice cube cold of his skin is exactly what I need. I lean in with all I'm worth, silently, making sure Stamp can't see, letting Dane know I'm here and I'm his . . . sort of.

When we get to my house, to Dad's house now, Dane slows to a crawl.

There's no wreath on our door, but on the other side of the bay window Dad's sitting alone at the breakfast nook staring at the empty chair across from him, a coffee cup on the table. His eyes are dry but vacant; suddenly the man who works with death for a living knows what it's like to feel it for himself.

I swallow and would gladly trade the rest of my days for a single tear. Half of me wants to race from Dane's truck, to sprint through the door, only for a second, a millisecond, to hug him, to straighten his collar, to warm up his cold coffee, to say, "Dad, I'm fine. I can't stay; I'll tell you why later, soon, but I'm fine. Don't be sad; don't miss me . . ."

But I can't. He would never understand, not the zombie stuff, not the Zerkers, not the Elders or the Sentinels or Stamp or Dane or . . . any of it, for that matter. He is a man of science, of brain cells and muscle fibers and time of death. His is not a world of fantasy or make-believe or fairy tales or graveyard rubbings.

No matter what I said, no matter that he should

simply trust me and not question his own daughter, no matter the pleading in my eyes, it wouldn't be enough to wrap his logic and rationale around. He would grab me instead, hold me, sit me down, force me to explain. He would question and pursue and expose me and Dane and Stamp and the Elders and the Sentinels for what we were: reanimated, the undead, immortals, the Living Dead—take your pick.

And they wouldn't allow that. He would cause more harm than good, even though his heart—his brain—would be in the right place. And in the end, some Sentinel, on the order of some Elder, would . . . *silence* . . . him. So, much the same way I had a choice with Stamp, I have a choice with Dad: save his life but make him sad, or tell the truth and send him to the gallows.

Just like with Stamp, the choice now is easy.

Okay, maybe not easy, but . . . simple.

He's still wearing his black suit from the funeral they never held for me, the funeral they never held because they couldn't find my body in the water and the rubble and the dozens of other corpses of my former teachers, classmates, rivals, and friends back in the gym.

Stamp's memorial service was easier. After I bit

him, Dane assured me he'd stay dormant through the weekend of the funeral. As usual, he was right. Long after the mourners went home and the over-worked cemetery staff left rows of white chairs waiting in the dark, I was there to greet him, brains, Sporks, and all.

And now we are ghosts, all three of us; truly dead and buried. And in our wake are those who cared for us the most and could never know the real truth. Dane's family, who never knew he was reanimated in the first place. Dad, assuming I was lost somewhere—somehow—in the electrical surge, death, and panic that marred this year's Fall Formal. And Stamp's parents, who buried their son and think he's still down there, six feet under, safe in his affordable coffin and only a few blocks away in Sable Palms Cemetery whenever they care to visit.

As Dane rolls gently by our front window, Stamp says quietly, "I never got to meet your dad."

I look at him, see the life behind his eyes, and say, "You would have liked him, Stamp."

"Yeah, but would he have liked *me*?"

"Oh yeah," I say.

Stamp nods halfheartedly, like maybe he doesn't believe me.

From the driver's seat, Dane whispers, "I never met your dad either."

And while Stamp is kind of still looking toward Dad's window, I sneak a peek at Dane and smile the kind of smile we used to share, in his trailer, out by the Dumpster during sixth period, when he was teaching me how to use a copper stake. And I mouth, and I mean it, "He would have liked you, too."

I don't think Dane believes me either. And, of course, he's right. *Stamp* was the kind of guy you brought home to Dad; not Dane. Stamp, the football star, the cocky kid, the kind of guy who'd stand around the kitchen and shoot the bull about sports scores and Dad's softball technique and the best charcoal to use for your Fourth of July cookout.

Dane was the guy you snuck in through the second-story window, or snuck out to see in the middle of the night, Dad's house rules be damned. The dark one, the rebel, the kind of guy who would gladly talk to your dad but have nothing to say. The guy your dad wouldn't understand; the guy your dad would gripe about before asking, "Why can't you date a nice guy, like Stamp?"

And how could you ever tell your dad the heart knows what it wants, and it wants . . . Dane?

Then Stamp says, as if all of this hasn't been going on, or maybe because it has, "Dane, take me by my house." It's not a question. In fact, it's kind of firm; and suddenly, I think Stamp is all back and knows *exactly* who Dane is.

Dane clears his throat, speeds away from my house like he's lighting out for the highway already, and says, "Stamp, listen, I don't think that's such a good—"

"Please, Dane," Stamp whispers, almost pleading now. "I just want to see them one more time. I know we're in a hurry; I know nobody can see me; I just *have* to see them."

Stamp doesn't have to give Dane directions. Palmetto Court is within spitting distance of Mangrove Manor, Dane's old trailer park. When we're deep enough inside the ratty, overgrown subdivision, Stamp says quietly, as if he's apologizing, "It's number 1791."

We keep driving until we find it. It's a sad little house, sadder now than ever. Stamp leans forward, nose pressed against the window, but Dane gently pushes him back against his wide bucket seat.

"We can't let them see you, Stamp," Dane reminds him, and now it's his turn to be the firm one giving orders.

For his part, Stamp silently nods and looks out the passenger window as best he can. The lights are on, even though it's late. His mom is washing dishes in the kitchen, the lines on her tired face visible even from the street outside. His dad is dusting the large pictures on the den wall facing the street; the pictures are all of Stamp. Stamp in Little League, Stamp in his football uniform, Stamp playing hockey in Wisconsin, Stamp on a ski slope, Stamp with family, Stamp solo.

"He loves that room," Stamp says reverently, as if to himself.

We idle in the street for as long as we dare, lights off, going less than a mile per hour, hugging the curb, until instinctively Stamp's mom looks up from her dishes and sees the truck slowly, suspiciously, cruising by.

"Go," shouts Stamp, leaning behind me.

Rubber peels as the truck speeds away. The last thing I see in the rearview mirror is Mrs. Crosby dashing out of the house and standing in the middle of the road, limp hair illuminated by a single streetlamp; she's still drying a dish, staring at Dane's taillights with a forlorn expression.

"This sucks," says Stamp, banging his head a few

times against the passenger side window.

"Sure does," I say.

Dane sighs. "I wish I could say it gets any easier, guys."

Stamp and I look at him, then at each other. Stamp reaches across my lap and grabs my hand. Dane looks out the windshield so intently it's hard to tell if he sees or not. Then he seems to kind of shrink away from my side, kind of melding into the driver's side window, and I know he does.

And still I return Stamp's grip, because that's what girlfriends do. And I settle, in my mind, for being Stamp's girl, because that's what girlfriends do. But even as I clench his hand tightly, I do so with an eye for Dane. Stamp is my boy because I'm the reason he's dead, and you don't turn your back on the guy you did that to.

He is my boy because we had something, once upon a time, when we were alive, still breathing. Sure, it was just one night, just one party, a party I never made it to. And then it was over, and Hazel moved in on him, and Stamp was weak—and I was cruel—and it was over, but not over, because then danger moved in and set its sights on Stamp, all because of me.

And you don't get someone killed and then ditch him for the guy who kissed you so hard you're still licking your lips, wondering if it was real and wishing you could relive it over and over and over again. And it was real; of course it was. And I remember it, so fondly, so powerfully. And it seems so strange that Dane was the first one to kiss me, even though I started out hoping, aching for that same favor from Stamp.

And he would have, I think, if I hadn't been stupid and gone out in the rain and gotten myself killed and reanimated and, after that, things hadn't gotten kind of hectic and, well, kissing hadn't taken a backseat to, you know, being dead and all. And the deader I got, the better Dane treated me. And the better Dane treated me, the closer we got.

Until we just kind of eased into each other, all the way. And for a moment we were a couple, then not a couple, and then suddenly we were on the run from any Zerkers that might still be out there, from the Sentinels, from the Elders, and it was Bonnie and Clyde all the way until . . . until . . . it was time for Stamp to rise from his grave and join the party.

And then two became three, and suddenly it was Maddy in the middle. And God help me, but even as Stamp holds one hand and stares out the window, I reach across to Dane and grab his arm; and the catch in his throat, the sudden shock and surprise is so strong and loud I'm sure Stamp hears it. But he doesn't; he merely stares at the scenery, blissful in the confidence that I am his girl and he is my boy.

And what the hell is going to happen next?

The minutes crawl awkwardly by; the miles slip slowly beneath Dane's tires. Out Palmetto Court, onto Marlin Way, we're nearly out of town when a government-looking van doing at least 80 miles per hour barrels past us in the opposite direction, straight into Barracuda Bay.

Dane looks intently in his rearview mirror, is still looking when two more vans just like it fly past.

He steps on the gas as we speed out of town.

"What was *that* all about?" I ask, letting my hand slip from his forearm as he wrestles with the steering wheel through the increased speed.

Clenching his teeth, Dane says, "Sentinels."

"Already?" I ask.

He nods, taps the newspaper I threw back on the dashboard, and says, "They have whole teams of Sentinels whose only job is to look for headlines just like this. For sure they're suspicious, and I'm sorry to say it, Maddy, but when they talk to your dad, find out they never found your body, and put two and two together, well, they'll come looking for us."

"For how long?" I ask, staring out into the night.

"As long as it takes."

Stamp's hand clenches tighter on my own. Is it wrong that, right then, at that very moment, Dane's would have made me feel a whole lot better?

Dane slowly applies more pressure to the gas pedal, sending us rocketing through the night and as far away from the Sentinels as possible.

"What will happen if they catch us?" Stamp asks a few minutes later, his eyes blank, his face forward, his hand limp in my own.

Dane lets out a sigh so long, so sour, I'm not even sure he's fully conscious he does it. Finally, as if to himself, he says, "I don't know, Stamp. I've never been on the wrong end of the Sentinels before. Chloe and I, well, we've always obeyed the zombie laws, always checked in whenever we moved, were always careful to toe the line, until . . ."

He lets his voice trail off, but I know what he was going to say: *until Maddy showed up and ruined everything.* I think of how many people have been altered, reborn, or lost in my wake: Hazel, the football team, Scurvy, all those teachers, Ms. Harrington, Mrs. Witherspoon . . . Chloe.

Now I could add Stamp and Dane to that list as well. The two people I cared about most in this world, aside from Dad, of course, and I'd hurt them both. First Stamp by getting him dragged into all this, then Dane by putting him on the wrong side of the Sentinels.

"I'm sorry," I murmur, barely able to hear myself.

Dane hears it and snaps, "Nothing to be sorry for, Maddy."

"Yeah, but . . ." I begin.

"Yeah, but nothing." He cuts me off. "You weren't the one who made the Zerkers go, well, berserk. It started with those girls in Home Ec and, the way they'd started stalking you, Maddy, you could have been next. And even if you weren't, it would have been somebody else. Maybe not this week, maybe next month, but soon enough they would have done whatever they wanted, and I'd still be in this truck, barreling down the highway, trying to get clear of their mess."

After a long, awkward pause that finds us five more miles down the empty highway, Stamp says, "Besides, whatever happened, we're in it now; in it together. All three of us, right?"

He looks to Dane until Dane solemnly nods.

Stamp looks to me, smiles benignly, his teeth already yellowing, his skin three shades paler, those dark circles charming under his chocolate eyes; I smile back, uncertain.

The tension in the cab of Dane's truck is palpable, all of us avoiding each other's eyes while secretly yearning for a look of approval from the person we want the most. I'm not very good at this; I've never been very good at this. It's always been hard enough for me to have one boyfriend, let alone two. And I don't know how long I can keep lying to one while pining for the other.

The partnership, on the surface, seems to comfort him. He clears his throat, energized, sits up a little, and says, "So, where will we go?"

Dane juts his chin toward the glove box and says, "There's a map of Florida in there. You know, in case of emergencies. For now I'm just heading south, away from the Sentinels, but we'll have to find someplace big and loud where we can disappear."

I peel out the road map, unfold it, and don't need a dome light to see the long, slender outline of Florida bathed in my banana yellow zombie vision. I start reeling off names: "Miami could be good; lots of people there."

Dane frowns. "Yeah, but everybody's so perfect there—and tan. I'm looking for someplace where we won't stick out."

I'm still moving my finger south along the map when Stamp says, "My dad almost got a job in the Keys before we decided to move to Barracuda Bay; that's as far south as we can go. He said he didn't take it, though, because when he went to visit, the place was full of freaks." He smiles at us both and says, "It could be just the place."

Dane nods, but I look at the place on the map and say, "Yeah, but it's the very southern tip of Florida. I mean, if the Sentinels come from north Florida down, they could trap us; we'd have nowhere to go."

Dane and Stamp nod.

"Good point, Maddy," Dane says.

Stamp says, "I didn't think of it that way."

My finger creeps back up the state while Dane says, "So maybe something more central, away from the coasts, away from the southern tip, something like—"

"Orlando?" I say, my finger landing there just as the inspiration strikes. "I mean, it's central to the state, right smack in the middle, there's an airport, tons of hotels, tourism's big, could be easy to blend in."

Dane looks unconvinced until Stamp says,

"Yeah, my folks took me to Universal Studios a few years ago. They have a whole part of the theme park designated for monsters and makeup effects from the movies. You know, the Mummy, Terminator, Beetlejuice, the Wolfman. We could get jobs there, be a part of the show, not even need to 'pass' because we'd already look the part."

Dane cracks a smile. "Monsters playing monsters. I like the sound of that. Maddy, we just passed mile marker 23 on Interstate 75. How far are we from there?"

I look at the map, moving my finger backward until we're just shy of Tampa. "It's 70, 80 miles tops. Start looking for signs for Interstate 4 going east, and according to the map it should take us right in."

Dane puts on his blinker, although there's not another car in sight this late at night, gets in the right lane, and turns onto I-4 a few miles later. The road signs for Orlando pop up almost immediately, the billboards a mile or so after that. Disney, Universal, SeaWorld, and about a million hotels. I think of a sea of tourists, Hawaiian shirts and sunburns, flip-flops and black socks, camera straps and floppy sun hats, and I smile.

It sounds like the kind of place you could easily

get lost in, like the kind of place no one would ask too many questions. The kind of place where a handful of zombies could start over, make a life, and hide out from the Sentinels.

At least, for awhile.

I look at Stamp, who's smiling, and Dane, who's also smiling.

At least, for awhile.

Then the reality of our situation seems to creep in, and the smile fades; the fear returns.

In between glances at his rearview mirror, Dane looks at me, trying to put on a brave face. But I know the look in his eyes, I can see the fear lurking there, and eventually he quits smiling altogether.

For now, at least, the romantic danger in the truck gives way to the immediate danger of armed Sentinels in pursuit. Instinctively I kind of pull away from Dane and slide my hand out of Stamp's grip (he's so preoccupied he barely notices). The anxiety is there, buried deep, but it's a bridge I can't cross right now—no matter who I end up running to on the other side.

As the bright lights of Orlando dawn on the horizon, as the sunny billboards promise "hours of fun" and "days of escape," I see our young, grim faces in a harsher light reflecting back from the windshield. We may be heading in a new direction, but the past is on our heels. And from the look on Dane's face, it's only a matter of time before it catches up with us.

MEDALLION
P R E S S

Be in the know on the latest
Medallion Press news by becoming a
Medallion Press Insider!

<u>As an Insider</u> you'll receive:

• Our FREE expanded monthly newsletter,
giving you more insight into Medallion Press

• Advanced press releases and breaking news

• Greater access to all of your favorite
Medallion authors

Joining is easy. Just visit our website at
<u>www.medallionpress.com</u> and click on the
Medallion Press Insider tab.

MEDALLION
P R E S S

Want to know what's going on with
your favorite author or what new releases
are coming from Medallion Press?

Now you can receive breaking news,
updates, and more from Medallion Press
straight to your cell phone, e-mail, instant
messenger, or Facebook!

Sign up now at www.twitter.com/MedallionPress
to stay on top of all the happenings in and
around Medallion Press.

For more information
about other great titles from
Medallion Press, visit
m e d a l l i o n p r e s s . c o m